ON THE
LAMB

ON THE LAMB

Tina Kashian

KENSINGTON PUBLISHING CORP.
www.kensingtonbooks.com

KENSINGTON BOOKS are published by

Kensington Publishing Corp.
119 West 40th Street
New York, NY 10018

All Kensington titles, imprints, and distributed lines are available at special quantity discounts for bulk purchases for sales promotion, premiums, fund-raising, educational, or institutional use.

Special book excerpts or customized printings can also be created to fit specific needs. For details, write or phone the office of the Kensington Sales Manager: Attn.: Sales Department. Kensington Publishing Corp., 119 West 40th Street, New York, NY 10018. Phone: 1-800-221-2647.

Kensington and the K logo Reg. U.S. Pat. & TM Off.

First Printing: March 2020
ISBN-13: 978-1-4967-2605-6
ISBN-10: 1-4967-2605-7

ISBN-13: 978-1-4967-2606-3 (ebook)
ISBN-10: 1-4967-2606-5 (ebook)

10 9 8 7 6 5 4 3 2 1

Printed in the United States of America

For my darling Gabrielle,
May you always follow your dreams,
have the courage to believe in them, and may
your star always shine bright.
I love you.

Chapter One

❦

"Saturday night is going to be one killer night out."

Lucy Berberian had just finished stacking menus on the hostess stand when Sally, a long-time waitress, bounded over. "It has been a while since our last beach bonfire," Lucy said.

Sally pulled her waitress pad from her apron pocket and set it on one of the tables. "It's been longer than a while. This winter seemed endless, and you've put long hours into learning the ropes here. You deserve to have some fun."

It was true. Since the summer, Lucy had worked overtime as the manager of Kebab Kitchen, her family's Mediterranean restaurant in Ocean Crest, a small Jersey shore town. But it was now early April. Winter had come and gone, along with numerous holiday festivities at the beach. A warmer breeze blew from the Atlantic Ocean, one of the first signs of spring at the shore. It was a long-awaited and delightful change. Soon Easter would arrive, along with town-wide egg hunts, church services, and family celebrations.

The swinging kitchen doors opened and Lucy's sister, Emma, carrying a tray of empty salt and pepper shakers, stepped into the dining room. "Are you two talking about our night out?" She eyed them as she set the tray on the waitress station.

"You bet," Sally said. "I've been telling Lucy she needs a break from work."

Emma slipped on a red waitress apron emblazoned with the Kebab Kitchen logo in black letters and tied it behind her. "Well, it was nice of your friend, Michael, to invite us to join his motorcycle-riding friends at their beach bonfire, Lucy. I know I'm tired of being cooped up inside. It's perfect timing, too, before the season starts and it becomes crazy busy in town."

Lucy knew what her sister meant. In a little over two months, Memorial Day would arrive, summer would officially start, and the small shore town would triple in size. A parking spot would be hard to find, even a metered one. But before then, one more townwide event would seize Ocean Crest—Bikers on the Beach.

Motorcycles from all over New Jersey and neighboring states would ride to the beach to raise money for injured veterans. It was a worthy annual cause, albeit a loud one. Her parents, Angela and Raffi Berberian, often complained about the noise of too many Harley-Davidsons roaring down Ocean Avenue.

Lucy didn't mind the noise or the additional

business for the town. The restaurant's neighbor and Lucy's friend, Michael Citteroni, ran the bicycle rental shop next door to Kebab Kitchen. He also owned a black-and-chrome Harley. Michael had invited Lucy and her girlfriends to a celebratory beach bonfire—the night out that Lucy was looking forward to just as much as her sister and Sally were.

Sally and Emma began filling the salt and pepper shakers and placing them on trays to deliver to the tables. It was the lull between the lunch and dinner shifts, and the family-friendly restaurant was quiet. Each table was perfectly set with a white linen tablecloth, sparkling glasses, a votive candle, and a vase of freshly cut flowers. Several maple booths situated in the corners were perfect for a couple's date night out. Cherry wainscoting added additional charm to the dining room. A low wall separated a waitress station from the dining area, and a pair of swinging doors led into the kitchen.

But it was the large bay windows that drew the eye and revealed the gem of the town—the spectacular ocean view. Seagulls soared above the water and a pristine beach stretched on for miles to the next Jersey shore town and beyond. In the distance was the boardwalk and the pier with an old-fashioned wooden roller coaster and Ferris wheel.

"Should I wear a bathing suit under my clothes at the bonfire?" Sally asked as she moved a vase aside to make room for the salt and pepper shakers.

Lucy shook her head. "I wouldn't. The ocean's too cold to swim and no one plans on braving a cold dip at night."

"Too bad. You mean no skinny-dipping like we all did way back in high school?" Sally teased.

"Good grief. Those days are over," Emma said. "But do you think Michael's friends are as good-looking as he is?"

Lucy rolled her eyes. "What kind of question is that?" Her sister was married to Max, a real estate guru in Ocean Crest, and they had a ten-year-old daughter, Niari.

"I know I'm a married lady. But I'm not blind," Emma insisted. Small-boned and rail-thin, with brown hair, at thirty-seven, Emma was five years older than Lucy.

The sisters had similar petite builds, but Lucy had deep brown eyes and shoulder-length, curly brown hair. The heat from the kitchen and the summer humidity made it even curlier. She would never call herself rail thin, and working with food all day—combined with her love of lemon meringue pie from Cutie's Cupcakes—were reasons she jogged the Ocean Crest boardwalk three times a week to stay trim.

Sally jokingly pushed Emma aside. "Well, I'm not married *or* blind." Sally was tall and willowy, with dark, pixie-style hair.

Lucy chuckled. How she loved these two. They made working at the restaurant fun.

"I invited Melanie Haven to join us," Lucy said.

Sally glanced at Emma. "Can you convince Melanie to bring along some candy?"

"Are you kidding? I already asked her," Lucy said.

Melanie owned Haven Candies on the boardwalk. When Lucy jogged the boardwalk, she longingly passed the candy store on her route. The salt-water taffy was a favorite with locals and tourists alike. As a kid, Lucy used to gaze wide-eyed in the window of the candy store as the candy maker stretched the taffy or made huge batches of fudge in big copper pots. Whenever fudge samples were handed out outside the shop, Lucy would sprint to snatch one.

The swinging kitchen doors opened and Azad Zakarian, the head chef of Kebab Kitchen, approached carrying a tray loaded with plates. "Ladies, I have tonight's specials for tasting. Mediterranean couscous salad and falafel as appetizers. Filet kebab and grilled grouper as main dishes. For the hummus bar, we have pine nut hummus, olive hummus, and traditional hummus."

Lucy's heart skipped a beat at the sight of both the food and the man. Tall, dark, and handsome, Azad cut an imposing figure in his crisp, white chef's coat. She'd recently taken a leap and started dating him again. According to Madame Vega, the tarot card reader on the boardwalk, it was either a wise decision or a dangerous one.

Lucy still wasn't sure.

The three women wasted no time in grabbing forks and tasting. The Mediterranean couscous salad was bursting with flavor from kalamata olives, cucumbers, and tomatoes in a lemon and olive oil dressing, and the falafel's fried chickpeas had just the right crunch. The filet kebab was perfectly seasoned and melted in their mouth, and the grouper was light and flaky.

"Yum. It's all delicious." She looked up to catch Azad's grin, and her gaze was drawn to the sexy dimple in his cheek. She cleared her throat and forced herself to look at the food. "Perfect timing. The hummus bar is almost empty."

"I'll do it," Emma said as she took the bins from the tray, then headed to the corner of the dining room where the hummus bar was located. It was one of the most popular features of the restaurant, and the varieties of hummus changed daily. There were vegetables for dipping, and fresh pita bread could be ordered from the kitchen.

Azad pointed to the other plates on the tray. Lines of concentration deepened along his brows, and Lucy knew he took his position as head chef seriously. "The grouper is fresh, straight from the fish market," he said. "I only hope we have enough for—"

A loud crash sounded from the kitchen.

Lucy started. "What the heck was that?"

Lucy pushed through the swinging doors and burst into the kitchen. Picking her way past the griddle, the commercial dishwasher, and the prep station, she passed through the kitchen and stopped short at the entrance to the storage room. Rows of metal shelving were packed with the essentials of Mediterranean cuisine—bags of bulgur, rice, spices, and jars of tahini and grape leaves.

In the corner, she spotted the orange and black cat, Gadoo, sprawled on his back, legs up. Her mother, Angela Berberian, was wielding a broom, her lips drawn in a tight line. A glass jar of tahini had shattered across the terra-cotta floor, leaving a sticky mess of sesame seed paste.

"Shoo!" Angela shouted as she shook the broom. "Out!"

If her mother wasn't clearly upset, Lucy would have burst out laughing. Angela was only five feet tall including her signature beehive hairdo. But Lucy knew not to make a sound. Her mother was like a marine sergeant in the kitchen—talented and disciplined. She liked the outdoor cat and always left him fresh water and kibbles outside the back storage room door, but Angela was a stickler for cleanliness and never permitted the feline inside.

"What's the cat doing in the kitchen?" Sally asked from behind Lucy's shoulder. Almost a foot taller, Sally had a good view.

"He snuck inside again. This time, he knocked over a jar and made a mess," Angela said.

"Is he dead?" Sally asked.

"No. He's faking," Lucy said.

"How can you tell?" Sally asked.

Lucy stepped into the room. "I've seen Gadoo do this before when he's scared. His chest is rising and falling. He's breathing."

"If you say so." Sally looked skeptical.

"Give me the broom, Mom," Lucy said.

When Angela didn't move, Lucy snatched it from her hands. "You're frightening him." She set the broom against the wall, then squatted down to pet Gadoo. He cracked open his yellow eyes. "Hey, Gadoo. You want a treat?"

The cat's ears perked up and he rolled over. He leisurely stretched, his razor-sharp claws spreading like mini spears, then sat up. Lucy grabbed a bag of cat treats from a nearby shelf and shook it.

Gadoo switched his tail, then sashayed over. Lucy wasted no time in pouring some chicken-leg-shaped treats into her palm and held them out for him.

"Not inside. Lure him out back," Angela ordered as she planted her hands on her bony hips.

Lucy opened the back storage room door and the cat followed. He ate from her hand and Lucy scratched under his chin when he was finished. His satisfied purring made her smile. Gadoo translated simply as "cat" in Armenian. Her mother had named him, and when Lucy had questioned her about it, Angela had responded, "A simple name is best. Why complicate it?" Perhaps she was right. The name Gadoo suited the feisty feline.

Lucy shook her finger at Gadoo. "You know better than to sneak inside while my mom is still here." She immediately stroked behind his ears to take away any sting in her voice.

Meowww. He looked up, his yellow eyes flashing in protest.

"Okay. At least wait until Mom leaves for the day before sneaking inside," Lucy warned.

The storage room door opened and Azad stepped outside.

Lucy stood. "Hey, Azad. Gadoo snuck inside. Mom had a fit."

Azad shrugged, and the outline of his broad shoulders strained against the fabric of his chef's coat. "He's been doing it more and more lately. He's looking for you."

Lucy glanced down at the cat, who began to wind a figure eight around her feet, then she looked at Azad. "I want to take Gadoo with me when I move out of Katie's house."

Lucy had been living with Katie Watson, Lucy's best friend since grade school. Katie was married to Bill, an Ocean Crest beat cop, and Lucy had been staying in the guest bedroom of their cozy rancher.

"Any prospects?"

"Max has a place for me to look at today." She'd been looking for a while and had almost given up hope of finding something within her salary range when her brother-in-law called to tell her he had a place to show her this afternoon.

Azad shoved his hands into his pockets. "I hear you and the ladies are going out Saturday night. Michael Citteroni invited you."

"You're not jealous, are you?" It was no secret that the two men never had seen eye to eye. Being business neighbors hadn't helped matters either.

He nodded, and a swath of dark, wavy hair fell casually on his forehead. Lucy's fingers itched to brush it back.

"Always. I'd be lying if I said I wasn't," he said.

"No need. Michael and I are just friends, re-member?" Lucy said.

She'd come to an understanding with Azad. Whatever male rivalry was between him and Michael, Lucy wasn't giving up a friend. Besides, it was clear where her heart lay.

She watched the play of emotions on Azad's face and was relieved when the corners of his lips tilted in a smile.

"I remember. Go have fun. But not *too* much fun."

Chapter Two

Max pulled up to the curb and put his sedan in Park. "This is it."

Lucy sat in her brother-in-law's car and stared out the passenger window at a two-story, tan building with white shutters. Well-tended hedgerows and blooming yellow daffodils and pink and white tulips added splashes of spring color. A two-car driveway and garage would make for convenient parking during the busy summer season.

"You never said it was this close to the beach. It must cost a fortune," Lucy said.

"Don't worry. This upstairs apartment comes with certain conditions. The rent is within your budget."

Something in Max's tone caught her attention, and she eyed him. He was dressed in a navy business suit and a striped navy-and-pink tie. Emma's husband was handsome, with brown hair and blue eyes, but he was also a born salesman, and she had a feeling he was keeping something from her. Of course, she'd been asking him to find her an affordable apartment in town—a difficult feat based on her salary. She'd almost been resigned to the fact that she'd live with Katie and Bill forever until Max had called. The location was ideal—only a two-block walk to Kebab Kitchen.

"What do you mean by 'conditions?'" Lucy asked.

"I told you the owner, Eloisa Lubinski, is in her eighties and a longtime widow."

"So?"

"Well, she's not moving out. She lives on the first floor and is looking for a tenant for the second floor."

Lucy's eyes never left his for an instant. "Okay. But what aren't you telling me? I get the feeling you're holding out."

"Mrs. Lubinski is in a bind. She's also a bit eccentric. Her nephew wants to put her in an assisted living facility and sell the house for a tidy profit. You're her last-ditch attempt."

"Last ditch at what? You want me to be her caregiver?" This wasn't something Lucy had considered, and she was surprised Max would think she would be a good fit. Nothing in her past had prepared her to take on such a big role.

Max shook his head. "No way! She's completely self-sufficient."

Lucy felt a moment's relief, but she knew not to let Max off the hook. "Then why does her nephew want to force her out?"

"He's a full-time landlord and has properties all over the Jersey shore. He's also her only living relative and sole heir."

Lucy shot Max a confused look. "I still don't understand. He wants to evict his own aunt?"

He shrugged. "Like I said, she can be eccentric. You have to meet her to understand."

Max killed the engine. They left the car and headed to the front door. Max knocked and waited. No answer. He knocked again. Still nothing.

"Mrs. Lubinski must be out. But it's okay. She left me a key." Max pulled a key from his shirt pocket and opened the door. Lucy followed him inside.

It was old lady décor. Sixties kitchen with a lime-green refrigerator, tiered curtains, wallpaper with roosters and matching decorative wall plates displaying more roosters. One of the cabinet doors had been left open to reveal a shelf liner with a print of—she could have guessed it by now—roosters.

It smelled like old lady, too. A combination of Jean Naté and BENGAY.

"Your rental is upstairs. I originally thought you had to share a kitchen, but the upstairs has its own. There's only one front door, but I thought you'd like that the upstairs comes furnished."

Having to enter through the main house was a deterrent, but an already furnished apartment was a plus. After working at a Philadelphia law firm for eight years, Lucy had quit after reaching the proverbial glass ceiling and had come home without anything other than suitcases of business suits, panty hose, and high heels, none of which she'd worn since stepping foot in Ocean Crest.

Thank goodness for small miracles.

She hadn't expected to stay in Ocean Crest, but family and friends, and an ex-boyfriend who'd turned into a current boyfriend—Azad—had a way of changing a gal's mind.

They climbed a set of stairs to the second floor, where Max opened a door and they entered the upstairs apartment.

"There's no lock on this door," Lucy said as she closed it behind them.

"No. That's part of the agreement, but Mrs. Lubinski says she won't intrude on your privacy."

Lucy wasn't sure how she felt about this part of the agreement, only that she wanted to be sure her privacy wouldn't be violated.

She followed Max into the kitchen. The table had a floral plastic tablecloth, but at least the refrigerator was white. Clear plastic slipcovers covered a plush pink sofa. In the bedroom, a light-blue bedspread embroidered with more flowers was draped over a queen bed. The bathroom was tiled in pink with a matching pink sink and toilet. The toilet tank was covered with a pink rug, and a crocheted toilet paper doll sat on top.

"It's a bit outdated," Max said.

"A bit?" Clearly, he'd slipped into real estate mogul mode if he was downplaying the place as only slightly outdated.

"I know what you're thinking, but there's more," Max said.

Lucy eyed him speculatively. "More plastic?"

"No, silly. More that I want to show you. Come look."

She followed him out of the bathroom and down

a hallway with a carpet runner covered with a plastic carpet protector. He opened pink vertical blinds to reveal sliding glass doors that led to a wood deck.

She froze. "Oh my gosh."

"This is what I wanted you to see," Max said.

It was beachfront and ocean view. Stunning. Nothing else mattered. The plastic-covered sofa, the blinding pink, the crocheted toilet paper doll. Nothing but this.

She opened the sliding glass doors and walked onto the deck and clutched the railing. She stood there, blank, amazed, and shaken.

It was late afternoon, and the sky was an amazing mix of pinks and blues. The sand dunes that protected the beach danced beneath a breeze, and seagulls circled above. The ocean was calm, an endless blue line in the horizon. She inhaled the scent of salty, fresh air. A gentle wind cooled her cheeks.

Patio furniture was arranged in one corner of the large deck, a glass-topped table and four chairs. A long, wooden staircase led from the deck directly down to the beach. She wouldn't have to leave her apartment from the front door to get to the beach. She could picture herself sitting outside every morning with a cup of coffee as the sun rose. She could also envision herself jogging the beach, the sand spraying the backs of her calves, the early morning rays kissing her cheeks.

She also understood why Max had said she'd have to enter through the front door. The deck stairs were a plus, but she couldn't get into her apartment this way unless she trekked through a lot of sand.

"Why doesn't Mrs. Lubinski want to live on the second floor and rent the first one?" She asked as Max joined her at the wooden railing.

"She prefers not to walk up and down the stairs. Didn't you notice the BENGAY smell?"

How could she miss it?

"She lowered the rent when I told her about you. She thinks you being here will hold off Gilbert," Max said.

She dragged her gaze away from the view to eye Max. "Who's Gilbert?"

"Her nephew."

Lucy knew better than to get involved with someone else's family business. She had her hands full with her own family and the restaurant. Her parents were supposed to be semiretired, but Angela and Raffi Berberian still managed to have their fingers in everything. Her father, especially, interfered whenever she wanted to make a change at the restaurant. He'd even given her a hard time when she'd sought to update the wooden shelving to stainless-steel in the storage room. Her father was the most stubborn man she knew.

Max led her back inside and closed the sliding glass door. "Well, what do you think about the place?" Max asked.

Lucy scanned the apartment, already envisioning the changes she'd like to make to the décor. "Yes. Definitely, yes. I'd be crazy not to take her up on—"

Footsteps sounded on the stairs from below, then a little old lady brandishing a baseball bat came tearing through the door. A growling shih tzu snarled at her feet.

"Out! I don't keep cash here!"

She wore a hot-pink velour sweat suit. A sweatband kept her steel-gray curls back from her face. Lucy took in the woman's full face of makeup, complete with slashes of blush across her wrinkled cheeks and bright pink lipstick. The dog's lower row of teeth flashed as it continued to growl. A topknot kept a tuft of hair out of its beady eyes.

Oh my God. Max had said eccentric, not crazy!

Lucy backed up a step until her hip jabbed the corner of the kitchen table.

Max raised his hands and bravely approached the pair. "Mrs. Lubinski! It's me, Max. I told you I was bringing someone to see the place today, remember?"

The lady halted, then lowered her bat an inch. "Oh. Why didn't you say so earlier? I thought I was being robbed."

Lucy tried not to gape. Robbed of what? Did she stash silver coins inside the lime-green refrigerator?

Mrs. Lubinski eyed Lucy up and down like a picky buyer at a yard sale. "What's your name?"

"Lucy Berberian."

"You smoke?"

"No."

"Drink?"

"Only on occasion."

"Have a boyfriend."

"Recently."

"See him often?"

"He works for me."

Mrs. Lubinski nodded once. "She'll do."

She'd gotten Mrs. Lubinski's approval, but her

little dog didn't appear to agree. The growling continued.

Lucy's head spun. Eloisa Lubinski's questions had come at her with the speed of a Gatling gun. "Um." It was all Lucy could manage as she pointed at the shih tzu.

Mrs. Lubinski bent to pet the little beast, and he stopped growling. "This is Cupid. He'll get used to you."

Cupid?

The aggressive little dog was as far from the Greek god of affection as one could imagine. Lucy cleared her throat and managed to find her voice. "One thing. I have a cat." She wasn't sure how Gadoo would feel about Cupid. Or Cupid about Gadoo. The house was only two blocks away from the restaurant, and Gadoo could travel back and forth as he wished. Another plus for the location. As for the landlady, the jury was still out.

Mrs. Lubinski scratched her headband. "A cat, humm. I don't like cats. Is he an outdoor or an indoor cat?"

Tricky question. Gadoo was mostly an outdoor cat despite his recent escapades of sneaking into the restaurant through the storage room door. She'd go with past history. "Outdoor."

"Well, as long as your feline stays clear of Cupid, we should be fine."

"Okay."

Apparently decided, Mrs. Lubinski turned and headed for the stairs. "I have a swim aerobics class in a half hour. You can move in today."

Chapter Three

"I can't believe you're moving out."

Lucy's stomach dropped as she looked at Katie. It was the following day, and boxes were scattered around them on Mrs. Lubinski's second floor. "Don't make me feel any worse than I already do."

Katie bit her lower lip. "I'm sorry. I knew this time would come, but I'm going to miss you."

"I'm going to miss you, too. But I'm not leaving Ocean Crest. I'm only a few blocks away from you and Bill. Now you can have a place to visit."

Katie had been Lucy's best friend for years and they'd survived Ocean Crest High School together. People had often wondered how they could have been so close—they were opposites in every way. Katie was a tall, blue-eyed, natural blonde, whereas Lucy had dark curly hair, brown eyes, and was five feet three inches tall after a strong cup of caffeine. Katie also grew up eating apple pie, and Lucy was a first-generation American with Armenian, Greek, and Lebanese roots.

"I can see why you were so excited," Katie said as she set down a box on the kitchen table and walked to the sliding glass doors that led to the deck and peered outside. "The ocean view is amazing." She turned away and eyed the plastic-covered couch. "Although the furniture needs a bit of updating. I can picture you and Azad relaxing on that plastic. You two just might stick to it permanently."

The two burst out laughing just as Lucy's parents came up the stairs, arms loaded. Her father, Raffi, held a box of dishes while her mother held clothes on hangers.

"What's so funny?" Angela asked.

Raffi gave Lucy a kiss on the cheek. Her father was a bear of a man, with a paunch and thinning, dark, curly hair streaked with gray. He could be highly opinionated and overbearing, but he was also affectionate when it came to his two daughters. "Where do you want these?"

"On the kitchen counter," Lucy said.

Angela eyed the place. "I don't like it, Lucy."

"Why don't you move back home, honey? You know you are always welcome," Raffi said.

"You can have your old bedroom. I kept it the same," Angela added.

Heck no.

She already worked in the family business, was dating the man her parents had always wanted for her. The last thing she needed was to return home. Before she knew it, they'd give her a curfew.

"We talked about this, Mom," Lucy said. "I want my own place."

"Fine," Angela said with a huff. "It seems safe."

Lucy stopped herself from rolling her eyes. "It's only a short walk from Kebab Kitchen. It's very safe."

Her father nudged her mother. "We'll go back to the car and get the last of your things."

As soon as her parents were out of sight, Katie stopped unpacking and went to the window. "They're talking about you."

Lucy joined Katie at the window to see her parents arguing and gesturing at each other. Lucy sighed. "Looks like my father is trying to calm down my mom. Eventually, she'll come to accept it."

"At least they showed up to help," Katie said.

Azad had offered to help, but with her parents here, they needed him to oversee the restaurant and kitchen for the lunch shift.

Hours later, all of Lucy's belongings had been moved in. Her clothes hung in the closet, and even her dishes—what few she had—were in the cupboards. After brief hugs and promises to visit them at their home soon, her parents departed. At last, Lucy was alone with Katie.

"Now we can officially celebrate." Katie reached in her bag and pulled out a bottle of wine and an opener. "Grab two glasses and meet me on the deck."

Lucy headed for the kitchen to search the cupboards. She found the two wineglasses she wanted just as Katie screamed.

Lucy rushed out to the deck to find a man facing Katie. Medium-built, he had blond hair and the beginnings of a goatee. He was well-dressed, in a navy sports coat and slacks, but had some sand on his black leather shoes. For a brief instant, Lucy wondered if he was a salesman, then dismissed the idea. A salesman would go to the front door and knock, not show up on the rear patio. Katie moved toward the sliding glass door, her face pale.

"Who are you?" Lucy demanded.

"I wanted to meet my aunt's new tenant." His voice was calm but firm.

She eyed him with renewed interest. "You're Gilbert?" Most women would find him attractive, but Lucy found him disturbing because he was standing on her deck.

A self-satisfied smirk crossed his face. "Good. She mentioned me. What's your name?"

"I'm Lucy."

He shot her a dark look, ignoring Katie, who stood watching the exchange with wide eyes. "Well, I just want you to know it won't work, Lucy."

"Pardon?"

"You staying here cheap. I know why my aunt's renting to you. She thinks with you here, I can't force her into an assisted living facility."

Lucy didn't appreciate his arrogant manner or his opinion of Eloisa Lubinski. The fact that he would force his aunt out of her own home told her, very clearly, what type of man Gilbert was. She'd come across men like this during her tenure at the firm, adversaries who had no empathy for others and who wanted to line their own pockets no matter the consequences.

She lifted her chin and boldly met his glare. "I don't know what you're talking about. From what

I've seen, your aunt is quite capable of living on her own. She even takes water aerobics."

He huffed. "She's cracked."

Lucy's eyes narrowed. "That's not very nice."

"She's my aunt. I can call her what I want." He pointed a finger at her. "As for you, I'll be seeing you often."

Lucy'd had enough of his threats, and she stiffened her spine. "I don't think so. I'm a legal tenant and you are not allowed to trespass here."

"We'll see about that." Gilbert turned on his heel and headed down the deck stairs and disappeared around the corner. She assumed he was headed to visit his aunt. Good luck. Mrs. Lubinksi wasn't home.

"What was that all about?" Katie asked.

Lucy turned to her friend. "Like he said, he wants to put his aunt in an assisted living facility. Apparently, he's her only living relative. He thinks she can't live alone."

"Is he right?"

"I don't think so. Max says Mrs. Lubinski is eccentric but not crazy or unable to manage by herself."

Katie eyed the pristine beach below. "This is prime real estate. He could get a good amount for it."

Lucy drew in her lips thoughtfully. "Despite what he said, I hope he gives up trying to evict his own aunt."

"If he bothers you again, call Bill. A man in uniform with a gun is always a great deterrent," Katie said.

"Good grief, I hope it doesn't come to that. My

mom will make me move back into my old bedroom."

Lucy's running shoes pounded on the boardwalk. She breathed in the salty air and let out a long breath. It was the following morning, and she'd begun her day with a jog.

After stretching on her deck, she'd run the short distance on the beach to the boardwalk ramp. She wasn't a natural-born runner like Katie, but since returning home to Ocean Crest, Lucy had made the effort to start jogging and had been committed to the exercise.

She'd come to love the early morning trek on the boardwalk. The Ocean Crest boardwalk was an eclectic mixture of shops and eateries. Tourists jogged, walked, and rode rented bicycles and surreys up and down the two-mile stretch. Pizza parlors, tattoo parlors, T-shirt shops, custard and French fry stands all vied for her attention during the summer season. Lucy waved to Madame Vega, the fortune teller and tarot card reader. She smiled at the Gray sisters as she passed the novelty shop run by two elderly spinsters.

Near the end of the boardwalk was Haven Candies. Saltwater taffy and homemade fudge was famous on the Jersey shore. Tourists were hard-pressed to walk by without making a trip inside the candy shop. Handmade fudge, and taffy, and chocolate-covered everything—blueberries, strawberries, Rice Krispie treats, Oreos, and Yodels—lured passersby. All were on display behind the shop's endless, glass counter. If you could name it, Haven Candies could dip it in chocolate.

Lucy stepped inside and the scent of chocolate wafted over her. As she gazed at the delights behind the glass counter, she could almost feel the added extra inches on her waist and hips. The candy store took temptation to a different level.

Behind the counter, Melanie Haven was serving a family of four, parents with two young girls dressed in beach cover-ups. In a white-and-blue-checked shirt and matching apron, Melanie was attractive, with short auburn hair, brown eyes, and a slim build. She had inherited the shop from her parents years ago.

Melanie had attended the same Ocean Crest High School as Lucy, but Melanie was older and had graduated a year before her. Since returning home, Lucy had been meaning to see Melanie, but time had gotten away from her. The bonfire was the first true opportunity to catch up with her friend.

Melanie waved to Lucy, then finished serving her customers. Lucy remembered Emma and herself as kids, staring wide-eyed inside the window of the candy shop as Melanie's father made fudge and stretched taffy.

A special was running today: buy a pound of fudge and get a pound free. The family's four pounds of fudge in white-and-blue boxes were rung up and placed in a bag bearing the shop's name and logo.

As the parents paid and left with their girls in tow, one of the girls peeked inside the bag, her eyes wide.

Lucy approached the counter. "Hi, Melanie. You ready for tonight's bonfire?"

"I wouldn't miss it. By the way, I heard you moved," Melanie said.

Lucy blinked. She hadn't told Melanie about her plans to leave Katie's home, but she shouldn't be surprised that she knew. Gossip in the tiny town traveled as fast as the speed of light. "I did. Mrs. Lubinski's second floor."

"Mrs. Lubinski?"

Was it her imagination or did a shadow cross Melanie's face? "Do you know her?" Lucy asked.

Melanie shook her head. "Not her, but her nephew."

"Gilbert?"

"Unfortunately, he's my landlord."

It was Lucy's turn to be surprised. She couldn't imagine having Gilbert Lubinski as a landlord. Did he show up unannounced on his tenant's decks on a regular basis? "You're kidding? He seems like a . . . like a—"

"Like a jerk," Melanie said.

"Well, yes."

Melanie made a face. "That's an understatement. Gilbert owns a lot of places, including a share of the Seagull Condos in Bayville."

"I didn't realize." Bayville was a town neighboring Ocean Crest. Lucy had driven by the Seagull Condos more times than she could count and knew they were four stories tall and full of units. If Gilbert owned part of that lucrative business, why bother with his aunt's home? Was he that greedy or strapped for cash?

"Most people don't know about Gilbert. He lies

pretty low, except with his tenants." Melanie reached behind the counter and held out a piece of wrapped candy. "Root beer taffy?"

"Sure." Lucy unwrapped it and popped it into her mouth; the taffy hit her tongue like a sugar shot. "Umm. No matter how often I indulge, I love this stuff. I remember the worst part of getting braces as a kid was giving up saltwater taffy."

Melanie chuckled. "I'll be sure to bring some tonight."

Chapter Four

Lucy spotted a row of parked Harley-Davidsons by the ramp leading up to the boardwalk. She counted ten bikes in all. Each motorcycle was unique. Some were personalized with the owner's name or initials painted on the sides, others had extra ornamental touches in shiny chrome, while others featured saddlebags to hold personal items. Not all the bikers were attending Michael's beach bonfire. Some were out walking the boardwalk, eating at restaurants, or enjoying the beach.

With Emma, Sally, and Melanie by her side, Lucy led them beneath the boardwalk and onto the beach. She carried takeout containers of shish kebab and Mediterranean couscous salad—the remains of Azad's dinner special. Emma brought chocolate chip cookies she'd baked with her daughter, Niari. Sally carried along a container of pulled pork and rolls from the Barbecue King, and Melanie had Haven Candies boxes containing an assortment from her shop. It was still light out and they easily spotted the teepee-shaped structure built of driftwood that, once lit, would be a bonfire on the beach. Taking off their shoes, they made their way across the sand toward the party.

Michael Citteroni came forward with a smile to greet the four women. "Hi, ladies. Thanks for bringing food."

Lucy eyed the ready-to-be-lit driftwood tepee. A nest of tinder was at the base—small twigs, dry grass and seaweed, and balls of crumpled newspaper. A shovel stood upright nearby, the blade dug into the sand. "You've been busy."

Michael gripped the handle of the shovel. "We dug a hole three feet wide, three feet long, and two feet deep. The bonfire will be a good fifty feet away from the sand dunes. Everything is just like your friend required." Michael grinned as he looked at Katie.

Katie nodded. "It looks just right." She'd issued the permit for the bonfire at the town hall, where she worked as head clerk.

"We also have enough wood to last all night." Michael nodded at a large pile of driftwood nearby, ready to be tossed, piece by piece, into the fire to keep it ablaze.

"Ladies, please make yourselves comfortable. We have plenty of beach chairs, and there's a table to place all the food. The coolers have water, beer, and wine. There's also a thermos of hot chocolate if you get chilly."

The sun was still up, but a cool April breeze blew from the ocean. Lucy was grateful for her rolled-up jeans and old Ocean Crest High School sweatshirt. The sounds of the ocean waves echoed through the night.

Two of Michael's friends were stacking additional driftwood on the big pile. When they spotted the women, they approached. "These are my friends, Pumpkin O'Connor and Craig Smith," Michael said, making the introductions. "We met at a motorcycle club three years ago and ride together whenever we can."

Pumpkin was a hulk of a man, with tattoos on his large biceps, slightly long, dark hair that brushed his collar, and a shadow of a beard. He wore a tank top and cutoff jean shorts with shredded hems. Craig, on the other hand, was tall, with a wiry build and short blond hair. He was clean-cut and as clean-shaven as if he'd just stepped out of a barber shop, and wore a navy T-shirt and khaki shorts.

"Why do you go by Pumpkin?" Sally asked.

"He has a big head. We dubbed him that years ago," Craig said, a twinkle of humor lighting his eyes.

"Knock it off." Pumpkin punched Craig on the arm. "You're giving these lovely ladies a bad image of me." He turned to the women and grinned, his straight, white teeth flashing. "What would all of you like to drink? I'm happy to fetch anything you'd like."

The women placed their orders, and Pumpkin traipsed off to get the drinks. Michael and Craig followed to help.

"Is he single?" Melanie asked.

"Which one?" Lucy asked.

"The tall, dark-haired one," Melanie said.

"Michael is, but he likes Lucy," Emma said.

Lucy gaped at her sister. "Not true! Michael and I are just friends. And he knows I'm seeing Azad."

"Hmm," Sally said. "Your sister has a point. I've seen you leave the restaurant to go next door and ride with him on his Harley-Davidson."

"As friends," Lucy insisted.

"I'd like a friend like that," Melanie said. "But I meant Pumpkin, not Michael. I like his name. It reminds me of fall, my favorite season."

"Sounds like a good enough reason to me," Sally said.

The men returned with drinks and everyone gathered around the unlit bonfire. "Would you do the honors?" Michael handed Lucy a lighter with a long handle.

"See. I told you." Emma elbowed Lucy in the side and whispered in her ear. "He didn't offer anyone else the opportunity."

Lucy shot her sister a scowl and a shut-up look, then took the lighter from Michael. "What do I do?"

"Just light the tinder," Michael instructed. "We already added lighter fluid to help."

Lucy ignited the lighter and reached in an opening at the base of the teepee and lit the tinder. A spark crackled, and then the tinder burned. Soon after, the bonfire was ablaze.

Everyone gazed at the sight. The heat warmed Lucy's cheeks, while a gust of wind blew the hair from her face. At first, Lucy worried the wind would put out the fire, but Michael and his friends kept adding dry driftwood to feed the flames.

The women gathered together on beach chairs and watched the bonfire.

"How about you, Melanie?" Lucy asked. "Have you been dating?"

Melanie shook her head. "No time. I'm always in the candy shop."

"I haven't met a man who doesn't like chocolate," Katie said.

"The only married ladies here are Emma and Katie. What do you two think? Shouldn't Melanie try to date?" Sally asked.

"Marriage isn't all peaches and cream. It takes work," Emma said.

Her sister's tone made Lucy wonder if she was having trouble with Max. She frequently complained that he worked long hours, especially during the summer.

Katie sighed. "It may be work, but marriage has its benefits."

Sally nudged Katie, and all the women chuckled.

"I didn't mean *those* types of benefits," Katie's said, her face turning bright red. "Although I won't deny that's a plus. I meant that it's nice never to be lonely."

Everyone grew silent as they contemplated the truth behind Katie's words. Lucy had only recently started dating Azad. Loneliness wasn't something she'd considered. She'd been too busy managing the restaurant, and before returning home, she'd been occupied working at the Philadelphia firm. But Katie was wise beyond her years. Loneliness wasn't a pleasant thought.

"I brought chocolate and vanilla fudge and saltwater taffy." Melanie opened one of the white boxes labeled "Haven Candies" she'd brought along. "Lucy's request."

Lucy reached for one of the boxes. "I claim the first bite of fudge."

"Your couscous salad is great, Lucy," Michael said as he approached, carrying a plate.

Michael knew Lucy had been taking cooking lessons from her mom, and from his words and the look on his face, it was clear he'd assumed she'd made the dish. Lucy didn't mention it was Azad who'd prepared the couscous salad. Michael wouldn't have been so free with his praise if he'd known.

"Craig brought his guitar to play. He's pretty good. Come and listen," Michael said.

Lucy was happy for the distraction and went over with the group to where Craig was playing. She was pleasantly surprised to discover that he wasn't just a talented guitar player, but he had a great voice, too. Everyone sat around the fire as he played and sang a variety of songs. Soon, people were singing along with him. Moods mellowed and problems were forgotten as the music flowed along with the calming sounds of the ocean.

The sun went down and a cool sea breeze blew in. A full moon appeared in the sky and illuminated the beach in a luminescent glow.

The beach at night was completely different from the beach during the day. Lucy loved both times, but there was something special about the evening. Some thought the beach was eerie at night. Lucy thought it was calming, yet dangerous at the same time. She'd skinny-dipped at night as a teenager. Katie had been with her, along with a group of high school seniors. It had been scary when a wave had knocked her feet from beneath her and she'd been pulled along by a strong undertow. A swimmer could easily lose her sense of up from down when that happened in the day, but at night, it was even scarier. Thankfully, Katie had been nearby and had helped her, but swimming at night wasn't something she'd ever attempted again.

No lifeguard, no swimming was her rule now Period.

Craig started a new song, and Lucy was pulled out of her reverie. The blazing bonfire was mesmerizing.

"Why haven't we done this more often?" Katie asked.

"It's the first bonfire of the year, remember?" Lucy pointed out.

"Not just this, genius. I meant a night out with friends," Katie said.

Lucy was about to respond when Melanie jumped to her feet and pointed in the distance. "What's *he* doing here?"

All heads turned to see a man with earphones, a headlight, and a metal detector scanning the beach. Ever since Lucy was little, she'd seen people do that. Her father, Raffi, had called them "metal heads" and claimed they were a bit strange. Who else would spend hours staring at the sand in search of loose change from tourists? A big score would be a lost wedding band or diamond ring.

But she'd never seen someone do this at night. Even with his headlamp and a full moon, she wondered how far he could see. Maybe the light from the bonfire helped. Had he known they would be here tonight? As if he knew they were watching him, the man removed his headphones to glare at them. A shaft of moonlight lit his face, and recognition dawned.

Gilbert.

A landlord who went looking for loose change? From what she'd heard, the man owned numerous shore properties. Why would he be looking for pocket change?

How weird.

It had to be his hobby, she rationalized. Like tennis or bowling or simply walking, but with an occasional monetary reward.

"I think he saw me," Lucy said.

Gilbert set aside the metal detector and began walking toward them. Lucy's anxiety rose the closer he came until he stopped directly in front of her.

"Hi, Gilbert. Did you come to crash the bonfire?" Lucy asked.

He scowled at her. "It's a free beach. I happened to be scanning when I just noticed that I have other business to conduct. I'm not one to waste an opportunity."

What other type of business did he have on a beach late at night? Was he still mad she was renting his aunt's second floor?

But instead of confronting Lucy, he turned his gaze on Melanie. "You're late with this month's payment, Melanie."

Melanie gaped, clearly taken aback, either at the demand or the sudden appearance of her landlord. She came alive and shook her head. "You're mistaken. I dropped off a check."

Gilbert glowered at her. "You paid the *old* rent. I told you I was raising it this month, remember?"

Melanie's face paled a shade. "I didn't think you were serious about this month! You never gave me a lease. It's almost double."

Gilbert snorted. "Your lease is up and it's now month-to-month. I can do what I want. If you don't like it, you're free to leave."

A flicker of apprehension crossed Melanie's face. "You know I can't leave at the drop of a hat. It takes time to find an affordable place in town, especially with the season right around the corner."

Gilbert's short bark of laughter lacked humor. "Not my problem."

Lucy had heard enough. Gilbert was ruining their evening and it was obvious someone had to help her friend. Lucy took a step forward. "Leave her alone. Now is not the time to harass Melanie about her rent."

Gilbert dismissed her with a wave of his hand, like she was an annoying sand flea. "It's not your business, Lucy."

"Lucy's right. Go away."

Lucy turned at the sound of the male voice to see Pumpkin standing behind her. Tall, tattooed, and broad-chested, Pumpkin could strike fear in anyone with common sense.

"This doesn't concern you either," Gilbert said, then frowned as he craned his neck to look the man confronting him in the eye.

Before Pumpkin could say a word, another male voice chimed in. "What's going on?" Craig had set aside his guitar and approached.

"Gilbert's giving Melanie a hard time. Something about raised rent," Lucy said.

"Come on, Gilbert," Craig said. "Don't you have anything better to do? Like going back to scanning the beach for lost dimes?"

"Like I told her," Gilbert hissed, pointing to Lucy. "You should all mind your own business."

Pumpkin folded his arms across his broad chest, and his tattoos stood out starkly like colorful snakes on his bulging biceps. "I'm making it my business. Unlike you, I was invited. You should leave." Next to the average-size Gilbert, Pumpkin's muscular frame cut an imposing figure.

Gilbert swallowed, then showed the good sense to back down. "Fine. But this isn't over." He hesitated only long enough to glower at Melanie, then walked back to fetch his discarded metal detector and stalked away.

"He really is a jerk," Katie said.

"Nah, never mind him," Craig said. "Let's not let anything or anyone ruin our evening. The bonfire is far from over."

"He's right. And we're making s'mores," Pumpkin said.

"I haven't had one of those in a long time." Lucy touched Melanie's hand. "Come on."

Everyone turned toward the bonfire but Melanie.

"Melanie?" Lucy asked over her shoulder.

Melanie shook her head. "No, thanks. I already own a candy store and make s'mores, fudge, and taffy. I'm happy with a plate of food. I'll just sit over there until you're all done." She filled a plate with small portions of food, including shish kebab,

Mediterranean couscous salad, pulled pork, and even her own candy, and carried a beach chair away from the bonfire.

"You sure? You're not still upset over Gilbert, are you?"

"No. I'm okay. I promise," Melanie said.

Lucy shrugged and rejoined the group to pick up a long stick, chocolate, marshmallows, and graham crackers.

Lucy pressed the melted marshmallow and chocolate bar between two graham crackers and took a bite. The crackers were crunchy and the chocolate and marshmallows melted in her mouth in sweet harmony. "Yum. I'll take a s'more to Melanie just in case she wants one. If not, I'll eat it for her."

She soon had another marshmallow melted and gooey, and with the hot s'more in hand, Lucy headed for where Melanie had moved her beach chair, but the chair was empty. Lucy scanned the beach for her friend, but Melanie was nowhere in sight.

Lucy cupped her hand over her mouth and called out, "Hey, Melanie! I made you a s'more."

A scream pierced the air.

Lucy felt as if her breath had been cut off. She scanned the beach, desperate to find her friend, and then she saw her. Melanie was on her hands and knees by a lifeguard boat farther down the beach.

Dropping the s'more, Lucy sprinted to her side.

The look on Melanie's face was chilling beneath the moonlight. Lucy followed her friend's gaze to see Gilbert sprawled across the sand. He looked asleep, with his mouth slightly ajar. Melanie had dropped her plate, and food and candy were at her feet. A piece of driftwood lay nearby.

"What is it?" Lucy asked.

"I thought he was asleep, but I called his name, then shook him. I think he's dead." Melanie's hand covered her mouth to stifle a cry.

Dread tugged low in Lucy's gut as she reached out to touch him. His flesh was lukewarm, and Lucy could find no pulse.

Oh, no. Gilbert was dead.

Chapter Five

Michael called 911 on his cell phone and the Ocean Crest Police arrived, followed by the paramedics. The police drove onto the beach in official Jeeps, the same vehicles that cruised the beach during the day. Their tires sprayed sand when they came to a halt by the body. Headlights illuminated the gruesome scene.

Bill Watson, Katie's husband, hopped out of the first Jeep. Tall and fit with a buzz cut, he was handsome, with a chiseled profile and blue eyes. He approached Katie and Lucy first. "You two okay?"

"We're fine," Katie said, then pointed to Gilbert. "He's not."

"Who is he?" Bill asked as he watched a paramedic press two fingers to Gilbert's carotid artery.

"Gilbert Lubinski," Lucy said, her voice low.

Bill's gaze snapped to Lucy's. "One of the town's landlords?"

"Yes."

Bill looked to the paramedic. "Is he dead?" The paramedic nodded.

Not good. Lucy already knew Gilbert was dead, but to have it officially confirmed made her stomach flip like a fish on a line.

Another Jeep arrived, and a man stepped out and came jogging toward them, his flashlight beam bouncing across the sand. Lucy immediately recognized him as Detective Calvin Clemmons—still Ocean Crest's sole detective until Bill finally could be approved and promoted from beat cop to detective.

In his late thirties, with a head of straw-colored hair, a bushy mustache, and a sharp profile, Clemmons was dressed in a gray suit, not an officer's uniform. The detective's gaze zeroed in on the body before looking to Lucy and Katie huddled together. "What happened here?"

"We're not sure," Lucy said.

Things had been frigid between Clemmons and Lucy when she'd first returned to town. A grudge against Lucy's sister, Emma, and her family, combined with Lucy's interference in Clemmons's past investigations hadn't helped. But after eating her mother's enticing cooking and a slice or two of baklava, the detective's relationship with Lucy had defrosted a bit.

Lucy hoped this new incident wouldn't set things back between them.

"It's Gilbert Lubinski," Bill told Clemmons as the detective went to the body. "The coroner has already been called," he added.

Clemmons snapped on a pair of gloves and bent

to examine the piece of driftwood that rested on the sand three feet from Gilbert's head. As he was examining the scene, more lights bobbed in the distance as the county coroner arrived. Dressed in a white coat with CORONER in bold, black print on the back, the man began to process the body.

Clemmons stood and directed his attention to Lucy. "You found him?"

"No. Melanie Haven did. I think she's in shock." Melanie stood two yards away, her arms wrapped around her body in a protective gesture. Her expression was a combination of terror and shock, her complexion the color of old parchment.

The detective's laser-eyed look homed in on Melanie. "Ms. Haven?"

No response.

"Ms. Haven." A bit louder this time.

Still no response.

Lucy walked to her and shook Melanie's shoulder. "Melanie?" she inquired, her tone soft.

A blink, then Melanie focused on Lucy's face. "Lucy, is he really dead?"

"I'm afraid so."

"How?"

"I don't know."

As if on cue, the coroner spoke to Clemmons, his voice loud enough for those close by to hear.

"Based on my initial examination, he was struck on the back of the head by that," the coroner said, glancing at the piece of driftwood, "but I don't think that's what killed him."

"Then what?" Clemmons asked.

The coroner raised a hand, a pair of tweezers

clutched in his fingers. Trapped in the tongs was a large, brown wad of *something*. "This was lodged in his throat. He was asphyxiated."

Lucy leaned forward to get a better look. At first, she thought it was the kalamata olives in her couscous salad, and her gut tightened. Then she recognized it. "Is that . . . is that saltwater taffy?"

"Root beer." Melanie's voice was weak but still carried.

Clemmons swung around, his eyes focused on Melanie. "What did you say?"

Melanie licked dry lips. "It's root beer saltwater taffy."

"How do you know that?" Clemmons demanded.

"Because I made it and brought it to the bonfire." Melanie's already sickly complexion paled another shade. Lucy worried she would vomit, or pass out, or both.

Clemmons stalked toward Melanie. "And did you know Gilbert Lubinski?"

"Yes. He was my landlord."

"What was your landlord doing at the bonfire?"

"He was on the beach when he saw us. He wanted to know about my rent."

"Your rent?"

Lucy placed a warning hand on her friend's arm, to no avail. Melanie, in shock, was uttering all that came to mind.

"He raised it and . . . and I was behind. We fought about it," Melanie said, her eyes never leaving Gilbert's body.

Lucy knew where this was heading. She also knew how bad it looked for Melanie. Behind Clemmons's beady gaze, she could see him connect the dots, and Melanie, like her candy, was in a sticky mess.

"This is the last box," Katie said.

The following morning, Lucy had awakened in her new apartment. Katie had promptly arrived to help unpack books, DVDs, and magazines and stack them on the built-in shelves next to the television.

"I'm getting a new TV. This one's ancient. Have you seen anything like it in a long time?" Lucy made a face at the wooden piece of furniture that held the TV.

Katie chuckled. "Other than out by a curb? It's vintage and reminds me of our high school years watching MTV together." At Lucy's laugh, Katie waved a hand. "Forget the TV, what about the pink, plastic-wrapped sofa?"

Lucy patted the sofa. "I'll keep it for now—minus the plastic."

Their lighthearted joking was a way to avoid talk of the tragedy at the bonfire last night. Finding Melanie standing over Gilbert's body on the beach wasn't something Lucy would be able to forget.

But Lucy was unable to ignore the topic for long. Biting her bottom lip, she sat down on the carpet. "What do you think about last night?"

Katie stopped stacking books on the shelves. "Other than the fact that our night out turned into a nightmare?"

"What did Bill say?"

"Not much. Bill's been working and also studying for his exam to become a detective. I don't need to ask him to know that Melanie's in trouble."

At this disturbing news, Lucy dropped the stack of magazines she was holding. "She's definitely on Detective Clemmons's radar, then?"

"This time I don't blame him. The evidence points to her."

Lucy sat back on her heels. "Why? Because Melanie and Gilbert argued on the beach regarding her raised rent, or because they didn't have a rosy landlord/tenant relationship to begin with, or because he was suffocated with her saltwater taffy?"

"All of it."

"But he was also hit on the back of the head with a piece of driftwood."

"You saw the piece of wood next to Gilbert. Melanie could have lifted it and struck Gilbert from behind. Plus, she was separated from the group and alone at the time of the murder."

"You don't honestly think Melanie killed her landlord over raised rent, do you?"

"Maybe there was additional motive we don't know about," Katie said.

Lucy rubbed her temples. "I can't imagine. But either way, I can't stop thinking about Gilbert. I'm having a hard time forgetting his face."

"A man was murdered, Lucy. It was frightening."

"It's not just that . . . I mean, it was scary, but he is . . . was Mrs. Lubinski's nephew."

"Your new landlady? What's she like?" Katie asked.

"Words cannot do Eloisa justice."

Just then, a low growling captured their attention. Lucy whirled to see Cupid standing at the top of the stairs, his white teeth flashing in a menacing snarl. A string of drool had gathered at his lower jaw and threatened to drip onto the carpet. His tail curled up, and his shoulders were thrust back in what looked like an attack stance.

In short, the small dog was terrifying.

The door to the first floor was partly open, and this time, Lucy realized she was at fault. She'd made numerous trips to her car for items and hadn't bothered to fully close the door.

It took seconds before Lucy realized it was Gadoo, not herself or Katie, who was the focus of the dog's attention. The black and orange cat sat outside on the deck licking his front paw. Lucy had cracked open the sliding glass door to let in fresh air, as well as enabling Gadoo to come and go as he pleased.

At the first sight of the vicious shih tzu, Gadoo's back arched and he hissed.

Oh, no.

It was clear the two pets were not going to make a smooth transition as roommates anytime soon.

Next up the stairs was Eloisa herself. Dressed in a black tutu with a black-and-white-striped, sequined top and black tights, she looked like a sparkling, senior citizen ballerina.

Lucy jumped to her feet and brushed her dusty hands on her yoga pants. "Hello, Mrs. Lubinski. This my best friend, Katie Watson. Her husband is an Ocean Crest police officer.

Lucy didn't know why she felt compelled to add that information. Perhaps she wanted her landlady to know she wouldn't throw wild parties with a friend like Katie around. Or, more likely, Lucy felt sorry for Eloisa because of her nephew's death and didn't quite know what to say.

Lucy swallowed and decided to address what had occurred on the beach last night. "I'm sorry about your nephew, Gilbert."

Eloisa's face fell, but then her skinny shoulders pushed back. "Gilbert didn't deserve to be murdered, but I knew that boy well enough to admit he had a knack for angering people, me included. He wanted to put me out to pasture, send me to a nursing home and take my house."

"Max told me."

Eloisa sniffed. "I still can't believe he's gone. Despite everything, it's very sad. That's why I'm dressed like this. It's the closest thing I have to mourning."

That was the closest? What else was in her landlady's wardrobe?

"He was my brother's only child." Eloisa pulled out a tissue from her glittery, cross-body handbag and blew her nose. Lucy hadn't noticed the bag. She'd been too focused on the tutu.

"After Peter died, Gilbert spent his inheritance buying properties," Eloisa said. "Most were good investments, but some were doozies. From what I heard, he wasn't a well-liked landlord."

Lucy recalled Melanie's red face as she argued with Gilbert over her raised rent. Then the image of Melanie's pale face hovering over Gilbert's lifeless body took its place. She couldn't imagine Melanie murdering anyone, even her landlord.

Lucy reached for a tissue box on the coffee table and handed Eloisa a clean tissue. "Do you know anyone who disliked him enough to want to kill him?"

Eloisa blew her nose, louder this time. "That's what the police asked me."

"The police were here?"

"Bright and early this morning. You must have slept through it."

Lucy'd returned to the apartment late last night and had been so tired, she'd slept soundly her first night here.

Eloisa pulled a business card from her handbag and put on her Minnie Mouse reading glasses, which dangled from a chain around her neck. "'Detective Calvin Clemmons,'" she read. "He paid me a visit this morning. He's good-looking, with his blond hair and mustache."

Lucy had never thought so, but Emma had dated him in high school, so she must have found him attractive. But then she had called him "Clinging Calvin" before breaking up with him. It wasn't very nice of her sister back then.

"Still, the sight of a detective on my porch gave me a fright. I would have had a glass of wine, but I no longer drink. Alcohol is bad for my nerves." She held out her hands. "See, rock steady. No shaking for my age."

"What else did the detective ask you?" Katie said.

"Well, for one, he wanted to know about my relationship with Gilbert. I told him the truth—that Gilbert wanted me out of here."

"You did?" Lucy said.

Eloisa's gaze turned from Katie to Lucy. "It's not a secret. Even your fancy real estate broker knew."

"Max is my brother-in-law," Lucy said.

Eloisa waved a hand, her glittering rings shining in the morning sunlight. "Whatever. Then the detective asked me if I was on the beach last night."

"That's easy. You weren't," Lucy said.

"I was."

"You were?" both Lucy and Katie asked in surprised unison.

"Not at the bonfire, but on the beach. It was my poker night with the gals. I won, left early, and walked home. You know what they say, 'Quit while you're ahead.' That damned Phyllis always wins, but last night was my lucky card night."

Lucy didn't think anything about last night was lucky but held her tongue.

"So, you walked home alone? At night?" Katie asked.

Eloisa's gaze narrowed on Katie. "What's wrong with that? I took a self-defense class with the county sheriff last year, young lady. I can handle myself. Plus, Ocean Crest is a safe, family town."

Katie stared, her blue eyes wide. Lucy bit her tongue harder. She didn't mention Gilbert, let alone any other crime that had occurred over the past summer months.

Lucy finally spoke up. "You walked on the boardwalk, then partly on the beach to get home?"

"It's much faster that way. I saw the light from the bonfire. Heard some music, too. You seemed to be having a grand time. If I didn't have a purse full of cash, I would have been tempted to join you."

"Cash? You could have been robbed," Katie blurted out.

Lucy eyed Katie. Her friend tended to cut to the chase, but failed to read a person's facial expressions to know when to quit.

Eloisa patted her small breasts. "All the Jacksons were safely tucked away. No one would have known."

This time Lucy did laugh, then swiftly covered it with a cough when Eloisa eyed her curiously.

"You told Detective Clemmons all this?" Lucy asked.

Eloisa nodded. "That's right."

Lucy would have loved to have been a fly on the wall. She could just imagine the stuffy Clemmons with his little notebook, scribbling down his notes as Eloisa Lubinski talked.

Eloisa whistled and Cupid obediently trotted to her side. "I'm off to take care of things for Gilbert. The funeral director needs clothes from his home. It's not a task I'm looking forward to, but there's no one else to do it."

Lucy sobered. "I can help. If you need anything, please ask."

As soon as Eloisa disappeared down the stairs into her own apartment with Cupid on her heels, Lucy left the door ajar. She may not want any surprise visits from the dog, but if her landlady needed her, she wanted to hear.

"She's something," Katie said.

"Her dog, too. But I like her." Lucy realized it was true. There was something refreshing about her new landlady.

"She does have spirit. And what girl doesn't like glitter? I'm jealous I can't wear it anymore. Not without people staring at me like I've lost my mind."

Maybe Katie was right and it was the clothes. Whatever the reason, Lucy felt protective of Eloisa Lubinski.

"She doesn't give a fig what people think. It's inspiring, actually." Lucy collapsed on the sofa, and the plastic crinkled beneath her. She really needed to remove the damned plastic. One task at a time. "You think Clemmons will consider her a suspect?"

Katie shrugged. "He's more focused on Melanie, but yes, he might. If Mrs. Lubinski told him she'd been walking on the beach and was close enough to see and hear the bonfire, even if it was only for a short while as she headed home, she was at the crime scene."

"It's crazy. Gilbert was struck on the back of the head with a piece of driftwood. You think she could have picked that up?"

"It wasn't a huge piece of driftwood."

Katie was right. Lucy had seen the driftwood. It wasn't big, but still . . .

Katie joined her on the sofa. "It still looks worse for Melanie. Lucy, how well do you really know Melanie Haven?"

Chapter Six

꩜

Pots simmered on burners, the industrial-sized mixer whirred, and mouthwatering aromas perfumed the air. Lucy and her mother were hard at work in the restaurant's kitchen, preparing for the day.

Soon the doors to Kebab Kitchen would open, and customers would rush in for lunch. They would be mostly a mix of Ocean Crest regulars and motorcycle-riding tourists from the Bikers on the Beach festival, but all the restaurant's guests would be hungry and eager to savor the Mediterranean specials of the day—lamb stew with rice pilaf, tabbouleh salad, and *choereg*, an Armenian sweet bread served with cheese.

"It's been a busy week," said Lucy. Standing behind a prep table, an apron draped around her neck, she was chopping fresh mint for the tabbouleh salad.

"The week of the motorcycle festival is always busy," said Angela, glancing over Lucy's shoulder.

"We don't get much of a break, and then the season will start."

"It's all good—right, Mom?"

Her mother picked up a chef's knife and began chopping with more energy than necessary. "Your father liked it. He just handled the paperwork. I had to do most of the cooking."

It wasn't the first time her mother had complained that she'd had it harder than Lucy's father over the thirty years Kebab Kitchen had been open. But Lucy knew Angela and Raffi had both labored hard when they'd worked full-time—her mother as head chef and her father as the experienced businessman who handled the ordering, inventory, invoices, timesheets, and payroll. Now they were semiretired, and Lucy was the manager and Azad was the head chef. Butch, their longtime African American line cook had stayed on to help. But it had been difficult for Angela and Raffi to completely relinquish their roles.

"Turn down the heat. You don't want to overcook the stew," her mom said.

Lucy set down her knife and lowered the gas flame. Her mother had been giving Lucy cooking lessons and, to everyone's surprise, mostly Lucy's, her dishes had come out not just edible, but tasty.

"I heard about what happened on the beach last night," Angela said as she worked.

Oh, no. Lucy knew how her mother worried about Lucy having put herself in danger in the past. Lucy had planned to tell her about last night, omitting any messy details.

"You read the paper?" Lucy asked. The *Ocean Crest Town News*, led by reporter Stan Slade, had printed the news this morning. Lucy didn't see eye to eye with Slade on most issues, but he'd reported the bare facts in the edition. The headline had read:

LOCAL LANDLORD, GILBERT LUBINSKI, FOUND DEAD ON THE BEACH. POLICE INVESTIGATING.

"I haven't seen the paper. Your father heard it from a customer at Lola's Coffee Shop this morning. God only knows why he likes to visit the coffee shop when he can make coffee here."

Lucy cracked a smile. "Maybe he likes the people, Mom. Lola Stewart's shop is always full of locals, not just tourists."

Angela snorted. "Maybe." She pointed a spoon at Lucy. "I'm just glad you, Emma, and Sally are all safe. Katie, too. What does Bill Watson know?"

"I haven't spoken with him yet, but Katie says he doesn't know much." Lucy checked that the stew was simmering, then replaced the lid on the pot. "Hey, Mom, what do you know about Melanie Haven?"

Angela resumed chopping. "The candy shop owner? She took over the boardwalk shop after her parents died. She remodeled the place and it looks nice. Townsfolk like her. Why?"

Lucy hesitated, not sure how much to tell, then decided it would be gossip soon enough. Nothing happened in a small town without word on the grapevine spreading as fast as lightning. "Melanie was with us last night, and I'm worried the police may consider her a suspect in Gilbert's murder."

Angela wiped her hands on a white dishcloth and turned to Lucy. "Really?"

"Gilbert Lubinski was her landlord. He wasn't always fair."

"Now, that doesn't surprise me. That man had his fingers in a lot of town rentals. Just ask Max."

Max? Why didn't she think of him? If anyone knew anything about shore rentals and housing in Ocean Crest, it would be her brother-in-law.

They worked side by side in silence as Lucy contemplated what her mother had told her. Lucy also had something else on her mind that she needed to discuss. "Easter is only a couple of weeks away, and I'd like to host Easter dinner in my new apartment this year. It will be a housewarming party and Easter celebration at the same time. I plan to invite Sally and Butch, Max, Emma, and Niari, and Katie and Bill. What do you think?"

Her mother stopped working to look at her. Lucy felt as if her breath was cut off, waiting for her response. Easter was the holiest of holidays, and her mother took every holiday dinner seriously. Lucy knew her mother was still put out by her moving into Katie's home a while ago, and now her own apartment. Angela and Raffi had made it clear that they'd wanted their daughter to move back home when she'd returned to Ocean Crest.

No way.

Lucy loved her parents, but she also knew they could be more than a tad overbearing. They'd probably wait up for her on Saturday nights.

"You want to host Easter? At that lady's second-floor home?" Angela asked.

"No, at *my* apartment, Mom."

Her mother drew her lips in thoughtfully. "Hmm. Will you serve lamb?"

"Of course." It wouldn't be a Mediterranean Easter without lamb. Her Armenian father would revolt if there wasn't lamb. Her mother was a mix of Armenian, Lebanese, and Greek, and she was just as discerning.

"Is Azad coming?"

"I haven't asked yet, but I plan to."

Angela nodded once. "Then we will come."

Lucy felt a thrill of triumph. It didn't matter that her mother wanted Azad at the Easter table so badly. She'd agreed to come, and that was an accomplishment in Lucy's eyes. She turned back to the stove before her mother could see the satisfaction on her face.

Months ago, her mother's insistence that she give Azad a second chance would have driven her crazy and she would have had a fast comeback. After all, Azad had broken her heart after college. But since then, he'd been quite persistent that he'd wanted a second chance to make things right, and things had heated up between them, in and out of the kitchen. She'd been unsure, but he had stayed to help as head chef when she'd needed him, which showed that he'd changed. Lucy hadn't regretted taking the leap into the romance department.

Of course, she didn't have to admit that to her mother or father.

They'd push for a wedding.

And Lucy wasn't *that* sure.

Half an hour later, the stew was ready and the

rice pilaf had cooked. The doors opened, and Lucy greeted customers from the hostess stand. The dining room looked quaint and cozy, with a vase of fresh yellow tulips on each table.

Lucy halted Emma on her way to take a customer's order. "Where's Max today?"

Emma clicked the pen in one hand and held her waitress pad in the other. "He said he would be on the boardwalk showing a potential buyer the minigolf."

Lucy tucked the information away. Soon all small talk stopped as the place got busy. Butch and Azad plated dish after dish, then called out numbers to Sally and Emma as their orders were ready for pickup. When Lucy had waitressed she'd been number six, her favorite number. It was an old-fashioned method, but an effective one. Lucy pitched in to help deliver meals to various tables as Sally and Emma were busy with orders or drinks.

"Food must be served hot or not served at all," Raffi Berberian always insisted.

Lucy scooped up a plate from the stainless-steel counter.

"Business is good today, Lucy Lou," Butch said with a wink from behind the cook's wheel.

"Just the way I like it," Lucy said.

Butch wore a checked bandanna on his head and had a gold tooth that flashed when he smiled. Tall, muscular, and broad, Butch had been the line cook at Kebab Kitchen since Lucy was in pigtails. He was one of the largest men she'd known, but he was friendly, soft spoken, and the last man to get in a bar fight or brawl.

Sally rushed over and took the plate from Lucy's hands. "Thanks, but I got this. Michael's here and asking for you. Looks like he wants personal service from our manager. Don't let Azad find out," she said with a wink.

Oh, brother. No sense arguing with Sally—once more—that she and Michael were only friends.

Michael sat at a table for two by the bay window overlooking the ocean. Lucy pulled out a chair and sat across from him. His blue eyes seemed even bluer with the sunlight streaming in the window.

"I wanted to be sure you're okay after last night," he said.

"I'm fine, but I'm worried about Melanie."

Michael was quiet for a moment, then nodded. "You should check on her."

"I plan to."

He opened his menu. "What do you recommend for lunch?"

"Lamb stew and rice pilaf. Tabbouleh for an appetizer."

He lowered his menu. "I'm starving already."

Lucy bit her bottom lip. She wasn't one to pass up an opportunity. She leaned forward and lowered her voice. "Hey, Michael. How well do you know your friends Pumpkin and Craig?"

"Like I said at the bonfire, we're motorcycle buddies and have ridden together for about three years. Why?"

She toyed with the strings of her apron. "It's just that both men got involved when Gilbert showed up on the beach."

"So? They were defending your friend."

Why was he sounding so defensive? "You're right. But it sounded like they *knew* Gilbert."

Michael shrugged and leaned back in his chair. "They probably did. Everyone knows everyone in Ocean Crest."

There was truth in that. It was one of the things that had initially bothered her when she'd first moved back home after quitting the firm. But the tight-knit community had soon grown on her. Neighbors looked out for one another, helped one another. Coming from the city, Lucy had quickly rediscovered the advantages of living in a small town.

Still, she wasn't about to give up on the suspects at the bonfire—and they were all suspects. "Pumpkin seemed most confrontational. What can you tell me about him?"

"Not much. He's a landscaper. Ask your dad. He put in the mulch beds and flowers here."

"He did?" She'd appreciated the blooming spring tulips and daffodils in front of the restaurant. For some reason, she'd thought her mother had planted them. She should have known better. Angela Berberian was talented in the kitchen, but she did not have a green thumb. Lucy recalled her mother purchasing an aloe vera plant to keep in the kitchen for small cuts or minor burns. The gardener who had sold it to her had assured her that they were easy plants to maintain. It hadn't lasted two weeks before rotting from overwatering.

"I don't mean to question you about your friends and—"

"Sure, you do."

The noisy conversation in the restaurant seemed a distant din as she focused on Michael's face. "Pardon?"

"I know that look in your eye, Lucy Berberian. Are you planning on investigating Gilbert's murder? Maybe with Katie's help?"

Just great. She wasn't sure how to answer that question, but Michael was a friend and she didn't relish lying to him. "I'm not sure yet." The truth. "I'll let you know."

"Well, if you want to know more, I have the perfect opportunity for you to talk with both Pumpkin and Craig."

"Another beach bonfire?"

"Nope. You haven't forgotten the big motorcycle ride down Ocean Avenue to Cape May, have you?"

The Bikers on the Beach Festival always had one big ride through the center of town and down the Garden State Parkway to Cape May. Friends and family sponsored each biker. It was part of their fund-raising efforts to benefit veterans.

"I haven't forgotten. Why?"

"Will you ride with me? Pumpkin and Craig will be there, too, of course."

Lucy's pulse pounded with excitement every time Michael asked her to ride on the back of his shiny, chrome Harley-Davidson. She'd gone from fear of the loud bike to loving the rides.

But to ride with him for the festival? It was customary for wives, girlfriends, or significant others to ride with the bikers. Azad wouldn't like it. Hostility radiated from both men when they were in the same room, but Lucy and Azad had moved past it. She was dating Azad, not Michael.

But the incentive Michael had dangled like a carrot in front of Lucy was as tempting as riding the Harley down Ocean Avenue. She'd get a chance to question both Craig and Pumpkin about Gilbert's death.

She grew aware of Michael's blue gaze as she contemplated his request. It was never really a question, was it?

"Yes, I'd love to ride with you."

Chapter Seven

Hours later, Lucy took a break after a busy lunch shift. It was usual for her to jog on the boardwalk or run errands or simply take an hour or two to herself before returning to the restaurant for a busy dinner shift. Her parents, Azad and Butch would cover for her.

Lucy went to the small office in the corner of the storage room and changed into navy shorts and a gray, faded Ocean Crest T-shirt. Even though it was April and there was still a chill in the air, she'd soon be sweating during her run. Her route was the same. She'd jog to the boardwalk ramp, run the length of the boardwalk, then make her way back on the beach. It was always harder to run on the sand. Even with a sea breeze, the sun blazed hotter, and her running shoes would sink in the sand and she'd have to exert more energy.

She made it to the boardwalk and chugged up the ramp. It was a pleasant spring afternoon and puffs of clouds dotted the blue sky. A rabbit darted across the path to the ramp and she smiled. Soon, Easter would be here and she looked forward to celebrating with family and friends. What could be a better housewarming than to host Easter dinner?

She set a steady pace. She loved the varied mix of shops on the Ocean Crest boardwalk. Different tourists and different items for sale on the racks outside the shops and the beautiful ocean view ensured her jogs would never be boring.

The boardwalk was busier than it had been in weeks. The shops always hoped for a boost in business during the Bikers on the Beach festival. Motorcycles weren't allowed on the boardwalk, but that didn't stop festivalgoers from walking the boards. Lucy spotted more than one Harley-Davidson T-shirt and leather jacket. The bikers weren't just men. Women bikers joined their male counterparts as they strolled from shop to shop, many sporting colorful tattoos on their arms and necks.

She passed two pizza shops, Harold Harper's T-shirt shop, and Madame Vega's psychic salon. She inhaled the scent of french fries and funnel cake. If she wasn't running to stay in shape, she would have indulged in fried food heaven. Lucy waved at the fortune-teller and Madame Vega, dressed in her signature blue turban with its large fake sapphire, waved back. A skinny, bald man with a T-shirt that read "DEA, Drink Every Afternoon," sat at a red, velvet-draped table as Madame read his tarot cards.

Lucy had never believed in the cards until a few months back, when they'd revealed more than she'd ever expected. She still didn't fully believe, but she no longer mocked the cards or doubted the longtime boardwalk psychic.

A loudspeaker blared, "Watch the tramcar please!" and Lucy jolted. She returned her attention to the boardwalk to see a bright yellow and blue tramcar heading in her direction. She moved to the side as the tramcar motored by. A Jersey boardwalk fixture, it carried twenty passengers—mostly senior citizens, parents, babies in strollers, or tired tourists—from one end of the boardwalk to the other. Two college students dressed in matching yellow-and-blue tops and black shorts worked the tram, one to drive it and the other to stand in the rear and collect the three-dollar fee. The loudspeaker and the endlessly repeating message could be an annoying inconvenience.

Lucy kept jogging, her running shoes pounding the boards. Since returning to Ocean Crest, she'd built up her endurance. The exercise was time to herself and her thoughts, and she'd often stop on the beach to sit on the jetty, watch the vast Atlantic Ocean, and sip from her water bottle.

But she had different destinations in mind today.

She spotted the hanging sign that blew in a current of ocean air: "Haven Candies." A young, pimply faced worker stood outside, handing out fudge samples. Lucy knew the part-time community college student who helped Melanie out between classes.

"Hi, Sarah,"

"Oh, hi, Lucy. Peanut-butter fudge today. Want

one?" Sarah held out a tray crammed with small cut pieces of fudge.

Lucy eyed the samples longingly. "What the heck. Why not?" She popped one in her mouth.

Heaven.

The creamy chocolate and peanut butter combo danced like a ballet on her tongue. She wanted another and eyed the plate like Adam must have eyed the forbidden apple in Eve's hand. That was the problem with sugar. One taste and she craved more.

"Melanie's inside and just about to make a batch of fudge."

Lucy glanced inside the candy shop's large bay window, and sure enough, Melanie appeared and picked up a large wooden handle and started mixing a batch of fudge in a copper pot. The sight of candy makers in the widows mixing fudge or pulling taffy was a tourist favorite. It was also a master sales technique, and customers would pour inside the shops to buy candy.

"Thanks, Sarah." Lucy forced herself to turn away from the temptation of the samples and made a beeline into the shop.

Melanie was stirring a pot of vanilla fudge mixture with a four-foot long, wooden paddle. Dressed in a white-and-blue-checked apron, a white hat, and a shirt emblazoned with the Haven Candies name and the logo of a piece of wrapped saltwater taffy, Melanie smiled in greeting. "Hey, Lucy! I'm making fudge. Want to help?"

"Sure."

Melanie's voice was cheerful, but there were dark circles beneath her eyes. Wisps of auburn hair escaped her hat to curl at her temples. It had been two days since the murder. Lucy would have come to check on Melanie sooner, but it had also been well after midnight before the police had allowed everyone to leave the beach and she was still recovering from the horrible events of that night. Detective Clemmons, along with the crime scene investigators, had to process the scene swiftly. No one would see crime scene tape on the beach. Everything, including any footprints, had washed away with the high tide.

Lucy was unsure how to ask about Melanie's welfare. Instead, she swallowed and then focused on the fudge. "What are the ingredients?"

"Twelve pounds of sugar, three quarts of cream, milk, and the chocolate wafers for chocolate fudge."

Twelve pounds of sugar! No wonder the fudge was so addictive. "What, exactly, are those?" Lucy asked, pointing to the bag beside the copper kettle.

"Pure chocolate wafers, no sugar. Try one."

Lucy popped one in her mouth and immediately wrinkled her nose. "Bitter!"

"Like I said, no sugar." Melanie added the wafers, mixed them in, then began to pull the fudge in the air in a three-foot ribbon of deliciousness.

Lucy watched, fascinated.

"Want to try?" Melanie asked. "There are aprons by the counter."

Lucy tied an apron around her waist and took the proffered handle from Melanie.

"Stir from front to back with the paddle, not in a circle," Melanie instructed.

Lucy began to stir the fudge in the copper kettle. It wasn't as easy as it looked and took a good deal of effort.

"Not in a circle, remember?" Melanie said.

She tried to pull the fudge with the paddle in a ribbon like she'd seen Melanie and other boardwalk candy makers do since she was a kid, but only succeeded in causing a mess and getting fudge on the pristine, white apron.

Melanie chuckled. "It takes practice."

"And stamina. I thought I was in shape from jogging. Your biceps must be like iron."

"I think I could hold my own in an arm-wrestling contest. Come to think of it, you should arrange one on the boardwalk."

Lucy was glad to see Melanie's first genuine smile. She waited until Melanie poured the fudge into square pans. "They'll cool overnight and then be ready to be cut and put behind the counter for sale." Melanie picked up two of the pans. "If you don't mind, can you carry the kettle into the back?"

"Of course." Lucy picked up the copper kettle and followed Melanie into the back of the shop. The kettle made a thud when Lucy placed it in the stainless-steel sink. "Gosh, it's heavy."

"Solid copper," Melanie said. "It's also old and was my parents' when they ran the candy store."

Lucy wiped her hands on a damp dish towel. "Melanie, the reason I stopped by was to check on you, and to be sure you are all right since the bonfire."

A pained expression crossed Melanie's face. "I can't believe Gilbert is dead."

"Have the police come around to ask you more questions?"

Melanie blinked, her brow furrowing. "No. Do you think they will?"

She did, but she also didn't see a reason to alarm Melanie. Not when her friend already looked ill. She decided vagueness was best. "I don't know." Lucy shifted awkwardly from one foot to the other. "Melanie, why didn't you want to make s'mores that night?"

Melanie untied her apron and hung it on a hook on the wall. "I told you. I make s'mores and fudge at the shop. I'm not tempted by candy like everyone else. It's just business to me. I thought to take advantage of having some time to myself on the beach."

Lucy believed her. "When you weren't with the rest of us, did you hear or see anything?"

"No. That's what I told the police."

"Nothing?"

Melanie's gaze held Lucy's. "No. You believe me, don't you, Lucy?"

"I do. But I heard you scream and ran to find you standing over Gilbert."

"I stumbled on his body," Melanie said in a low, troubled voice. "I screamed because I was shocked. Wouldn't anyone be to find him like . . . like that?"

Something flashed in Melanie's eyes, but it was gone as fast as it appeared. Was it a quirk of the sunlight from an overhead window, or something else? Was she reliving the horrifying moment?

Lucy watched her friend carefully as she responded. "Yes, I'd be, too."

Melanie began to wipe down the counter with a wet rag, her movements rapid and uneasy. "I know it looks bad. Everyone saw me arguing with Gilbert over my rent. I was by myself while the group made s'mores. I found his body. And the coroner pulled out a wad of my root beer saltwater taffy from Gilbert's throat."

When she summed it up like that, it sounded even worse. Lucy could just imagine what County Prosecutor Marsha Walsh would declare at a summation during a criminal trial. Lucy'd had more than one encounter with the smart, wily prosecutor at Kebab Kitchen in the past, and she didn't want another.

Melanie tossed the rag into a bucket and turned back to Lucy. "Can you do something for me? Can you look into who killed Gilbert?"

It was Lucy's turn to blink in surprise. "Me?"

"You've done it before, and I don't trust the police. Detective Clemmons thinks I killed him. He is looking for more evidence before he arrests me. I just know it. But I didn't kill Gilbert!"

The thing was, Lucy believed Melanie, but not entirely. Instinct told her that her friend was keeping something from her, but what and why?

Why not tell the police if it could help clarify things and take away any suspicion from herself? Why ask Lucy to investigate?

Even though her inquisitive mind had already started asking questions, it was still unnerving for Melanie to request that she investigate.

Melanie stepped close. "Please!"

Whether it was the desperation in Melanie's eyes or Lucy's own nature to help others, she found herself saying, "I can't promise anything, but I'll try."

After leaving Melanie's shop, Lucy continued with her jog. She wasn't sure what to make of her meeting with Melanie. She'd stopped by to check on her, and had been surprised at Melanie's plea for her to find the killer.

Lucy's instincts had told her something was off with Melanie. She wasn't sure what, but she'd learned over the years not to ignore the gut feeling in her stomach. Maybe she should backtrack and pay a visit to Madame Vega to see what the tarot cards might tell her.

No. She didn't have time to indulge. She had one more stop in mind. After running past a dozen more boardwalk shops, she spotted the flashing sign that read BOARDWALK BLACK-LIGHT MINIGOLF. Four apartment units were located above the minigolf, and Lucy knew that both year-long renters and seasonal renters occupied the units. She'd once asked Max about the units, but with their ocean views they were out of her price range. It wasn't too upsetting. She didn't want to live above a boardwalk shop. During the summer nights, the noise from the boardwalk and the screams from the roller coaster on the amusement pier could be heard blocks away.

She entered the place. Inside a small lobby, a woman with dyed auburn hair who was chewing a

wad of bubble gum and reading a fashion magazine sat behind a money-collecting booth.

"Hi," Lucy said. "I'm not here to golf, but to see
Max. I was told he would be here."

The woman glimpsed away from her magazine
to wave at Lucy. "Go on inside. The place is empty
this time of day."

Lucy stepped inside and blinked as her eyes adjusted from the bright sunlight to the darkness.

A large room showcased the neon putting
green. Holes were featured all around an outside
ring on an artificial felt green. Each hole glowed
in bright, fluorescent colors beneath ultraviolet
black lights. She glanced down at herself. In her
gray T-shirt and dark shorts, she was completely invisible, except for her glowing, white shoelaces.

The woman in the ticket booth had been right;
the place was empty. Lucy stepped onto the green
and walked from hole to hole. She'd played this
indoor course more than once and was familiar
with the displays—a turning windmill, a spinning
waterwheel, a medieval castle with a drawbridge
ramp, and others for a total of nine holes. All the
glowing holes required some skill with a player's
putter to progress to the next challenge.

The last hole featured a clown. If the ball landed
in the clown's mouth, the ball would be captured
in a trapdoor, and the player couldn't play additional rounds without purchasing another game.
The first player of a group to reach the clown
would win the round. The clown's curly, red hair
and garish scarlet lips glowed eerily, while its white
face shimmered an unearthly white. The clown

had always creeped her out as a teenager. Looking at it now, it still did, and gooseflesh rose on her arms.

Don't be a ninny!

She was older and wiser now. Clowns shouldn't scare her, even glow-in-the-dark ones. Taking a deep breath, she approached it hesitantly. She reached out to touch it, just as something smacked her hard in the center of her back and sent her flying forward.

Chapter Eight

❦

"Ouch!" Lucy stumbled forward to catch herself on the clown's glowing, red nose.

What the heck was that?

She whirled to see a dark figure running toward her.

Not a figure. A man.

Panic welled in her chest. She struggled to her feet as footsteps pounded toward her.

A firm hand settled on her arm. "I'm so sorry! I didn't see you. Are you all right?"

Eyes wide, Lucy focused her gaze on the man's face—then on a head of fair hair and the tall, wiry build. Recognition dawned. "Craig?"

"Lucy?" He dropped the putter he'd been holding in his free hand and it made a dull thud on the green felt.

"What are you doing here?" Her sluggish mind raced to put two and two together. He must have been golfing and hadn't seen her in her dark clothing.

Craig offered a hand and helped Lucy to her feet. "I'm meeting a real estate broker to buy this place. I figured I'd try my hand at the course while I waited. I apologize; I didn't see you."

Lucy took a couple of breaths to calm her racing heart. The clown, the stinging in her midback, and the shock of a dark figure racing toward her left her unsteady. "You're meeting Max? To buy this place?"

"Yes. Do you know him?"

"He's my brother-in-law."

"Go figure. Ocean Crest is a small world."

It sure was. Lucy brushed dirt from her shorts.

"Come on. Let's get out of this glow-in-the dark area so we can talk." He took her arm and steered her toward the exit. Both of them squinted at the brightness.

Peering back inside, Lucy could still make out the scary clown. She suppressed a shiver.

Craig eyed her from head to toe. "Are you sure you aren't hurt?"

"My back may be a little sore tomorrow, but I'll be okay." She was suddenly conscious of her old T-shirt and shorts with her hair pulled back in a ponytail. She suspected tendrils of her curly hair had escaped and probably looked like a frizzy halo in the shore humidity. She resisted the urge to smooth the wisps.

"I'm so sorry. I was taking a run through the course. I thought the place was empty," he said.

Craig was one of Michael's motorcycle-riding friends and a good guitar player, too. She'd never guess he'd enjoy minigolf.

"It's not your fault and I'm not exactly dressed to stand out," she said.

"Truth is, I didn't expect to see you so soon after what happened at the bonfire," Craig said.

"That was a tragedy, but I never had a chance to thank you and Pumpkin for standing up to Gilbert and helping Melanie. She's a friend," Lucy said.

"Any friend of Michael's is a friend of mine."

She thought about the evening. The way Craig had addressed Gilbert that night had made it seem like he'd known Gilbert, or had at least been somewhat familiar with him. But how? She was just about to ask him when another male voice caught her attention.

"Lucy, what are you doing here?"

Lucy whirled to see Max approach. Dressed in a button-down blue shirt and a red tie, a frown marred his brow. Her brother-in-law did not look happy.

"Hey, Max. I came here to see you, when I ran into Craig," Lucy said.

"Craig is looking to purchase the minigolf and the four apartments above it. I'm showing him the property," Max said.

He'd already told her he was thinking of buying the minigolf, but she'd forgotten about the apartments. Why would he want the four apartments that came with the business?

Lucy turned her attention to Craig. "I know we recently met, but I'm still surprised. At the bonfire, I learned you're a guitar player, a singer, and a motorcycle enthusiast, but not this," she said, waving her hand toward the nine-hole course.

"Tourists love the blacklight minigolf. What else is there to do during the season when it's raining and not a good beach day? Parents line up to bring their kids here," Craig said.

He had a good point. If there was a cold or drizzling day, there wasn't much to do on vacation at the Jersey shore except see a movie, hang out in a cramped hotel room, or play minigolf. The fact that the place was neon and indoors made it go-to entertainment during a rainstorm.

"The apartments above the place are an added incentive. I've been a landlord for years," Craig said.

"Really?" The only other professional landlord she'd known had been Gilbert Lubinski.

"Too bad your night out with your lady friends and Michael at the bonfire was ruined by Gilbert," Craig said.

"I wouldn't say Gilbert ruined our evening. The man was murdered," Lucy said.

Craig looked contrite. "You're right. I shouldn't be so cold. After all, we were business partners."

He was surprising her more and more. "You were?"

"We both owned equal shares of the Seagull Condominiums in Bayville. Have you heard of the place?" Craig asked.

Melanie had mentioned the condos, but Lucy had no idea Craig had been Gilbert's partner and owned a share. Bayville was close to Ocean Crest. As its name suggested, the town bordered the bay, not the ocean, and as a result, it wasn't as big with the tourists, but it was only a short drive to Ocean Crest and the beach. The Seagull Condos was a large, four-story complex. If there was no vacancy at the Sandpiper Bed and Breakfast in town or another close-by motel, a family could rent one of the condominiums during the season. Other residents lived in the units year-round.

Lucy recalled how Craig had acted the night of the bonfire when Gilbert had confronted Melanie about her rent. Pumpkin had stepped in, but Craig had also told Gilbert off.

"You didn't act like partners on the beach," Lucy pointed out.

Craig shrugged. "Ah, well. Gilbert and I didn't always see eye to eye."

"Business partners don't have to be friends to be successful, Lucy," Max said.

If they weren't friends, what had they been? Enemies? Rivals? And with Gilbert dead, who received the other half of the condominiums? They must be pretty valuable.

"Now, what did you want to talk to me about?" Max asked, his voice tense.

Lucy's gaze snapped to Max. It was clear he didn't want her to interfere with a potential sale. She got the message loud and clear. "Oh, no biggie. I wanted to invite you and Niari to dinner at the restaurant tonight. The special is lamb stew." Lucy wouldn't mind seeing her niece for dinner.

"Sounds good," Max said. "We can talk then, okay?"

"Good luck." Lucy was fine with the dismissal. She'd learned more than she'd hoped for. Giving a jaunty wave to both men, she headed for the boardwalk. She tried not to glance back at the clown on her way out.

*　　*　　*

Katie stopped by Kebab Kitchen after leaving work at the town hall that evening. She sat in one of the maple booths, plopped down her purse, and sniffed the air. "What smells so good in here?"

"Lamb stew. Want some to take home to Bill? My mom's in the kitchen, and she'd be happy to pack him a large takeout container."

"He'll be thrilled. He thinks your mother is all the bomb."

"She loves to feed people and is always trying to stuff food down my throat. If Bill moved in with my mom and dad, he'd gain ten pounds in a week."

"He wouldn't care." Katie placed her elbows on the table and leaned forward. "Now tell me again what both Melanie and Craig said. Starting with Melanie."

Lucy had already filled Katie in on both of her boardwalk visits. "Melanie wants me to investigate Gilbert's murder."

"That's a pretty big ask, even for someone with your history of solving crimes," Katie said.

"You mean *our* history of crime solving." Lucy rubbed her chin. "But you should have seen Melanie. She looked desperate."

"You still think she's innocent?"

Lucy fingered the napkin on the table as she considered the question. "I do. But there's something she's not telling me or the police."

"Such as?"

"I don't know. It's just a gut feeling."

Katie pursed her lips. "We need to dig deeper. Meanwhile, I looked into Craig Smith. He really was partners with Gilbert, and they each owned half the Bayville Seagull condominiums."

"I still can't believe it. They didn't seem to have anything in common." Thinking back to the night of the bonfire, they had seemed somewhat hostile. Not as angry as Pumpkin had acted toward Gilbert, but certainly *not* friendly.

"It gets better. Craig made several offers to buy Gilbert's share of the condos, but he refused. Gilbert then turned around and was in negotiation to sell to another buyer. Craig must have been furious, because three months ago, the Bayville police were called to break up a fight between the two."

Lucy looked at her in surprise. "How do you know that?"

"A few strokes of the keyboard at the town hall. All county police reports are public record."

"Craig didn't tell me *that*."

"I'm not surprised. It's motive for murder."

Lucy pursed her lips in thought. "So, who gets the other half of the Seagull Condos now?"

Chapter Nine

Dating a chef had its advantages. Azad knew food, and he also knew which restaurants offered the best cuisine in South Jersey. In the past, he'd taken Lucy to Le Gabriel, a French restaurant that required reservations months in advance.

Lucy wasn't sure what to expect the following evening, but when Azad showed up at her apartment with a full bag of groceries in each arm, she knew she was in for a treat.

"I thought we could eat in and I could cook for you."

Unsure where they were headed, she'd dressed with care in a light blue blouse and a gray pencil skirt. Azad looked good in a navy golf shirt. The color flattered his olive complexion and dark eyes and the tailoring emphasized his broad shoulders. She'd always found him attractive, even back in high school, and after spending eight years in Philadelphia and returning home to Ocean Crest, he'd grown even more handsome.

She held back a sigh. She was no longer a starry-eyed teenager. She was a grown woman in an adult relationship.

Gadoo came out from the bedroom to meow a big welcome and then rub against Azad's leg.

"Hey, Gadoo. Looks like you've made yourself at home here," Azad said.

"I think he misses you," Lucy said.

"No, he's happy to finally be with you full-time without your mom kicking him out of the storage room."

The cat meowed again as if to agree with Azad's comment, then padded off to curl up by the pink couch in the cat bed Lucy had purchased for him.

Lucy followed Azad as he set the bags on the kitchen counter. "What's on the menu?"

"It's a surprise." She watched as he unpacked the bags and the mysterious ingredients were revealed.

Shrimp. Scallops. Fresh ginger and shallots. Red and green peppers, broccoli, and mushrooms. Teriyaki and soy sauce.

Definitely not Mediterranean cuisine. Her curiosity grew.

"It's an Asian fusion dish I used to make where I worked," he said as he pulled out a bottle of white wine.

Azad had worked in a fancy Atlantic City casino restaurant as a well-paid *sous* chef before coming to Kebab Kitchen as head chef. She'd always wondered why he'd agreed. Was it because he'd always been fond of the small, family feel of the place? Or because her parents had given him his first job as a busboy, and his second as line cook in his teenage years, and then he'd felt indebted to Angela and Raffi as adoptive parents?

Or was it because of her?

He'd hoped to buy the place one day, but his plans had not come to fruition when Lucy had decided to stay in Ocean Crest and take a stab at managing the place. Azad had taken it in stride and had accepted the position as head chef.

He heated oil in a skillet and it began to sizzle. Meanwhile, he used a chef's knife to swiftly mince the ginger, shallots, and vegetables. Soon the delicious aroma of seafood stir-fry filled the apartment.

Lucy inhaled. "It smells great."

Azad kept mincing. "Can you pour some wine?"

She found two wineglasses and before she could ask, he took the opener from her, popped the cork, and handed the bottle back to her.

Lucy clutched the bottle. "You must think I'm useless in the kitchen."

Azad resumed working. "Not at all. I've been watching you and your mom in the kitchen. You're a good student."

He'd been paying attention. Lucy felt a swell of pride. "My hummus is good. Good enough to serve in the restaurant's hummus bar."

He halted to look at her then, his dark eyes unwavering. "I never doubted you."

This time, it was more than just pride Lucy felt. The invisible knot of attraction grew between them. She wanted to kiss him and show her gratitude.

Instead, she sipped her wine. "Hey, Azad. I'd like to host Easter here this year. It will be a housewarming party and Easter all rolled into one. Will you come?"

"I wouldn't miss it. I assume you're serving lamb?"

Of course he knew what she'd serve. A Mediterranean Easter wouldn't be complete without lamb. "My parents wouldn't come if I didn't."

"If you need help cooking, let me know," he said as he mixed the stir-fry.

Yes, dating a chef definitely had its advantages.

Lucy's stomach grumbled as Azad filled two plates. "Where would you like to eat?"

She glanced at the kitchen table, then decided she wanted a cozier atmosphere and led him to the coffee table before the pink sofa. She'd removed the plastic cover beforehand.

"It's more comfortable here." And more intimate sitting side-by-side.

Azad handed Lucy a pair of chopsticks. "Um, I'm not that good at using these." She held them awkwardly.

"I'll teach you."

They both chuckled at her failed attempts to grasp a piece of shrimp, then he scooted closer to show her how to properly hold the chopsticks. She didn't quite master them, but she managed to finish her meal without getting food on her clothes.

Afterward, they poured more wine. She wanted to tell him about her plans to ride with Michael through Ocean Crest for one of the bikers' events. But when he placed an arm around her shoulders and leaned in for a kiss, the thought flew from her head. He tasted like wine, ginger, and tantalizing male, and she leaned into him, comforted by his warmth and the hardness of his chest.

She sighed, kissed him back, and grasped a fistful of his shirt. The springs of the couch protested. She ignored the sound and tugged him closer.

A low growl sounded nearby.

Azad jerked back. "What was that?"

Cupid stood in the corner of the room. Gadoo left his cat bed and arched his back and hissed.

Not again! It was just a matter of time before a full-blown animal fight would take place to determine which one was the boss of the place. Her bet was still on Gadoo.

Lucy took one look at the cracked-open door leading to her landlady's downstairs living quarters. Her pulse raced, and not in a good way. "Mrs. Lubinski!"

Eloisa must have already been halfway up the stairs, because the door flew wide open and her landlady stood in the doorway. Lucy's eyes widened, both at her sudden appearance and her dress. The woman wore a full-length, sequined blue gown and tiara. She also wore a full face of makeup and fake eyelashes.

"Cupid!" Eloisa shouted.

The small shih tzu backed up one step, but kept growling at the cat. Gadoo hissed and his tail stood straight on end.

"Cupid!" Eloisa barked again, more forcefully this time.

The dog's ear's lowered and he reluctantly trotted over to his owner's side. As soon as Cupid had turned his back, Gadoo sprinted to the sliding glass door. Azad was already there and held it open for him. The cat took off down the deck stairs like a shot.

Eloisa reached down to pat the shih tzu's top-knot. "Cupid doesn't care for your kitty."

No kidding. Lucy's gaze returned to the tiara. Where the heck was she going dressed like that?

Eloisa's eyes traveled up and down Azad and her painted lips curled in a smile. "Well, well. Is this your chef?"

Lucy made the introductions. "This is Azad. Azad, this is my landlady, Eloisa Lubinski."

Azad came forward to shake Eloisa's hand, his dark eyes twinkling. "My pleasure."

Eloisa looked up, her plucked brows nearly disappearing into her hairline. "Wowee. I see why you pay him to stay with you."

Lucy choked. "It's not like that. He's the head chef at the restaurant I manage."

"Uh-huh. You still pay him to stay around, right?" Eloisa said.

Azad grinned from ear to ear. "She sure does."

Lucy didn't know who was more annoying, her landlady or Azad.

"Would you like a glass of wine?" Azad asked.

"She doesn't drink," Lucy said.

Eloisa blinked her fake eyelashes. "I'd love one."

Lucy glared at her. "But you said—"

Eloisa cut her off with a wave of her hand. "I know what I said, but a lady can change her mind, can't she?"

"Of course." Azad had reached for a glass in the cupboard and poured the wine.

Eloisa accepted the glass from him and broke

into a wide-open smile. She sipped her wine. "I could use a big, strong man to help me from time to time."

Azad bowed. "I'm at your service. All you need to do is ask Lucy to contact me, and I'll come over in a flash."

Lucy struggled not to roll her eyes. Really? She needed a big, strong man to help *her*, and her landlady was interfering. She reached for her own wine and drank. She knew Azad was being nice. Her landlady was alone and had recently suffered the loss of her nephew. Even if Gilbert hadn't treated her well—had treated her terribly, in Lucy's opinion—he was still family.

Now that Cupid was under control and Gadoo was somewhere roaming the streets, Lucy took a breath and calmed her racing pulse. "Mrs. Lubinski, you look . . . nice. Were you headed out?"

"Ballroom dancing at the senior center."

"How nice," Lucy said.

"I wasn't going to go this month. Gilbert hasn't even been buried, but my girlfriends convinced me. Said it's important for me to be with people right now."

Lucy felt even more sympathy toward her landlady. The gown, the tiara, the makeup, they could all disguise a grieving woman. Eloisa had said she wasn't particularly close to Gilbert, but that didn't mean she didn't mourn his passing.

"Easter is coming. It's the first time in my new apartment and I'm hosting my family and friends. If you don't have plans, I'd love for you to join us," Lucy said.

Eloisa turned to Azad. "Will you be there?"

"I will," Azad said.

"Count me in."

A car honking sounded from outside. Eloisa drained her glass and handed it to Lucy. "That's Phyllis. Don't want to keep her waiting. All the senior men will be taken if we don't get there on time. No sense ballroom dancing without a partner." She hurried to the door leading downstairs. Cupid was hot on his owner's heels.

Lucy made sure to firmly close the door behind her. It may not be a lock, but she didn't want any more intrusions from Cupid.

God knew, there'd been enough as it was.

Chapter Ten

"Your landlady is a hoot," Azad said.

"She has a crush on you," Lucy pointed out.

"She has spirit. I like her a lot, too."

"Don't let it go to your head."

Azad chuckled and led Lucy back to the couch. "Let's finish our wine."

Lucy needed no encouragement. She settled on the couch and rested her back in his arms. She was about to confess before they'd been interrupted. She turned in his embrace and looked up at him. "I need to tell you something. You know about the Bikers on the Beach ride down Ocean Avenue and to Cape May?" At his nod, she continued. "Michael asked me to ride with him and I plan to."

She took a deep breath and waited for him to respond. Her heartbeat escalated as Azad remained silent. She knew that she didn't have to ask for permission, but it was better if he knew her plans in advance. It was also best if she knew what his reaction would be. Instead of protesting or agreeing, he surprised her by tightening his arms around her.

"If we're confessing things, you should know something about my relationship with Gilbert," he said.

She was taken aback at the change in conversation from riding on the back of Michael's Harley-Davidson to Gilbert. "I didn't know you had one."

"We weren't buddies, but we weren't enemies either."

"Okay. Tell me."

Azad's expression stilled and grew serious. "Gilbert wasn't just a landlord, he was a loan shark of sorts."

A soft gasp escaped her. "A loan shark? You mean he lent people money at high-interest rates?" At least, that's what she'd read about loan sharks in the Atlantic City newspapers.

"Yes."

"And you were one of his customers?" she asked.

"Yes."

She recalled that Azad's loan application had been rejected by the Ocean Crest Savings and Loan when he'd sought to purchase Kebab Kitchen in the past. But that was well before Lucy had returned home and decided she wanted to manage the restaurant. She also remembered the bank's CEO had been murdered, and Azad had been a prime suspect. Thankfully, the true murderer had been found and everything had worked out for Azad . . . and Lucy.

But this was different.

"I know what you're thinking," Azad said.

She hoped not.

"I didn't borrow money from Gilbert to buy Kebab Kitchen. I borrowed it to fund part of my culinary school education. I received grants and federal loans, but it wasn't enough. Culinary school is expensive. I needed an additional five thousand to get me through, and I didn't want to ask your parents. They helped me enough in the past, and I know they're not cash rich. Word on the grapevine was that Gilbert Lubinski was the local man to go to for money."

This was news to her. She'd known Gilbert was a businessman, a landlord, and a nephew who wanted to kick out his eightysomething-year-old aunt and sell her ocean-view home for a tidy profit. But she'd never heard he'd loaned towns-folk money.

"Do you know of others in town who borrowed cash from him?" she asked.

Azad shrugged. "I don't know. It's not like Gilbert advertised or anything. His interest rates were higher than the bank's."

"Did you pay him off?"

"A while ago. I made a good salary working in Atlantic City as a *sous* chef."

He must have made more than what Kebab Kitchen paid him now. It was another mystery why he'd stayed to help. The way he was looking at her told her she'd had something to do with his decision. A tiny thrill raced down her spine.

"I don't know who else borrowed from Gilbert, but I know there were others. I didn't mail a check but paid him in person. Gilbert always came to my apartment to collect the monthly payments."

She wondered if Katie had heard anything about

Gilbert's loan-shark activities. Or Bill. She didn't think so. If the police knew, wouldn't Bill have mentioned it to Katie?

"You sure you don't know of anyone else in town?"

"Come to think of it, one time when Gilbert came over to collect a payment, his briefcase tipped over on my kitchen table and I spotted one of the file-folder names."

She sat up. "Who?"

"Kevin Crowley, the owner of the boardwalk tramcars."

"Mr. Crowley borrowed money from Gilbert?" Lucy asked.

"That's the name I saw." He leaned back on the sofa and studied her. "You're not thinking of digging into this, are you?"

He once told her she'd had a tell, a twitch by her left eye, and that he could figure out when she was lying. Azad had known her since before high school. There was no sense lying to him. "I'm thinking about it."

"I also know it's in your mind to question things. Always was. Even before law school," he said.

He *did* know her.

He took her hand in his larger one. "I know I can't tell you what to do, only to be careful doing it."

His understanding made her feel good, and she was glad to be with him. "Thanks for telling me about Gilbert and for dinner. It was delicious."

Azad stood and helped her to her feet.

She swallowed tightly, suddenly nervous. "Do you want to stay?"

He shook his head. "Not yet. Let's take it slow. I don't want to rush anything, and I want us to get it right this time."

Her chest tightened at his thoughtful words and the intense look in his gaze. She knew it wasn't that he didn't want to stay, only that he was thinking of their relationship. Their future.

She walked him to the door. He held his arms open, and she eagerly stepped into his embrace. His kiss was sweet and enticing at the same time. He pulled back to look into her eyes. "By the way, it's fine with me if you ride with Michael. I'm no longer insecure about us."

Early the following morning, Lucy knocked on Katie's front door. Dressed in workout gear of capris and a tank top, Katie opened the door. Her blond hair was pulled back in a messy ponytail. Loud music sounded from inside.

"I'm interfering with your workout." Lucy knew Katie exercised to DVDs most days.

"Cardio kickboxing." She stepped aside and held the door open. "Come on in and you can join me."

Lucy glanced down at her work uniform of black slacks and a button-down white shirt. "I'm not dressed for it."

"No matter. We can talk sleuthing. Bill's home."

Lucy followed Katie into the kitchen. Katie disappeared to turn off the TV and the pulse-pounding workout music. Lucy planned on telling her friend what she'd learned from Azad last night. She still couldn't believe Gilbert loaned out cash on the side. She'd known he was greedy. Who else would seek to toss out their elderly aunt from her home? But his greed went even farther. The tramcar owner was a place to start.

Lucy sat at the counter and spied a box of pastries from Cutie's Cupcakes. She flipped open the box to find an assortment of pastries.

Katie returned to the kitchen. "Hey, you found my stash."

"Is this why you're working out?"

"No way. I bought them for Bill."

As if she had summoned her husband, Bill, dressed in his work uniform, entered the kitchen. His blue eyes twinkled when he spotted Lucy.

"Hi, Lucy. We both miss having you around. Do you like your new place?" Bill asked.

"I miss the company, but it's nice to have my own space," Lucy said.

"We're coming over for Easter," Katie said. "Lamb, right?"

"Medium-rare. Just the way you like it. Azad said he'd help," Lucy said.

"Really? Then it will be much more delicious than if I cooked Easter dinner." Katie took a breath, then her blue eyes searched her husband's face. "Bill, tell Lucy what you've learned."

An expression of pained intolerance crossed Bill's features. "Katie . . ."

"I'm not asking for anything that will cause a conflict of interest for you," Katie said.

"Fine. There's no conflict because Calvin Clemmons is working the case, not me. I won't be a full detective for another month or so. But I know you two will nag me until I tell you something, so I can tell you what Clemmons is going to release to the press today. The coroner has confirmed that Gilbert Lubinski suffered a hit to the back of the head from the driftwood you saw near the body, but that's not what killed him. He died from suffocating on a wad of saltwater taffy."

They'd overhead the coroner at the bonfire, but for it to be official made it all seem much worse.

"Are you saying the murderer hit him with the driftwood and then shoved a piece of taffy down his throat until he stopped breathing?" Katie asked.

"So it seems," Bill said.

"Do they have a list of suspects?" Lucy asked.

"You mean other than your friend Melanie Haven?" Bill said.

"Melanie didn't do it," Katie said.

"How do you know?" Bill asked.

"Lucy's intuition," Katie argued.

Lucy's intuition also told her Melanie was hiding something, but that didn't mean she'd killed Gilbert. She decided to keep quiet about that for now.

Bill shot his wife a sidelong glance. "I don't think Lucy's intuition is admissible in a court of law."

"Gilbert was business partners with Craig Smith. They each owned half of the Seagull Condominiums in Bayville," Lucy said.

"The police know. You two do realize that we investigate, right?" Bill said.

Katie folded her arms across her chest. "Craig and Gilbert fought over a potential sale of the condos. There's a Bayville police report detailing the event."

Bill spoke without a hint of boastfulness. "We know that, too."

"Then you should be looking into Craig Smith, not just Melanie," Katie argued.

Bill glared at his wife. "If Clemmons had stopped investigating leads, then Melanie would be behind bars."

Lucy couldn't argue with that logic. She also wanted to tell him that Gilbert had been a town loan shark and that he'd loaned money to Kevin Crowley, the tramcar mogul, but held her tongue. She needed to talk this over and confirm it with Katie first.

"Is there anything else you can tell us, Bill?" Katie asked.

"Other than to stay out of it?" There was a bitter edge of cynicism in his voice.

Katie wasn't the least perturbed by it. She kissed her husband on the cheek. "Yes, other than that."

The show of affection had its desired effect. Bill's brow smoothed and he smiled down at his wife.

She is smooth! Lucy would have to learn how to calm Azad in the future. What could it take? A brush of the lips, a full-blown kiss, a massaging of the shoulders? Lucy wouldn't mind trying any one of those tactics.

"If it's any consolation, we're looking into Gilbert's wife, Sophia Lubinski," Bill offered.

Lucy blinked in surprise. "We didn't know he was married." She couldn't comprehend how anyone had found Gilbert's overbearing personality charming enough to marry.

"They were in the final processes of a nasty divorce. No life insurance, so no motive there," Bill said.

Another thought occurred to Lucy. "But as his wife, she'd inherit his half of the Seagull Condos. That's motive, isn't it?"

"Could be. I'm sure Clemmons will look in to it." Bill picked up his officer's hat and car keys from the counter. "I want to tell both of you to keep your noses out of this, ladies, but I also know better by now. Just promise that you'll stay out of trouble."

They nodded in unison.

As soon as Bill left for the station, Katie reached for one of the pastries in the box. "Give me a second to change, then we can talk more, especially about Sophia."

Lucy shook her head. "Forget about changing. Do you have any workout clothes I can borrow? A T-shirt and shorts? I wouldn't dream of fitting into your pants. I'd trip over them."

"Sure. Why?"

"We need to go for a boardwalk run."

Chapter Eleven

Lucy and Katie ran side-by-side. Katie was over six inches taller, and Lucy had to pump her legs faster to keep up, but months of training made it possible to stay in sync. It was before nine, and already a throng of early-morning joggers, walkers, and bicycle riders were on the boardwalk. The roller coaster on the pier was still; the rides wouldn't start until noon.

Lucy mulled what they'd so far learned. Craig and Gilbert had fought over the sale of the condos. Gilbert had been going through a nasty divorce that hadn't been finalized, and chances were his wife, Sophia, would inherit his share of the condominiums.

Then there was the information Azad had provided about Kevin Crowley. That was the reason she had dragged Katie to the boardwalk this morning.

They ran past the Breakfast Shack, and Lucy breathed in the tantalizing smell of freshly brewed coffee and toasted bagels when she heard, "Watch the tramcar, please!" blare from speakers from behind her.

"It's just on time," Katie said.

Lucy turned to see the oncoming bright-yellow-and-blue boardwalk tramcar. They halted by the iron railing, and Lucy raised her hand to wave at the approaching vehicle. The tramcar slowed, then came to a stop.

Together, Lucy and Katie stepped onto the tram and walked down the center aisle. Passing senior citizens, and parents with infants or toddlers in strollers, they finally spotted an open seat. They slid across the bench, their sweaty skin sticking to the plastic seat. The college-aged girl, who was dressed in the signature yellow-and-blue top and black shorts, approached, and they both paid with five-dollar bills. The girl reached in the money-belt tied around her waist and gave them change. Then the tramcar jerked forward as it began its crawl up the boardwalk. Walkers and bicyclists scrambled to get out of the tram's way.

"Does this thing stop at the end of the boardwalk?" Katie asked.

Lucy shrugged. "I don't know. I've never ridden it."

Katie shot Lucy an incredulous look. "Really? You grew up in Ocean Crest and you never rode the tramcar?"

"I guess I always jogged or walked, no matter how tired I was. If you've been on it, you should know where it stops," Lucy argued.

Katie glowered at her. "I've always ridden it back toward my home, not in this direction."

Lucy assumed the tram would stop at the very end of the boardwalk. She leaned back on the bench and glanced at the scenery. To the right was the ocean and the pristine Ocean Crest beach. A few beach walkers enjoyed a pleasant morning stroll as seagulls soared above. To the left, the boardwalk shops became a colorful blur as they drove by. Lucy spotted Madame Vega smoking a cigarette outside her psychic parlor. She waved and Madame waved back.

"Are you seeing the psychic regularly for romantic advice?"

Lucy's lips curved in a smile. "What makes you think I need any advice?"

Katie looked at her with renewed interest. "Ah, your date night with Azad went well? Did he spend the night?"

Lucy felt her cheeks grow warm. "Azad wants to take things slow."

"He must really like you. Either that or he fears for his job."

Lucy rolled her eyes. "Oh, brother. Now you sound like my landlady. She brought up the employer/employee relationship."

"She has a point," Katie said. "If you ask me, I think Azad likes working as head chef at Kebab Kitchen. I don't think he wants to go back to being a *sous* slave for some bigwig Atlantic City chef."

Lucy's brow furrowed as she contemplated Katie's words. She often thought of why Azad had stayed to help her as head chef after her parents announced they wanted to ease into retirement. She couldn't have managed the restaurant without him. She knew he felt strongly about the place, and he'd once mentioned that the restaurant was hard to leave. Once again, she pondered his motives. Had he stayed for her parents, the pull of the family restaurant, or her?

"I guess I haven't thought about it that way," Lucy said.

"Don't look so glum. I meant it as a compliment. Azad chose you, not a celebrity chef in a five-star restaurant," Katie said, then glanced ahead. "Look, we're coming to the end."

The tramcar slowed, then came to a stop by a custard stand.

Just off the end of the boardwalk was the municipal pier, where trash and recycling were stored until it could be transported to the county landfill. A small Bobcat and other construction equipment were parked on the pier, along with tramcars that weren't currently in use. From what she could see, three tramcars were parked there now.

"Let's get out and see if we can find Kevin Crowley," Lucy said.

She waved to the attendant. They hopped off the tramcar onto the boardwalk. The tramcar made a U-turn and headed back the way it had come, all the while blaring, "Watch the tramcar, please!"

"Ugh, I think I'd go insane if I had to work on the tram and listen to that message all day long," Lucy said.

"I may complain about working at the town hall, but it's heaven next to that," Katie said.

"Come on."

The municipal pier was a short walk from where they'd stopped. Rows of dumpsters and recycling containers were lined up like silent sentinels on one end. Three yellow-and-blue tramcars were parked in the middle of the pier. She walked by each tramcar, and didn't see a person in sight. It was eerily silent here, no tourists or cyclists or joggers.

Lucy sighed, disappointed. Her idea had amounted to a dead end. "No one's here. Maybe we should leave."

Katie placed a hand on her arm. "Not yet. What about that trailer at the end of the pier? Someone could be inside."

"What trail—?" Lucy's question died as she spotted the white-and-gray trailer beyond the row of dumpsters. "Good eye. I would have missed it."

Lucy wrinkled her nose as they passed the smelly dumpsters. In just a few weeks, they would be full to the brim with trash from all the tourists. She would never want to work in a trailer this close to the smelly receptacles. The only saving grace was that the trailer was located at the very end of the pier, and a steady gust of refreshing ocean air blew away most of the stinky smells. A few feet from the trailer, steps led to the beach.

Lucy approached the trailer, knocked twice on the door, then waited alongside Katie.

Nothing.

"Too bad. No one's here," Katie said.

Lucy reached for the door handle and found the trailer unlocked. She cracked it open an inch, then glanced over her shoulder. "Let's take a look."

Katie bit her bottom lip. "Are you serious?"

Lucy tugged on her arm. For all her love of

crime and detective television shows, Katie could get cold feet when faced with snooping.

"We'll make it quick. We won't have a better opportunity. If you're nervous, stand outside and keep a lookout. I'm going in," Lucy said.

Katie stiffened and shook her head. "No way! Two can search faster than one."

Lucy was relieved to have her friend's help. She opened the door and stepped inside the trailer. Katie was right behind her. It was a small and narrow space. An oak desk and filing cabinet occupied almost half the trailer. A stack of papers piled on the corner of the desk were held in place beneath a stone paperweight. Two plastic folding chairs were in front of the desk.

"You look at the papers on the desk, and I'll look in the filing cabinet," Lucy said.

Katie was already reaching for the paperweight. "What are we searching for?"

"Anything that mentions Gilbert Lubinski, especially any loan papers."

Katie began sifting through papers, and Lucy opened the top drawer of the filing cabinet. She flipped through neatly labeled file folders and spied invoices from mechanics to repair the tramcars, to timesheets for the employees who worked on the trams.

"There's nothing here," Katie said.

"I'm not finding anything unusual either."

Katie neatly stacked the papers and placed the paperweight on top. "I have a bad feeling about this. Let's get out of here before we're discovered."

"All right."

Katie reached for the doorknob just as voices sounded outside the trailer. Wide-eyed, they looked at each other.

"Oh, no," Katie said.

Lucy's gaze flew to the back of the trailer, but there was no entrance or exit other than the one they'd come through.

Crap.

"What do we do?" Katie whispered.

Lucy's mind whirled. The voices were directly outside; their options were limited. Hide or 'fess up to snooping.

"Sit in front of the desk," Lucy said.

"What?"

Lucy pulled out one of the plastic chairs. "Sit. We can claim we were waiting for him."

Seconds later, the door opened. A balding, middle-aged man with brown hair and a thick mustache walked inside. He was dressed casually, in a short-sleeved, collared shirt and blue jeans, and carried a clipboard in his right hand. He halted when he spotted them. "I didn't realize I had company waiting for me."

Katie stood and extended her hand. "Hello, Mr. Crowley. I'm Katie Watson, and this is Lucy Berberian. We're with the township, and we are planning to run a series of articles in the *Ocean Crest Town News* about local business owners. We were wondering if we could interview you. You'd be our first."

Lucy masked her surprise. For someone who'd had the jitters about searching the trailer, Katie had come up with a great lie and backed it with bravado.

At the mention of an article, Mr. Crowley's hostility at finding two intruders in his trailer visibly eased. He pumped Katie's hand, then Lucy's. "Kevin Crowley at your service. Please sit."

Lucy's heart pounded as she resumed her seat. Mr. Crowley sat behind his desk, his chair springs squeaking as he leaned forward and folded his hands on the desk. "What would you two like to know?"

A small notepad and pencil materialized from Katie's purse. She flipped open the notepad. "How'd you start this business?"

"I didn't. My daddy did. Tramcars are the family business. Everybody needs a ride now and then," Mr. Crowley said.

"Very true. We grew tired during our jog and rode your tramcar today," Lucy said.

"Good to hear," Mr. Crowley said. "I've been thinking of raising the three-dollar fee to four-fifty."

"That's a big hike," Katie said.

"More tourists visit Ocean Crest every summer. My trams usually run full during the season," Mr. Crowley said.

Lucy took a breath and asked the question that had been on her mind. "Have you heard about the murder of Gilbert Lubinski on the beach?"

He hesitated, his eyes meeting hers. "I have. All crime is a shame, let alone a murder," he said.

"Did you know Gilbert?" Lucy asked.

"Not particularly. I run a tramcar business. He was an Ocean Crest landlord. We didn't socialize."

"You knew he was a landlord?" Katie asked.

Mr. Crowley steepled his fingers on the desk. "Ocean Crest is a small town. Business owners are familiar with each other. One of my college-aged workers needed an apartment rental. I sent her to Mr. Lubinski."

"That was thoughtful of you," Katie said.

"Why all the questions about Gilbert? I thought you were interviewing me for an *Ocean Crest Town News* article." He leaned forward in his seat and glowered at them. "Come to think of it, why are you doing the interviewing and not Stan Slade from the paper?"

Oh no. Time to go.

"Like I said, I work for the township," Katie said. "We are conducting preinterviews to determine who we want featured by the *Town News*. I'll then reach out to Mr. Slade for a full-blown interview."

Suspicion glinted in his gaze. "And my interview has to do with Gilbert Lubinski?"

If there was one thing Lucy had learned in law school, it was to never show nervousness or weakness to an opponent. She tilted her head to the side and met his gaze. "A murder is big news anywhere, let alone our own small town, Mr. Crowley. People want to know how local businessmen like yourself are faring. That's the only reason for our inquiries."

Mr. Crowley regarded her, then nodded. "Although I'm sorry for his family, I'm faring just fine. Business hasn't suffered."

Both Lucy and Katie stood. It was time to make a hasty exit.

"Thanks for your time," Lucy said. "We will be in touch about the interview."

* * *

Lucy waited until they were back on the boardwalk before turning to Katie. "For not wanting to search Mr. Crowley's trailer, you sure thought fast on your feet. An interview for a *Town News* article about local businessmen? How'd you think of that?"

"I don't know," Katie said, kicking a small shell out of her path. "It just sprang to mind. Something I saw on an episode of *Hawaii Five-O*. You recovered pretty quick yourself when you told him murder is big news and that people want to know how it has effected local business."

"I wish I could point to a crime TV show."

Katie halted by the custard stand and pulled out a ten-dollar bill from her shorts. "After that close call, I need sugar. I'm buying. Don't whine about the calories."

"I'd never complain about custard." Lucy smiled at the college-age boy behind the counter as she ordered. The custard was a Jersey shore favorite.

Minutes later, they were seated by a bench overlooking the ocean and licking their own cones. Lucy had ordered an orange-and-vanilla twist—one of the custard stand's most popular combinations. Katie's tastes were simpler; she enjoyed a vanilla-and-chocolate twist in a sugar cone.

An ocean breeze teased tendrils of hair that had escaped Lucy's ponytail. In the distance, she spotted the jetty she often stopped at during her jogs. The limitlessness of the Atlantic Ocean was calming and had a way of making even the most complex problems seem small. Today, the ocean was calm and puffs of cloud dotted the sky.

"What do you think about Mr. Crowley?" Lucy asked.

"He said he didn't interact with Gilbert, but then he referred his employee to Gilbert for an apartment. Sounds like Kevil Crowley knew Gilbert a bit better than he'd like us to think."

"It doesn't mean he murdered Gilbert," Lucy said. "What he said was also true about business-people being familiar with each other. My parents know many of Ocean Crest's business owners. My dad always says, "It's a small world; don't misbehave.""

"We didn't find anything to link him to Gilbert, especially any loans. And he wasn't on the beach the night of the bonfire."

"Not that we saw him. Did you notice how close the trailer was to the steps leading to the beach? He could easily have walked onto the beach that night," Lucy said.

"You're right. It was dark. We weren't exactly looking for others."

Lucy licked her cone. "He had opportunity, but like you said, no motive—or none we know of."

"We're no closer to finding suspects. Detective Clemmons still has Melanie Haven on his suspect list," Katie said.

"If only the coroner didn't pull a wad of her taffy out of Gilbert's throat." Lucy finished her custard and tossed a napkin in the trash can. She hated to think of Melanie as a murderer. She couldn't picture it. But she also couldn't shake the nagging feeling that Melanie was hiding something.

They began jogging back and passing all the shops they had seen on their way during the tram-car ride. This time, Madame Vega had a customer in her salon. She sat at a table and was reading a man's palm, not tarot cards.

"Madame's a jack-of-all-trades, isn't she?" Katie said.

"I don't know about palm reading, but she's skilled with tarot cards."

"Maybe I need to see her to talk about Bill. She might have insight on when he'll be promoted to detective," Katie said.

They came to Haven Candies. Sarah was outside handing out fudge samples again. Lucy was determined to avoid the loaded tray. Custard *and* fudge and she'd have to run every day this week.

"Look! Taffy."

Lucy's gaze followed to where Katie pointed. The saltwater taffy machine was pulling taffy like a large, yellow elastic band in the window of the candy shop. Lucy wondered what flavor it was.

Lucy waved to Sarah, then headed inside the candy shop. Melanie was arranging boxes of salt-water taffy on a table.

"Hi, Lucy. Hi, Katie," Melanie said with a smile.

"What kind of taffy are you pulling in the window?"

"Banana taffy. You want to try a piece when it's done?"

"We just stopped by for a quick hello. But we also have some questions. We heard rumors about Gilbert Lubinski," Lucy said.

Melanie slipped a hand inside her apron pocket

and worried her bottom lip. "What kind of rumors?" Melanie asked.

"Rumors that Gilbert wasn't just a landlord, but that he lent money to locals in town. Have you heard of anyone borrowing money from Gilbert?"

"No."

Lucy studied Melanie's expression carefully. "Melanie, have you ever borrowed money from Gilbert?"

"No! He was my landlord. Nothing else." When Lucy and Katie stayed silent, Melanie rushed on. "I would never borrow money from that horrible man. He was unfair to deal with as a landlord; I couldn't imagine him as a lender." She shivered, as if the thought repulsed her.

Her reaction seemed sincere. Yet Melanie must have had trouble paying her rent if she was arguing with Gilbert about raised rent at the bonfire. Lucy knew firsthand that owning a business was tough work, and that there were months a business didn't earn a profit. Certainly, the winter months at the Jersey shore weren't as profitable as the summer season. And if a business had a hard summer due to weather, a lag in tourism, or any other factor, it would be doubly difficult.

Lucy picked up a box of chocolate nut fudge. "I know you're busy. I'll take one of these for my mom. She loves your fudge."

"It's on the house." When Lucy opened her mouth to protest, Melanie pressed the box into Lucy's arms. "I insist."

"Then you have to visit Kebab Kitchen soon for baklava."

Melanie smiled. "I look forward to it."

As soon as they returned to Katie's house, they filled large glasses of ice water. Lucy leaned on the laminate counter in Katie's kitchen as she sipped.

"We're no closer to finding any leads. We didn't find anything incriminating in Kevin Crowley's trailer, and Melanie had no idea about Gilbert's unethical lending habits. So where do we go next?" Lucy asked.

"Sophia Lubinski," Katie said.

"The wife on the verge of divorcing Gilbert?" Lucy asked.

"She doesn't have to go through the trouble of a nasty divorce now, does she?" Katie pointed out.

"True. But Bill said Gilbert didn't have a life insurance policy."

"If the divorce wasn't final, then chances are Sophia inherited Gilbert's share of the condos," Katie said.

Lucy had already considered this, but something else was bothering her. Sophia's motive needed to be fleshed out. "Not necessarily. There could have been a prenuptial marital agreement preventing her from getting her hands on those condos."

"Even so, we may be overlooking another motive. Maybe Sophia hated Gilbert enough to want to kill him. It's not that far-fetched. Bill always says spouses and significant others are often the killers. *Columbo* and *Matlock* had plenty of spousal murderers, too."

Lucy chuckled. "Good to know television backs up the real cops." Before Katie could protest, she said, "but you're right. We should question Sophia."

"Great minds think alike. We need to find out where she'll be and corner her when she's not expecting us. Any ideas?" Katie asked.

Lucy tapped her foot. "My landlady might know her schedule. She was her aunt-in-law, right?"

"It's worth a try," Katie said. "But you'd better make sure Gadoo isn't around when you ask her. For all her dog's bark and bravado, your cat's claws just might make mincemeat of him."

Chapter Twelve

It turned out Lucy had to wait to talk to Eloisa. Her landlady had an active social calendar—much more active than Lucy's. She wasn't home all day and Lucy had to return to work.

After a busy lunch service, the dinner shift started steady. Guests began tumbling in and didn't let up for hours. Lucy helped seat customers and then walked around the dining room, stopping at each table to be sure all the guests were enjoying their meals. Azad had prepared sole stuffed with Mediterranean herbs, along with rice pilaf and freshly baked pita bread. And Butch had added *tan*, a cold yogurt drink, to the dinner menu.

After the dinner service had slowed and only a few customers remained drinking coffee and enjoying pieces of baklava, Lucy walked into the storage room with a clipboard in hand.

"The dreaded inventory?" Azad asked as he glanced up from where he'd been searching the stainless-steel shelves for an item.

Lucy wrinkled her nose. "It's Saturday. I have to finish taking inventory so that I can prepare our ordering on Sunday and have everything ready for our suppliers bright and early Monday morning."

His lips curled in a slow, sexy smile. "How about we go out sometime next week as a reward? We can hit Mac's Irish Pub."

Lucy's pulse pounded at his smile and his offer. "Mac's sounds great."

He plucked a big bag of rice from the top shelf like it was thistledown. Her gaze traveled to the muscles in his biceps. Azad had always worked out, but he seemed to be in better shape now than when he was in college.

"I'll leave you to your fun task." He winked, then returned to the kitchen.

Lucy scanned the rows of shelves. Just great. She disliked inventory and estimated it would take at least a couple of hours to complete tonight.

The office door in the corner of the storage room opened, and Raffi Berberian stepped out. He smiled when he spotted her and came close.

"I thought you'd gone home by now, Dad," Lucy said.

"I was finishing up the insurance paperwork."

"I'm supposed to do that now."

"Nonsense. Your mother and I are easing into retirement. We aren't ready for a nursing home."

"I didn't mean it that way," Lucy protested.

He took off his reading glasses and tucked them into the pocket of his shirt. "I know, sweetheart." He glanced at the clipboard in her hand. "Do you need help with the inventory?"

The faster she got out of here, the sooner she'd be able to question Eloisa about Sophia's whereabouts. But she was the manager now, and inventory was a big part of her job. "I can manage."

His eyebrows drew together and he leveled an all-too-familiar parental look of concern her way. "Don't be stubborn. It's Saturday night. Don't you have a date with Azad?"

Stubborn? When it came to stubborn, Raffi Berberian's picture should be displayed by the word's definition in the dictionary. Rather than argue, Lucy bit her tongue. "No. We are going out another night."

"Ah. You just want to go home."

"I do. I could go home a lot faster if we used an electronic inventory system."

"We talked about this, Lucy. Our system works just fine. I did it this way for thirty years," he said.

She swallowed her frustration and aimed for a calm and logical tone. "Times have changed, Dad. Taking notes by hand and then cross-referencing everything with our supplier's orders is archaic and time-consuming. Inventory and ordering can be completed simultaneously with a computer system. It would be so much easier to carry my iPad instead of this clipboard."

Raffi shook his head. "If it isn't broken, don't fix it."

"Oh, please. You said that about replacing our old, wooden storage room shelving with this new stainless-steel shelving and it all worked out. Adding dining room ceiling fans worked out, too."

"The shelving took too long to install. And installing ceiling fans was a much smaller job than changing our entire inventory and ordering system."

Granted, the shelving had taken longer than she'd expected. But it wasn't her fault. The factory that made the shelving had gone on strike, and then the local handyman she'd hired to install the shelves had thrown out his back. It had been nearly impossible to find another one during the summer season. Thankfully, Azad had stepped up and put the shelving together. It had been another way he'd shown her how much he cared.

"Dad, it will save countless hours. You entrusted me with managing the place, so why do we have to butt heads over every little change?"

Raffi's dark, earnest eyes searched hers. "Fine. Get some estimates. I promise to consider them."

She kissed his cheek. "Thanks." For all his stubbornness, her father was softhearted when it came to his daughters and his wife. She just needed to remind him of the long-term benefits versus the costs.

A thought occurred to her as her father stood by her side. He'd survived in a tough business for thirty years and had been a fixture in the Ocean Crest business community. She'd told Katie that all business owners were familiar with one another in the small town. She'd been referring to tramcar owner Kevin Crowley at the time. But Raffi and Angela Berberian had been around even longer.

"Hey, Dad, do you know anything about Haven Candies on the boardwalk?" Lucy asked.

"Sure. The finest fudge and saltwater taffy around," Raffi said. "The parents founded the candy shop around the same time your mother and I opened Kebab Kitchen."

Lucy tapped her pen on the clipboard. "That long ago? Melanie Haven, the daughter, now runs the candy store."

"I guess the older sister didn't want it," Raffi said.

Lucy's fingers ceased tapping as she looked at her father in surprise. "Melanie has an older sister?"

"Yes. I think her name is Rhonda. She's about ten years older than Melanie. Rhonda reminds me of your own sister in a way. Emma likes working here as a waitress, but she doesn't have the business savvy or interest to manage the place."

Lucy didn't think about Emma. She was too preoccupied thinking about what she'd just learned. Melanie had never mentioned an older sister before, and because Rhonda was that much older, Lucy wouldn't have known her when she went to high school with Melanie years ago. But was it important?

"Dad, where's Rhonda now?"

Raffi shrugged. "Last I heard, she married a wealthy salesman. I don't even know if she's living in town."

Lucy didn't know if this information was relevant or not. She made a mental note to tell Katie. Meanwhile, she had to tackle the inventory and then seek out her landlady and learn everything she could about Gilbert's mysterious wife, Sophia Lubinski.

*   *   *

Tracking down her elderly landlady was proving to be a challenge. Eloisa still wasn't home when Lucy returned that night. Lucy changed into sweatpants and an old Ocean Crest High School sweatshirt, then scrubbed her face free of all traces of makeup. After a busy lunch and dinner service, then inventory, she was exhausted. All she wanted was to collapse in front of the television with a glass of wine and cuddle with Gadoo. Instead, she peeked outside whenever a pair of headlights shone through the window in anticipation of Eloisa's arrival home.

It had been ten o'clock when Lucy had last looked outside. Where could the woman be?

She poured herself a glass of white wine and looked at the couch, but at the last minute, she longingly glanced outside onto the deck. Rather than sit inside to constantly get up and peek out the window, she'd enjoy her deck. Besides, she could hear Eloisa's car park in the driveway if she was already outside.

Lucy carried her wineglass and opened the sliding glass door. Gadoo followed. She sat on one of the patio chairs and the cat leaped onto her lap. She stroked Gadoo's soft fur as he purred.

"Don't get too comfortable. As soon as Mrs. Lubinski's home, you have to stay upstairs. No more confrontations with Cupid."

Gadoo's yellow eyes cracked open.

"I mean it. I won't have any more battles. You two need to learn how to get along."

Gadoo turned up his nose as if to say, "Don't hold your breath."

The moon cast an iridescent glow on the ocean. The calming sounds of waves eased her nerves and left her with her thoughts. A cool blast of air blew in from the ocean, and Lucy was glad for her heavy sweatshirt. She sipped her wine and glanced over the sand dunes, past the dark beach and beyond.

A shadow crossed the path from the dunes toward the beach and took the form of a man. He hesitated, then glimpsed up at the deck before turning back around. Because he was dressed in dark clothing and a beanie hat, Lucy couldn't make out his face, but she had the distinct feeling he was hiding in the dunes, looking at her.

Weird.

Gooseflesh rose on her arms. Was he watching her? Or was she imagining things?

"Do you see that, Gadoo?"

The cat's yellow eyes glowed in the moonlight, then he leaped off her lap to prowl the deck. He stopped by her feet and arched his back.

The cat's behavior was as unnerving as the appearance of the mystery man on the beach.

Lucy blinked and leaned a bit forward in her chair. The figure turned and, for a heart-stopping moment, stared straight ahead—at her. Then he disappeared into the darkness.

She pushed back the chair and stood. "Time to go inside." Her heart beat fast and she didn't breathe easy until she and Gadoo were both inside and the sliding door was shut and locked.

She was acting paranoid. The beach was far below her second-floor patio. Maybe the stranger had spotted the outside patio light and noticed her sitting outside. He hadn't looked at her for very long, not even a full minute. He was probably out for an evening stroll on the beach for solitude.

She pushed her uneasiness aside. She had a different agenda in mind for tonight, one that involved her landlady and not a possible beach stalker. Besides, she was safe in her upstairs apartment.

Headlights flashed through the window, and Lucy jumped up to peer outside. "Finally!" She scooped up Gadoo and dropped him on the pink sofa. "Sorry, Gadoo, but you have to stay here. It's for your own good." Gadoo shot her a menacing look, then began licking his paw.

Lucy waited until she heard the downstairs door open, then cracked open the door leading to the first floor.

"Mrs. Lubinski?"

Cupid immediately started a high-pitched barking.

Good. Better than a doorbell.

Lucy crept down the stairs, all the while keeping a lookout for the killer little dog. "Mrs. Lubinski?"

"If the hot water heater is broken, you have to wait until tomorrow. I won't call for an emergency plumber." A disgruntled voice drifted up the stairs.

Lucy wasn't deterred. In the kitchen, Eloisa was filling a teakettle with water at the sink. She was dressed in a flowing pink dress with lace-up sandals. Lucy didn't know how she wasn't cold. It was a chilly April evening.

"It's after ten o'clock. Where were you?" Lucy asked.

Eloisa shuffled to the cabinet and reached for the shelf holding the mugs. "You're my tenant, not my mother."

"I was worried. Besides, there's something I want to talk with you about."

Cupid yawned and settled on a round, red dog bed in the corner of the kitchen. The shih tzu must be getting used to her. Either that or he'd decided she wasn't much of a threat.

"I was at purse blingo," Eloisa said.

"Blingo? What's that?"

Eloisa looked at her like she was an idiot. "Blingo is where all the prizes are designer handbags. The Protestant church hosts it once a month for charity. You have to have heard of it. Do you live under a seashell or what?"

Lucy struggled to maintain her temper. "I've been working at the restaurant. I guess I haven't had much time."

"Humph. How about some green tea and then you can ask me what you want?"

Lucy eyed the mug. "Is it decaf?"

"It is. Don't worry. It won't interfere with your beauty sleep."

The teakettle whistled, and Lucy turned off the stove as Eloisa fetched another mug, a box of tea, and a sugar bowl. Lucy poured the hot water and joined her at the kitchen table.

After adding enough sugar to cause diabetes, Eloisa looked at Lucy. "Okay. Shoot."

Lucy sipped her tea, unsure of how to bring up the subject without upsetting the woman. "I keep thinking about finding Gilbert. I know you must be mourning your nephew's death, and—"

"Like I said. I'm not surprised. That boy had a habit of angering folks around town. And we weren't the closest of relatives. The only time Gilbert visited me was to tell me I was too old to live by myself. I saw through his phony concern. He only wanted my house."

Lucy shifted in her seat. "That must have been horrible."

"You're looking into things." It was a statement, not a question.

Lucy blinked in surprise. Eloisa Lubinski may be in her eighties, but her mind was sharp as a tack. What to say? She could deny it, but she knew Eloisa would doubt her answer. She decided on the simple truth. "I am."

"That candy seller is your friend. Word on the street is she's the number one suspect," Eloisa said.

"Melanie didn't do it."

"The police have me on their list, too."

"What? Why?" Lucy asked.

"I told that detective I walked home on the beach the night Gilbert was killed. If that cop has any brains, he has to consider me."

Lucy understood that Detective Clemmons was doing his job. In the past, she may not have agreed with him, but she understood why he was keeping both Melanie and Eloisa on the suspect list. She didn't have to like it or agree, but she understood.

On the other hand, she would also think Clemmons would quickly eliminate Eloisa as a suspect. There was no way she could have killed her own nephew, even if he was a jerk.

"Has Detective Clemmons asked you to come to the station to answer more questions?" Lucy asked.

"Not yet."

"If he does, will you promise to tell me?"

"Why?"

"So I can find you a lawyer," Lucy explained.

"You're a lawyer. You do it."

If she had a dime for every time someone asked her *that*, she'd already be rich. "I'm a patent attorney. I've never practiced criminal law. They're very different. It would be like going to a podiatrist for brain surgery."

Eloisa lowered her mug. "I already have a foot doctor who shaves my corns. Come to think of it, Doctor Ted is single. Not as good-looking as your dark-haired chef, but if things go south between you two in the kitchen, bagging a doctor is never a bad idea."

Lucy gaped at her. "Mrs. Lubinski! I'm not talking about dating your podiatrist. I'm talking about the police dragging you into the station and interrogating you. Now, promise me you'll tell me."

Eloisa waved a hand. "All right. Don't get your panties in a knot. I promise." She picked up her mug and slurped her tea. "Now, if you're sticking your nose in the murder, who do you think did the foul deed?"

Eloisa's pointed gaze made Lucy squirm. "I wanted to ask you about Sophia, Gilbert's wife."

"That rat trap? She is a money-grubbing lady. If there was anyone greedier than Gilbert, it was Sophia. Those two deserved each other."

Harsh words, but Lucy suspected they were true.

She didn't know Sophia Lubinski, but if Eloisa thought she was greedy, Lucy didn't doubt it.

"You think Sophia killed Gilbert?" Lucy asked.

"I'm not saying that, but it wouldn't surprise me if she did. Those two were like cats and dogs going through their divorce. She hired an aggressive divorce attorney and told Gilbert she was taking him to the cleaners. He said she wouldn't get a dime from him. Thank God they didn't have kids."

Hatred was a strong motive, but if Sophia wanted to take him to the cleaners and get as much cash out of the marriage as she could, what else was she after? "My friend Katie said there wasn't a life insurance policy."

"Gilbert let it lapse. She was angry as a hornet about that, too. But the woman should finally be satisfied. She gets Gilbert's share of some ritzy condominiums he owned in Bayville."

So, there wasn't a prenuptial agreement. Lucky Sophia! The divorce hadn't been finalized, and as Gilbert's wife, Sophia would be his legal heir. Real estate prices at the Jersey shore had risen over the past decade. Max was always spewing out figures whenever he visited the restaurant. Lucy suspected the Seagull Condos were worth a tidy sum.

At Lucy's silence, Eloisa nudged her arm. "You think Sophia killed Gilbert?"

"I'm not saying that, but I'd like to talk to her," Lucy said. "Do you happen to know her schedule?"

"She's a yoga fanatic. Rises early every Sunday morning and goes to the Yoga Palace."

Perfect. Tomorrow was Sunday, and she knew how to get to the place. Lucy drove by the Yoga

Palace on her way to Holloway's, the town's family-owned grocery store. She'd never been inside the yoga studio, but it was an opportunity to observe Sophia and, hopefully, ask her a few questions.

She jogged the boardwalk and considered herself fit. How hard could yoga be?

Chapter Thirteen

"**I**'m going to die." From the doorway, Lucy gasped as she watched the instructor as she led the class into its fifth downward facing dog.

Katie chuckled, but the sound held little mirth. "I've never liked yoga."

They had arrived at the Yoga Palace at five forty-five in the morning. The attendant must have stepped away from the front desk, and Lucy and Katie had wandered inside and stuck their head inside a doorway to observe a class.

"I'm surprised you don't like yoga," Lucy said. "You were always athletic in high school."

"Athletic, yes. But flexible?" Katie shook her head. "Not so much."

"Then this will be a challenge for both of us. Whatever the instructor is doing makes them all look like pretzels."

A voice from behind them made both Katie and Lucy jump. "Welcome to the Yoga Palace. Is this your first time?"

Lucy whirled to see an attractive, middle-aged woman with a French braid, wearing a Yoga Palace T-shirt and black tights, standing behind them.

Lucy cracked a smile. "It is our first time. Our friend, Sophia Lubinski, recommended the Yoga Palace and claims it's the best on the Jersey shore. She mentioned a free trial."

The woman's face lit up. "How nice! I'll be sure she gets our referral bonus. Please follow me."

They trailed behind her to the front desk. "Do you know if Sophia has arrived this morning?" Lucy asked.

"Not yet. Do you two have mats or yoga blocks?" the woman asked, a chipper tone to her voice.

"No," Katie said. "Do we need them to try a class?"

"Don't worry. You can borrow ours. If you decide to join today, you get a ten percent discount, plus a new yoga mat," the woman said.

One look at the yoga room and Lucy had decided to stick to jogging on the boardwalk, but Katie was convinced they could glean something from Sophia.

The five o'clock morning class ended and a stream of women began filing out of the yoga room.

"Oh, look! Here comes your friend now," the woman said as she glanced out the front door. "I'll leave you all to catch up. Excuse me while I make sure everything is set for your class." She bounced away.

The front door opened and Sophia entered. Dressed in spandex pants and a tight athletic bra, her bleached-blond hair was styled in a high pony-tail and she wore makeup. A purple yoga mat was tucked under her right arm. She headed straight for the yoga room.

"Time to get flexible," Katie said.

Lucy followed Katie into the room and they set up their mats on either side of Sophia. Sophia didn't appear to notice. She had slipped off her Crocs and begun a series of impressive stretches on her mat. Lucy wouldn't have been surprised if she split the seam of her tights.

Lucy slipped off her running shoes and socks and made a pretense of stretching, all the while watching Sophia out of the corner of her eye.

"Are you Sophia Lubinski?" Lucy asked.

Sophia froze in a straddle and looked at Lucy. "Yes. Do I know you?"

"No. But I'm sorry about your loss. We knew Gilbert," Lucy said.

Sophia's gaze shuttered. "Oh. Thanks."

Just then, the instructor entered. She was a tall, fit and athletic woman who sat with her legs crossed and addressed the crowd. "Good morning. Let's start by meditating for a full minute. Shut your eyes and empty your thoughts of worries and troubles and focus on a positive day ahead."

They all sat in silence for a minute. Lucy cracked her eyes open and observed Sophia. The woman's lip gloss glimmered beneath the fluorescent lights.

"Now we can begin," the instructor said. "Move into a downward facing dog. Our first position of the day may feel stiff until we warm up."

"You must be fearful," Katie said.

Facing downward, Sophia turned her head to look at Katie. "Fearful? Of what?"

"Your husband was murdered. Aren't you afraid the killer will come after you?" Katie asked.

Sophia swallowed. "The thought had never entered my mind."

"Move smoothly into a plank position," the instructor called out.

Lucy held the plank pose. Thirty seconds . . . a minute . . . a minute and a half. Her arms started to shake.

"Now lower and arch your back in the cobra position."

Thank goodness. She needed more abdominal workouts. But her relief didn't last when the class went through numerous other difficult positions.

"You think Gilbert's murderer will kill again?" Sophia asked.

Clearly, Lucy's question had been working on Sophia's mind. "Most serial killers don't stop with one murder," Lucy said.

"Serial killers!" Sophia squeaked.

People turned to stare at them. "Shh," the instructor called out. "On your backs for bridge pose."

After a full minute, Lucy's lower back began to scream in protest. How long could they hold this ridiculous pose?

"Don't worry. My husband is a police officer," Katie added. "He says most serial killers are captured by the third murder."

Sophia's face flushed and she began to tremble, but Lucy didn't think it was from their uncomfortable position.

The instructor glared at them this time, then shouted a bit too loud, "Warrior pose."

Lucy rose and copied the instructor by standing with her feet apart and her arms stretched out to her sides. It was a more comfortable pose. But it wasn't to last.

"Now we will test our standing balance with the tree," the instructor said. "Stand with your feet together and place your right foot on your inner left upper thigh. Press your hands together in prayer and close your eyes and breathe."

Lucy could barely lift her foot above her calf without wobbling. Katie was having a harder time. Tall and thin, she had trouble with balance and looked like she would topple over at any second. Sweat beaded on her brow. After several unsuccessful attempts to stand on one foot, she gave up and rested the toes of her right foot on the ground.

A full hour later and after five more challenging positions, the class was finally over. The instructor placed her palms together and said, "Namaste."

Sophia rolled up her mat and glowered at Lucy and Katie. "I don't remember seeing either of you, and I was familiar with most of Gilbert's friends and acquaintances. Come to think of it, there was never a mention of a serial killer from the police. Who are you really?"

Lucy clutched her own rolled-up mat under her arms. "We were on the beach the night your husband was killed."

Sophia stood taller. "So? Maybe one of you two did it."

"That's funny, because the police always suspect the spouse," Katie said.

Lucy wanted to slap a hand over Katie's mouth. They wanted Sophia to talk, not clam up in anger.

"Are you kidding me? In Gilbert's case, there's a list a mile long of people who disliked him," Sophia said. "He wasn't exactly well-liked."

"Do you know of anyone who disliked him enough to murder him?" Lucy asked.

"There's an entire building full of people. You should talk to his tenants in the condos he owned just outside of town."

"As his wife, don't you inherit part of those condos now?" Katie asked.

A murderous look flashed across Sophia's face. Maybe Lucy was wrong and Katie had it right. Get her mad enough to see what she'd do or say.

Sophia planted her hands on her hips and narrowed her eyes. "If you're looking to pin his murder on me, you're out of luck. I wasn't near the beach that night."

"Where were you?" Katie asked.

"Let's just say I have a fondness for bikers. I was at Mac's Irish Pub hanging out with the motorcycle riders for the festival. A dozen people saw me. Just ask Mac MacCabe himself." Sophia tossed her ponytail, then sashayed out of the studio.

Once outside the Yoga Palace, Lucy collapsed in the passenger seat of Katie's Jeep and sipped her water bottle. She'd be sore for a week, but it had been worth every second.

"Did you see how angry Sophia became when I mentioned she'd inherit the condos?" Katie asked.

"How could I miss it? I had to force myself not to back up a step and drag you with me just in case she lashed out," Lucy said. "She has to have muscles from that yoga class. She's strong enough to clock her husband with a piece of driftwood and knock him out. Suffocating him afterward would have been easy. It all fits, except for her alibi."

Katie tapped her fingers on the steering wheel. "You believe Sophia's story about being at Mac's Irish Pub the night her husband was killed?"

Lucy rested her water bottle on her knee. "I don't believe a word out of her mouth, but I can double-check her alibi. Azad wants to take me to Mac's Pub one night. I can ask around to see if people remember seeing her at the pub the night of the bonfire."

"Good for you. I want the juicy details of your date night with Azad, too."

Lucy rolled her eyes. She was looking forward to her date, but she wasn't prepared to talk to Katie about everything when it came to her relationship with Azad. She may have known Azad most of her life, but every moment between them was now too new. "We're taking it slow, remember?"

"Whatever. That's the same line Bill gave me back in high school."

"Everybody's hormones were raging back in high school," Lucy argued.

Katie and Bill were the only couple she knew who were still together from high school. Katie had been obsessed with crime-fighting shows even back then, and when Bill had announced he was going to the police academy instead of college, Katie had been crazy for him.

Katie shot her a sly look. "And your hormones aren't still in full swing?"

She had a point. Why else would she catch herself sneaking glimpses of Azad's chest when he reached up for an item on the storage room shelf or his biceps when he chopped vegetables with record speed in the kitchen? He looked good, plain and simple. "I'm a bit older and wiser now," Lucy said in her defense.

"Fine. I'll give you that. But I still want details afterward."

"Whatever. Let's not talk about my relationship with Azad, but what we learned about Sophia."

Katie rubbed her chin with a thumb and forefinger. "You're right. I say it doesn't matter if Sophia does get Gilbert's share of the Seagull Condos. If Sophia's alibi checks out, we're at another dead end."

"I'm not ready to throw in the towel. Sophia did give us a bit of a lead when she told us to talk to Gilbert's tenants. They may give us some clues. But meanwhile, tomorrow is the motorcycle festival's ride down Ocean Avenue. I'm riding with Michael."

Katie almost dropped her keys. "You are? What about Azad?"

"He knows. I told him. Azad understands that

Michael and I are just friends. Besides, Pumpkin and Craig will be there, too."

"You plan on asking them questions?" Katie asked.

"I suppose I have a double motive for riding with Michael."

"You are sly, girl. Let me know what you find out."

Chapter Fourteen

Lucy sifted through time sheets on the desk in the restaurant's office. She'd risen extra early on Monday to get through paperwork and payroll so that the rest of her morning would be free. No one else was in the restaurant and it was quiet. Kebab Kitchen didn't open until lunchtime, but there was always paperwork to handle behind the scenes. Running a restaurant wasn't always glamorous.

She pushed back her chair and banged her elbow on the corner of the filing cabinet. It was a ridiculously small office, but they needed every square inch of the storage room for the restaurant's supplies. A desk, a filing cabinet, and shelves just about fit in the office. The desk was littered with papers and the shelves were full of samples that suppliers often gave to her father to try out new products. Her mother had always been picky about the menu, and her father had ended up donating most of the canned goods and boxed products to the local food pantry.

Now that Angela was semiretired, Azad was the one to go through the samples. He turned out to be just as selective, and it would be Lucy's job to gather everything and drive to the food pantry.

But she wouldn't make that trip today.

A familiar thrum pounded in her veins. She'd be doing something else this morning. Something infinitely more exciting than payroll.

She left the office door just as a low knock sounded on the storage room door. Reaching for the doorknob, she found Michael standing outside. His dark hair brushed the collar of his leather jacket and his blue eyes were ringed with dark lashes.

"It's a beautiful day for a ride." He leaned casually against the doorframe.

"It is," she said. The weather could swing either way at the Jersey shore in April. Rainy and cloudy or sunny and warm. Today, not a rain cloud dotted the blue sky.

"You ready?" he asked.

Lucy scanned the asphalt. "Where's your motorcycle?"

"At the bike shop. We're meeting Pumpkin and Craig there, too."

She'd dressed for riding with a pair of jeans and a long-sleeved shirt. She followed Michael outside, locked the door, then walked with him across the restaurant's parking lot to the fence that separated Kebab Kitchen from Citteroni's bicycle rental shop. They strolled along the fence to the sidewalk, then stepped onto Michael's property.

His Harley-Davidson was parked in the driveway. The garage door was open, and Lucy spotted rental bicycles, tricycles, and four- and six-person surreys parked inside. Michael's father, Anthony Citteroni, owned the bicycle rental shop and Michael managed the business.

Anthony was a famous fixture in town and owned many businesses, including Laundromats, trash services, and the bicycle rental shop. He was a bit shady, and if the rumors were true, he used these businesses to launder money from his other—not so legal—Atlantic City activities. Lucy had met Anthony on several occasions, but no matter how often she encountered Michael's father, the man still sent a nervous chill down her spine.

When Anthony needed someone to run the bicycle shop, Michael had stepped up to help with the family business. It was one of the things Lucy had in common with Michael, other than coming from ethnic families who could be overbearing at times. As business neighbors, they'd formed a unique friendship.

An extra helmet with a skull and crossbones painted on its sides hung by its strap on the Harley's handlebars. Michael helped Lucy secure the helmet's strap beneath her chin. "Pumpkin and Craig will be here any minute."

Michael sat on the motorcycle, and Lucy climbed on the back of his bike just as two motorcycles pulled into the driveway and stopped beside them.

"Hey, Lucy! Good to see you again." Pumpkin's long hair stuck out from the back of his helmet. He wore a T-shirt, and an eagle tattoo was visible on his large biceps.

Craig sat tall on his motorcycle. "Ready to ride?"

In response, Michael's bike roared to life. Lucy's

pulse leaped with excitement as the three Harleys drove out of the parking lot and down Ocean Avenue.

Soon the loud roar of dozens of motorcycles pierced the crisp morning air as they joined a long line of riders of men and women. The ride was a tradition of the Bikers on the Beach Festival. A woman with a bullhorn stood behind a table with a banner that read, "Donations for Veterans." Dotting the street were food trucks and vendors selling a range of items, T-shirts, sweatshirts, leather vests and jackets, and other apparel, as well as banners and handheld American flags. The food trucks offered egg, bacon, and cheese sandwiches; croissants, bagels, and pastries to satisfy the morning riders and spectators.

The bullhorn crackled. "We're only a thousand short of our ten-thousand-dollar target. Don't wait to donate!"

"My father said he'd donate a grand," Michael said.

"Wow! That's generous," Lucy said.

Michael's leather jacket creaked as he shrugged his shoulders. "He served in Vietnam."

"I didn't know." Lucy had never suspected that Mr. Citteroni had served in the military. He'd never mentioned it.

"He doesn't talk about it, but I know it weighs heavily on him. He lost good friends." The helmet blocked her view and she couldn't see Michael's expression clearly, but the tone of his voice was telling. It was the only time he'd spoken of his father in a sympathetic voice.

She'd never look at Mr. Citteroni the same way again.

"My parents donated, too." Lucy didn't know why she felt compelled to offer this, but she felt grateful for all those who served in the military, past and present. She'd known the motorcycle riders collected donations for veterans, but she'd always thought they just wanted a reason to ride their loud motorcycles at the shore.

Now, she was looking at them through different eyes.

The woman with the bullhorn walked to stand at the front of the pack. She raised an American flag, engines revved, then she waved the flag, and the riders took off. Lucy held on to the sides of Michael's leather jacket as he rode down Ocean Avenue. Out of the corner of her eye, she spotted Pumpkin and Craig beside them.

A crisp flurry of air ruffled her shirt, and she breathed in the fresh ocean air. The first time she'd ridden with Michael, she'd been anxious and tense. She'd only agreed because he'd had information she needed to solve a crime. But something magical had happened during her first ride—her fear had flown away along with the wind. Then they'd ridden at night, and she'd been entranced by the stars that had glittered like diamonds in a black, velvet sky. They'd passed the boardwalk, and the bright lights of the Ferris wheel had blurred into a colorful array of jewels.

But today, they were riding in daylight, and a brilliant goldenrod sun shone in the sky. As they turned onto the Garden State Parkway toward

Cape May, the large group of riders separated. Pumpkin and Craig rode in front of Michael, and the three stayed together. Lucy's grip relaxed and she enjoyed the ride.

Once again, she was riding with Michael to gather information from his friends about a murder. Her motives were the same, but her hesitation to climb on the back of his bike was long gone.

They picked up speed as they drove off the ramp and onto the highway. She felt like one of the seagulls that circled above, flying and free. She could see the drivers' faces as they rode, and knew they weren't going faster than the speed limit. Too soon, they came upon the sign for the Cape May exit, and Michael veered off toward the ramp. Pumpkin and Craig followed.

She spied the Cape May lighthouse in the distance. Michael had taken her there months ago and they'd climbed the spiral staircase, all one hundred and ninety-nine steps, to the top for a spectacular ocean view. They weren't headed there today.

They rode down wide streets lined with hundred-year-old sycamore trees and passed lovely Victorian homes that looked like exquisite gingerbread houses. The historic homes with their wraparound porches with rocking chairs and exquisite woodwork made Cape May a tourist attraction. They passed a dozen of the houses, many with brightly painted spindles of burnt sienna, violet, indigo, and bright pink.

Most of the riders would enjoy a day in Cape May before returning to Ocean Crest. Some would visit the lighthouse and the beach, others would eat at the dozens of well-known restaurants, while others would simply stroll the streets and enjoy the Victorian homes.

Michael pulled into the lot of an old-fashioned ice cream parlor. Pumpkin and Craig stopped beside them.

"Ice cream and a motorcycle ride all in one afternoon? You're spoiling me," Lucy said.

Michael lowered the kickstand. She stepped off the bike first, then he followed. He helped her remove her helmet and hung it on one of the Harley's wide handlebars, his own on the other. "I know you want to talk. What better place than here?"

The Freezy Cone was crammed with tourists and locals on the pleasant afternoon. The scent of freshly baked waffle cones drifting on a puff of air made Lucy's mouth water. She'd been here before as a college student, and the place was known for its dozens of homemade flavors. By the time they made it to the front of the line, she was drooling. She ordered a double scoop of mocha chocolate delight topped with chocolate syrup and rainbow sprinkles in a waffle cone.

At her first taste, her eyes closed in pure delight. "Oh my gosh, this is so good."

Michael, who had ordered chocolate chip cookie dough ice cream topped with extra whipped cream, nodded. No need for words.

She hadn't eaten at the restaurant and she had a monster appetite, but this ice cream needed to be eaten slowly and appreciated. A family of four left a picnic table, and Lucy and Michael quickly occupied it. She was careful to avoid the sticky caramel sauce that had been left behind on the end of the bench. They waited for Pumpkin and Craig to order and join them.

"We hadn't planned on ice cream, but who's complaining?" Pumpkin said as he dipped his spoon into his banana split.

Craig's ice cream sundae wasn't as big but looked just as tempting.

Michael eyed Lucy above his own cone, and a corner of his lips turned into a grin. She knew that look. He watched her, his blue eyes a combination of amusement and intrigue. He was anticipating her questions.

Lucy swallowed a spoonful of sweet mocha chocolate. "Pumpkin, I noticed the landscaping at Kebab Kitchen. The daffodils and tulips are very pretty. Do you do it on the side?"

Pumpkin lowered his spoon. "No, it's my full-time business. Pumpkin's Landscaping. Haven't you seen my trucks around town?"

She hadn't, but she nodded.

"Yeah, well, I do a lot of business outside of town, but my client base is growing in Ocean Crest. Your mom hired me for Kebab Kitchen's flower beds."

"You must be good. My mom is very picky."

"Not as picky as others in Bayville."

She stuck her spoon in her ice cream and eyed him. "Wait. You said Bayville? Any connection to the Seagull Condos Gilbert partly owned?"

Pumpkin snorted. "Nope. I did work for Gilbert, but it was for the two side-by-side townhomes he owned in Bayville."

Gilbert had owned yet another piece of property? Lucy's thoughts turned back to the night of the bonfire. Gilbert had showed up and started harassing Melanie, but *both* Pumpkin and Craig had come to her defense. She'd learned Craig had been equal partners with Gilbert with the Seagull Condos. But she'd never suspected Pumpkin had known Gilbert as well.

"Were you business partners with Gilbert, too?" Pumpkin snorted. "Not on your life."

Craig spoke up. "Pumpkin was spared the pleasure. I was the one who had to deal with Gilbert Lubinski as a partner."

Lucy couldn't envision the pair working together. Craig seemed levelheaded and kind. Maybe he'd had it with Gilbert strong-arming his tenants and that was why Craig wanted to buy out his share. Or maybe there was a different side to Craig, a more violent one. According to Katie, Craig and Gilbert had fought badly enough for the Bayville Police to show up and write up a report.

It made Lucy look at Craig in a different light. He had been at the bonfire and could have slipped away when the group had been making s'mores. Everyone had been drinking, and no one would have noticed if someone had left for a short period of time. Craig may not be as muscular as Pumpkin, but he was certainly strong enough to lift a piece of driftwood and strike Gilbert on the back of the head, then suffocate him.

Pumpkin cleared his throat and Lucy's attention returned to him. "Gilbert hired me to handle the landscaping for the townhomes. In the beginning, I thought it would be good, steady work. There was always something to do year-round, flowers and mulch in the spring and summer, weeds and leaves in the fall, and snow removal in the winter. But he turned out to be a big pain in the butt."

"What do you mean?" Lucy asked.

"He didn't pay on time."

She couldn't fathom this. Gilbert had a steady stream of income from his tenants. Or had he been strapped for cash? Was that why he'd raised Melanie Haven's rent?

"What'd you do when he didn't pay?" Lucy asked.

Pumpkin's face broke into a wide grin and revealed a gap between his two front teeth. "I dug up his flowers. Had fun doing it, too."

"You didn't just stop doing the work?"

Pumpkin scoffed. "He owed me over a grand. I did stop, but damned if I was going to drive by the place and see my hard labor, knowing I didn't get a dime for it."

In a convoluted way, his argument made sense. "How did Gilbert respond? Did he pay your bill?"

"Nope. He showed up at my greenhouse raving mad and threatened to set it on fire. I laughed in his face. If there was one thing about Gilbert, he was all hot air and couldn't pack a solid punch."

She didn't know many men who were physically bigger than Pumpkin O'Connor. Still, Gilbert couldn't have been all hot air. Not if he'd gotten into fisticuffs with Craig. And not if some Ocean Crest residents had owed him money and were fearful of him.

Lucy took another bite of ice cream as she studied the two men before her. "Did either of you two borrow money from Gilbert?"

Craig looked at her in surprise. "No. Where'd you hear that?"

Lucy shrugged. "Gossip travels like wildfire in town."

"I'd never borrowed a dime from him," Pumpkin said.

"Me either," Craig said.

Michael spoke up for the first time. "It looks like it's going to rain. We'd better head back."

Lucy glanced at the sky. A few dark clouds hovered overhead and blocked much of the sun. She'd been so engrossed in questioning the two men before her, she hadn't noticed.

The rest of her ice cream had melted into soup. It was for the best. She'd lost her appetite after listening to both men. Her mind was racing instead. Craig had been partners with Gilbert with the Seagull Condos. Pumpkin had provided landscaping services for Gilbert's townhomes and was unpaid for his work. Both men had reason to dislike Gilbert.

But was that motive enough for murder?

Were a few unpaid bills for daffodils and tulips enough to kill someone in cold blood?

Craig had the stronger motive. As business partners, he'd been mad that Gilbert rejected his offer and gone behind his back to sell his share to another. But could she envision him as a killer?

She wasn't certain, and if there was one thing she'd learned, it was not to jump to conclusions without all the evidence.

Pumpkin and Craig headed back to their motorcycles. Michael touched Lucy's arm. "Did you learn what you needed?"

She may have gotten answers today, but she was left with even more questions.

Chapter Fifteen

The Ocean Crest Town Hall was a redbrick building located in the center of town across from the library. It was also connected to the municipal court and police station, but had its own separate entrance. Katie often joked she could visit Bill at work if she could just walk through the wall that separated them. As town clerk, Katie handled everything from taxes to zoning to renewing dog and cat licenses.

Lucy found Katie refilling a mug of coffee in the break room. "Can you take a lunch break?"

"Sure. Why?" Katie set down her mug on a laminated counter crowded with sugar packets, powdered creamer, and tea bags. An open box of muffins from Cutie's Cupcakes rested by the coffee machine. One lonely muffin was left inside.

"I spoke with Pumpkin and Craig during our motorcycle ride to Cape May. There's a lot going on in Bayville. We should check it out."

"I'll fetch my purse and keys."

Lucy held up her own keys. "No worries. I'll drive."

Fifteen minutes later, Lucy spotted the sign for WELCOME TO BAYVILLE. Katie sat in the passenger seat of Lucy's Toyota, directing her from her cell phone GPS. "Turn right here."

The light turned yellow and Lucy stopped.

"You should have let me drive," Katie said. "We would have been there by now."

Katie tended to drive like a NASCAR driver and push the lights. "We're not in Ocean Crest. You'd get a ticket."

"You think I'd use Bill as an excuse to get out of a speeding ticket?"

"It can't hurt to be married to a cop in town."

Katie rolled her eyes. "I always drive the same, in or out of town."

"That's why I wanted to drive." The light turned green and Lucy made the turn. A tall building came into view, along with a sign that read "SEAGULL CONDOMINIUMS." "Besides, we're here."

Lucy turned into a spot for visitors and put her car in Park. "We're in luck. Tenants are out and about." An older, white-haired couple walked hand in hand. A young mother in yoga pants and a sweatshirt pushed a stroller. A man in a business suit rushed to his car.

Katie unfastened her seat belt and reached for the door handle. "Let's see what they have to say about their deceased landlord." She walked toward the mother, then made a show of glancing into the stroller. "What a cute baby! How old is she?"

The young mother pushed a stray lock of dark

hair from her forehead and beamed. "Nine months today."

"She looks like an angel sleeping." Katie's gaze traveled from the sleeping baby to the mother. "Have you lived here long? My friend and I are thinking of renting," she said, motioning to Lucy, who stood behind her.

"We've been here a year. It's convenient to my husband's work. He's a plumber. It's also a close drive to the beach. I'd live in Ocean Crest if I could afford it."

Lucy took a step forward. "Maybe someday you will."

"What about your landlord? Do you like him?" Katie asked.

"He's okay. Or I should say *was* okay." The mother lowered her voice. "He was murdered."

"Wow!" Katie feigned a horrified expression. Lucy followed suit and placed a hand on her chest.

The baby woke from its sleep and began to fuss. The woman began rocking the stroller back and forth. "The former landlord's business partner seems much better."

"What was wrong with the one who died?" Lucy asked.

"Grumpy. You could never be a day late. He harassed my neighbor, Janet, over it. He couldn't just evict her. There are landlord/tenant laws he had to obey. But Janet had a toy poodle, and he said he was changing the rules and not allowing pets. She was quite upset."

"What happened?"

"The weirdest thing was, her dog died a week later. He was only two years old and didn't have any health problems. To this day, Janet swears Mr. Lubinski had something to do with it. She claimed he poisoned her dog somehow in retaliation."

"That's awful!" Lucy's reaction was real this time. If anyone harmed Gadoo, she'd be devastated.

Devasted and furious.

Pets were a part of the family. Killing one was akin to murdering a relative. Was that motive for murder?

"What happened to your neighbor?" Lucy asked.

"Janet was pretty heartbroken. She'd never married and that dog was like her child. She moved to California about six months ago. But you don't have to worry. The new landlord, Craig Smith, is much nicer."

If Janet had moved cross-country a half year ago, then she couldn't have killed Gilbert. As for the remaining landlord, Craig had to be an improvement over Gilbert. Lucy found him pleasant and could envision him as a professional landlord—not someone who'd threaten eviction over a few days' late rent, and definitely not someone who would harm a pet.

"Thanks for sharing," Lucy said.

The woman waved, then pushed the stroller toward the entrance to the condominiums. A man who was departing held the door open for her to pass through.

Lucy looked at Katie. "Gah! A dog murderer. What's worse?"

Katie tapped a foot. "There's no proof Gilbert poisoned her dog."

"No. But he wasn't well-liked even here, was he?"

Lucy hadn't met a single person who'd liked Gilbert. Eloisa Lubinski didn't speak ill of him, but she did say he'd provoked a lot of people. Which led to another thought. "The funeral is tomorrow. Can you go?"

Funerals in Ocean Crest were well-attended, especially when one of their own was the deceased. A murder was big news, and the town would be abuzz. Lucy had hated funerals ever since her grandmother died several winters ago. She had been devastated by the loss, and she still had bad memories of watching the coffin being lowered into the cold ground while she stood shivering by her mother's side.

"Bill has to work Tuesdays," Katie said. "Let's go together."

Before Lucy could express her gratitude, her cell phone rang. She dug into her purse to pull it out and glanced at the screen. She didn't recognize the number, but it had a local area code. "Hello?"

"Lucy, it's Melanie."

"Melanie? Where are you?"

"I'm at work. I just got a phone call from Detective Clemmons. He wants me to come in to the police station for more questioning."

Lucy's grip tightened on her phone. She'd expected this, but she still felt a sinking feeling in her stomach. The evidence pointed to Melanie, and Clemmons was doing his job. But she also knew the crafty detective could easily wheedle information out of Melanie that could incriminate her enough to slap a pair of handcuffs on her right then and there in the station.

Melanie was out of her league.

"You need to call an attorney. Clyde Winters handles criminal cases in town. He's old but still on his game." Azad had used Mr. Winters in the past, and the attorney had served him well.

Melanie's voice was strained. "No. I don't want an attorney. I'm innocent and have nothing to hide."

Lucy tamped down her frustration and struggled to keep a calm tone. "Melanie, I don't think that's wise. Just reach out to him and—"

"The reason I called you was because I need you to let Sarah into the candy store. I like Sarah, but she's a part-time college student and is sometimes forgetful. I don't trust anyone with the key, but I trust you. Will you do it?"

This wasn't what Lucy expected and she was caught off guard. How could she refuse? "Okay."

"The spare key is hidden in a ceramic seagull just outside the back door."

Seriously?

"I know it's not exactly a fake rock with a key, but close. Will you do it?" Melanie asked.

"Of course. I can be there in twenty minutes," Lucy said. "But Melanie?"

"Yes."

"Be very careful of what you say to the detective."

As soon as Lucy hung up the phone with Melanie, she called home and asked her parents to stay at Kebab Kitchen to help until she could return. She then dropped Katie off at the town hall and headed straight for Haven Candies. Each boardwalk shop had back stairs that led to a storage room. This way, business owners could receive deliveries and come and go without having to enter their stores from the crowded boardwalk. To secure the shops from the boardwalk entrance at the end of the day, the owners would lower rolling security gates.

Lucy arrived at Haven Candies and began to climb the flight of stairs that led to the back storage room. At the landing, she spotted the ceramic seagull. She picked it up and turned it over to discover a small compartment in the belly of the seagull. Sliding the little door open, she found the key. Melanie was right. It wasn't exactly a fake rock, but close. It was also perfect for Ocean Crest because almost every house had shells, crabs, fish, or seagull lawn ornaments.

She'd have to wait until Sarah arrived for her shift. Meanwhile, she could help. Lucy found an apron emblazoned with HAVEN CANDIES, tied it around her waist, then fetched the trays of fudge from the back room that Melanie had prepared the previous day.

She was in the middle of the task when Sarah showed up. "Lucy? What are you doing here?"

"Hi, Sarah. Melanie had to run an errand," Lucy fibbed. "She asked me to open the shop until you arrived."

Sarah stared at Lucy blankly. "An errand? She never misses a day of work. What kind of errand could be that important?"

Lucy's mind whirled as she thought of an excuse. She knew Melanie wouldn't want to reveal the truth to Sarah. Pressed for a response, Lucy blurted out the words before she could think. "Um. She got a call from her sister."

"Rhonda?" Sarah's brow wrinkled. "I didn't even know they were on speaking terms."

Lucy's initial anxiety was quickly replaced with curiosity. Her father had mentioned that Melanie had an older sister. Lucy had thought Melanie was keeping something from her regarding Gilbert's murder, but she didn't know if it had anything to do with her sibling. Now was the time to learn a bit more.

"Sarah, what do you know about Rhonda?" Lucy asked.

Sarah had reached for her own apron, and then began cutting the fudge and placing it in small boxes which would be displayed for sale. "Rhonda's about ten years older than Melanie. She came to the candy store a few times. I asked Melanie why she ended up running the candy store and not Rhonda."

"What'd she say?"

Sarah shrugged, then stacked boxes of chocolate fudge in one pile and chocolate nut in another. "Rhonda had no interest and married some rich salesman. They live on Sandstone Street, the fancy new homes in town. She likes her stuff and doesn't want to work. She also said Rhonda never felt an emotional connection to the family business and wanted to sell it."

This sounded somewhat similar to Lucy's own family. When Lucy had left the city law firm and first returned home to Ocean Crest, her parents had wanted to sell Kebab Kitchen. Lucy, who hadn't wanted to stay home, had been shocked and felt a stab of regret at the news. But Emma had agreed that their parents should sell. Her sister's acquiescence had surprised Lucy almost as much as her parents' announcement. If Lucy hadn't come around to decide to manage the place, would Emma have been happy to see the restaurant sold off?

Sarah wiped her hands on a towel and met Lucy's gaze. "They also fought a lot in the past. To tell you the truth, I'm glad Rhonda stopped coming around. It was upsetting."

"Did they fight about the candy store?"

"No. They never fought about this place."

"Then what?" Lucy asked.

"Something to do with Rhonda's husband."

Her husband?

"How do you know it was her husband?" *And not her lover?*

"His name is Noah. He came in here once or twice and was friendly. When the sisters fought, his name always came up."

Lucy thought about everything she'd learned. What could the sisters have been fighting over? Did Melanie dislike Rhonda's husband, or was it the other way around?

And, more importantly, did the sisters' bickering have anything to do with Gilbert's murder?

Chapter Sixteen

The Catholic church on the corner of Ocean Avenue and Shell Street was crowded. The family had decided to hold the funeral directly after the viewing, and many townsfolk showed up to pay their respects for one of their own. Gilbert's family consisted of Eloisa, his wife Sophia, and distant cousins who had traveled from out of town.

The funeral hadn't yet begun, and Lucy and Katie were near the end of the condolence line at Gilbert's viewing. Lucy spotted Eloisa, standing next to Gilbert's casket, her head slightly bowed. Her blue eyes were watery, her powdered skin looked as fragile as old parchment, and for the first time since Lucy met her, she looked her age. She'd dressed in a simple black dress that fell to her knees and low-heeled pumps. No lace, frills, or sequins. The only accessory that expressed her usual flamboyant style was a black feather boa draped around her neck.

Sophia stood beside her aunt-in-law. Gilbert's

widow was dressed in the height of fashion in a low-cut black dress with a wide slit up her thigh. Her bleached-blond hair was loose and contrasted against the black, and her full lips glistened with the same shimmering lip gloss she'd worn in yoga class.

Sophia was first in line, and Lucy and Katie approached Gilbert's widow together.

"We're sorry for your loss," Lucy said.

Sophia's heavily mascaraed lashes widened. "I recognize you two. You're from the Yoga Palace."

Katie didn't miss a beat. "We told you we were Gilbert's friends."

Sophia's painted lips curled in a knowing smile. "Right. The whole town is here. Have you asked anyone else questions like you asked me?"

"We didn't plan on asking questions. We wanted to do yoga," Lucy said.

"Hard to believe because I haven't seen either of you at the Yoga Palace since that morning. I also asked the receptionist. You never joined after your free trial."

Lucy tried not to grimace. "It was harder than we thought." By the look on Sophia's face, she wasn't buying any of their story now, just as she'd come to suspect their intentions on the day of yoga class.

Sophia looked beyond Lucy's shoulder. "That detective is here. Maybe I'll ask him about you two."

Lucy glanced at the pews to see Detective Clemmons seated a few rows back. Thankfully, he was talking to Ben Hawkins, the town barber, and wasn't paying attention to them.

Time to move on.

Katie didn't seem perturbed. She squared her shoulders and met Sophia eye-to-eye. "You can speak to whomever you like. We are just paying our respects."

Katie tugged on Lucy's arm, and together they moved down the line.

Lucy lowered her voice to a whisper. "Why antagonize her?"

"I wanted to see her reaction. She doesn't seem upset, just mad."

"Probably because she claims to have an alibi," Lucy said.

They stopped talking as they came to Eloisa. Rather than say the customary "I'm sorry for your loss," Lucy met her landlady's gaze and said, "How are you holding up?"

"I didn't think it would be this sappy, but Gilbert's lying there in the casket and all I can think about is his last demand to oust me from my home. He claimed I had dementia." She blew her nose in a tissue.

Lucy squeezed her hand. She couldn't figure out if she was relieved or sad. Grief did strange things to people. But for the first time, Eloisa seemed frail. Lucy didn't like it. She wanted her feisty landlady back. "Now that Gilbert's gone, you don't have to worry about anyone trying to evict you from your home anymore."

"I know this sounds crazy, but I'll miss the bastard. He was my only nephew." She turned to gaze at the casket and then blew her nose once again. "Do you think the police will figure out who killed him?"

"Detective Clemmons won't stop until he has a suspect arrested," Katie said.

I only hope it's the right suspect, Lucy thought.

"Bah! I know I'm on that detective's list. I don't trust the police, but you two seem to have your heads on your shoulders. How close are you to finding the real killer?" Eloisa said.

Lucy stared. "Mrs. Lubinski . . . we're not the police—"

Eloisa waved a hand and lowered her voice as she lifted her head to stare at the pews. "It could be anyone here."

Lucy followed her gaze to the townsfolk who crowded the church pews. Katie had been right. When one of their own passed, the citizens of Ocean Crest showed up en masse.

Lucy spotted Melanie four rows away. Lucy was surprised she was here. She was one of the main suspects and Detective Clemmons was in attendance. Or did Melanie think it would look even worse if she didn't come? Sort of an admission of guilt?

Melanie wore black slacks, a black silk blouse, and a small black hat, but it was her face that drew attention. She looked like she was going to burst into tears at the slightest provocation. Why? She hadn't liked Gilbert. She had no reason to grieve his loss so deeply unless she feared she would be arrested any minute for his murder. Lucy never had had a good opportunity to ask Melanie how her questioning had gone in Detective Clemmons's office. Lucy had let Sarah into the candy shop, then had to return to Kebab Kitchen to work. The questioning couldn't have been too bad. If it had, Melanie would have been dragged away in handcuffs or arrested by now.

So why did she look so forlorn?

Lucy's gut tightened with the all-too-familiar feeling that Melanie was hiding something—something important that had to do with Gilbert's murder.

Lucy spotted Kevin Crowley, the boardwalk tramcar owner. His presence wasn't unusual, but her gaze lingered on his expression. He checked his watch twice and appeared impatient.

His words sprang to mind: *All business owners are familiar with one another. It's a small town.*

But was there more familiarity there? Had Gilbert loaned money to him and Kevin couldn't pay the entirety back plus the exorbitant interest? Alongside Katie, Lucy had searched his boardwalk trailer for evidence of loan documents, and they hadn't found anything. But a rushed twenty-minute search wasn't all-encompassing.

Michael sat in the back pew with Pumpkin and Craig. She liked both of Michael's friends and didn't want to think of either of them as killers, but each had a possible motive. Craig hated his former business partner and had publicly fought with him, enough for the police to come and break up their fight. He wasn't as mild-mannered as she'd thought. Then there was Pumpkin. Did he lose his temper when Gilbert failed to pay for his landscaping services and decide to take it out on Gilbert once and for all?

Lucy glanced at Sophia, who was standing beside Eloisa. The widow was receiving condolences from the current mayor, the town pharmacist, Theodore Magic. She sniffled and dabbed at the corners of her eyes. Lucy thought it a wonderful performance. She didn't look like the same woman who'd threatened to summon Detective Clemmons, the woman who'd been in a heated divorce with her spouse. Had she offed Gilbert in order to gain his share of Jersey shore property?

Or had another of Gilbert's tenants killed him?

Eloisa tilted her steel-gray curls toward Sophia and lowered her voice. "The murderer could be the person standing at the front of the line."

Lucy didn't know what to say to that. Despite Sophia's claims of innocence, she was on Lucy's list of suspects until she could confirm Sophia's alibi the night of the bonfire.

The priest stepped up to the altar and the organist began playing. The viewing was ending and the funeral service was about to begin.

"You two keep digging," Eloisa said. "Find the real killer."

An hour later, the services had concluded and Lucy and Katie were ready to leave the cemetery.

"Mrs. Lubinski doesn't look so hot," Katie said.

"She just buried her nephew," Lucy said as she walked beside Katie. They passed rows of gravestones as they headed to Lucy's car. A tall mausoleum stood between them and the parking lot. The gray stone facade appeared like a gloomy specter and made a shiver travel down her spine. Lucy's beloved grandmother's gravestone was located just beyond the mausoleum.

At least it was spring and the weather was pleasant. A warm wind blew across the cemetery.

"That's not what I meant when I said Mrs. Lubinski doesn't look great," Katie said. "She obviously doesn't get along with her niece-in-law. Sophia kept shooting her nasty glares."

Lucy sighed. "It's sad, if you ask me. I'm growing to like my landlady more and more. If only Cupid and Gadoo would settle in."

Katie was silent as they rounded the edge of a tall gravestone. "There's no luncheon to follow the service either. I'm hungry."

This was something Lucy could remedy. "Come to Kebab Kitchen. I'll fix you a plate of shish kebab, pilaf, and hummus."

"You've convinced me."

They made it to the mausoleum and Lucy spotted the black hearse parked by the curb. Eloisa hadn't wanted to arrive in the hearse and had driven to the church with Lucy and Katie, but she would be traveling back home with Sophia in the gloomy vehicle.

As they rounded the corner, angry voices sounded. Lucy looked up to see Melanie arguing with a woman. Melanie gestured wildly with her hands, her face screwed in an angry expression. The other woman had blond hair, much lighter than Melanie's auburn curls, but their features were strikingly similar.

Lucy grasped Katie's arm and held her back. Thankfully, Katie understood and crept around the corner of the stone mausoleum and stayed out of sight.

"I can't believe you're here," Melanie said, her voice tight with anger.

"Why wouldn't I come?" the woman said.

Melanie's voice hardened. "Because it's Gilbert's funeral and you wanted him dead. Don't you have any shame?"

The blond woman rolled her eyes. "Oh, please. As if I'm the only one. You had no love for him either, and from what I've heard, his wife hated him with a passion, too."

Katie glanced around the corner of the mausoleum, then whispered to Lucy, "They look a lot alike. You don't think she's . . ."

Lucy risked her own glance, then turned back to Katie. "It has to be Rhonda, Melanie's sister."

When Katie opened her mouth to ask a question, Lucy pressed a finger against her lips and shook her head. Katie fell silent. Together, they peered around the corner and listened.

"Where's Noah?" Melanie asked.

"He's around," Rhonda answered nonchalantly.

"Will you ever tell him the truth about your online gambling problems and your loan from Gilbert?"

Rhonda tapped her high heel. "No sense now. Gilbert's dead."

"You have no conscience."

Rhonda smirked. "You should talk. You're not the moral, upstanding person everyone thinks you are. Wasn't it your taffy they pulled out of Gilbert's throat?"

Melanie's eyes grew wide. "You can't be serious?"

Lucy's heart pounded as she eavesdropped on the two women. She looked at Katie and whispered, "Oh, my gosh! Rhonda borrowed money from Gilbert."

Lucy spotted a movement from the corner of her eye. A man in a dark suit walked toward the sisters. He was heavyset with thick brown hair and sideburns. The two sisters jumped apart when they spotted him.

Rhonda waved the man forward. "Noah, we were just catching up." She placed a hand on his arm, her blood-red fingernails curling like talons on his sleeve.

Noah's brow furrowed in concern as he looked at Melanie. "You okay, Melanie? I know Gilbert was your landlord."

"Oh, I'm fine. It was just a shock," Melanie said, her voice unsteady.

"I had a long conversation with the wife. Sophia seems to be taking it hard," Noah said.

At the mention of Sophia, Melanie froze, and her gaze darted to her sister.

Rhonda's lips curled in a smile as she looked up at her husband like nothing untoward had occurred. "Noah, why don't you pull up the car, and I'll meet you?"

"Of course." Noah placed a kiss on his wife's cheek and departed.

Melanie's expression turned into one of pure disgust as she looked at her sister. "He has a right to know. You had no problem coming to me for money when you couldn't make Gilbert's outrageous interest payments."

Rhonda planted her hands on her hips and faced her sister. "You offered to help me, remember? How should I know you'd put yourself behind on your own rent and Gilbert would come knocking on your door? His death serves your purposes as well as mine."

"You're such a bitch."

"Oh, please. You hated Gilbert."

"I didn't hate him."

"No? Not enough to kill him?"

Melanie glowered at her sister. "Get away from me. I never want to see you again." She spun on her heel and headed in the opposite direction.

A Lexus pulled up at the front of the parking lot. Noah was in the driver's seat. With a huff, Rhonda turned and walked to her husband.

Lucy let out a held-in breath. "That was disturbing. In order to pay off her online gambling debts, Rhonda had borrowed money from Gilbert."

Katie whistled. "Of all people."

"And when Rhonda couldn't pay, she went to Melanie."

It was clear that Melanie was furious with her sister. And Rhonda had kept her gambling problem and debts secret from her husband, Noah.

"Melanie asked me to help find Gilbert's real killer," Lucy said. "My gut kept telling me that Melanie was keeping a secret, but I couldn't imagine what she was hiding."

"Both Melanie and Rhonda had their own reasons for disliking Gilbert. By helping Rhonda, Melanie had also inadvertently taken on her sister's debts. Do you think Melanie killed him?" Katie asked.

Lucy hesitated as the awful thought that her friend may have murdered Gilbert in cold blood settled in her mind. "I don't know anymore. But

I'm sure she didn't tell Detective Clemmons everything we just learned when she was called in for questioning. If she did, she might not be walking around free today."

Katie rubbed her chin with her thumb and forefinger. "We're missing something important."

"What?" Lucy asked.

"Do you think Sophia knew about Gilbert's side business as a moneylender?

It was a good question. They were married, and one could assume that Sophia knew about her husband's moneylending, but what if she didn't? They were in the middle of a heated divorce. "Maybe Sophia discovered her husband was hiding income on top of everything else and she went crazy?" Lucy said. "She could have lost her temper and killed him in a rage. It's a public beach. Anyone could have snuck near the bonfire that night."

"Except she claims she wasn't on the beach and that she was at Mac's Irish Pub and has a rock-solid alibi. Do you believe Sophia?"

Lucy's didn't hesitate. "No, but I plan on finding out tonight."

Chapter Seventeen

Lucy flipped the switch of the restaurant's ten-gallon commercial coffee urn to brew. Within minutes, the aroma of freshly brewed coffee made her mouth water. But what she really craved was one of Lola Stewart's steamed cappuccinos. Her father went to Lola's Coffee Shop every morning for coffee and conversation. Her mother often complained about her father's caffeine habit, but Lucy made a mental note to go to Lola's soon.

"Are you ready for our date tonight?"

Lucy turned to find Azad leaning on the kitchen's long, stainless-steel prep counter, his arms folded across his broad chest. He grinned, and the tempting cleft in his chin made her want to press a kiss there. He looked confident and sexy in his chef's coat.

What was it about a competent male in the kitchen?

Her mother religiously watched Cooking Kurt, the handsome celebrity chef on the cooking channel. Lucy had never understood her mother's fascination until she'd seen Azad chop vegetables with lightning speed, his muscles flexing beneath his coat with every stroke of his chef's knife.

Lucy swallowed hard and stepped away from the urn, all thoughts of coffee fleeing from her head. "Is a local band playing?" The last time he'd taken her to Mac's Irish Pub, the Beach Bums had performed.

"Not tonight. I thought we could sit by the bar, share a drink, and talk."

"That sounds nice."

They closed the restaurant half an hour early that night so that they could both go home and dress for their evening out. The bar was beach casual, but Lucy took care with her appearance and wore a pale pink sundress and wedge sandals. Her dark curls were loose down her back.

Azad arrived at her apartment in jeans and a white button-down shirt with shirtsleeves rolled up in a casual manner. His hair was still damp and a dark lock rakishly fell across his forehead. He looked like a pirate.

"You look amazing," he said.

A zing traveled down her spine. "You look nice yourself."

He tucked her arm in his and escorted her to his truck. The pub was only five blocks away and she could hear the music and the crowd when they pulled into the parking lot. The pub was a local favorite and featured a large selection of microbrews and classic beers on tap, as well as a good selection of wines, some from the local winery in Cape May.

He held open the door and Lucy stepped inside

the pub. The smell of beer and fried bar food wafted to her. A long, mahogany bar, its surface polished but nicked from years of use, ran the length of one wall. The place was crowded with locals and others Lucy recognized as bikers from the motorcycle festival. Men and women sat at tables, drinking beer and watching a Phillies game on a large-screen television above the bar.

Azad pulled out stools from the bar, and Lucy and he each took one.

A gum-chewing barmaid slid cardboard coasters advertising domestic beers before them. "Hi, Lucy!"

"Hi, Candace. How's Brandon?"

"He just started as a freshman in high school this year."

"Wow! Already?"

"I can't believe my baby boy is so big," Candace said with a wide grin.

Candace had graduated from high school with Katie and Lucy. She'd also become pregnant her senior year and dropped out. It was a shock to all the students. But Candace had decided to keep the baby and had finished her high school degree at night school. She'd worked at Mac's Irish Pub all through that time and had made her way up from waitress to bartender to assistant manager. Mac McCabe depended on Candace.

Candace turned her attention to Azad. "Hey, Azad. How's the cooking?"

"Good. You should stop by tomorrow night. It's shish kebab night."

"I wouldn't miss it. Now, what can I get you two?"

They ordered two beers on tap. As they waited

for Candace to pour their beers, several men walked by and slapped Azad on the back in greeting. Two others waved at him from their tables. Azad waved back.

It seemed as if almost everyone in town knew Azad. It was something she'd gotten used to since returning home. The small-town camaraderie had bothered her in the beginning, but she'd come to appreciate the townsfolk and the way people felt close to one another.

Candace delivered their beers, and Azad held out his glass to Lucy. "To a nice night out with my favorite lady."

"To a fun night out with my favorite chef." Lucy tapped her glass to his.

They sipped their beers, and she felt a ripple of excitement at the admiration in his dark eyes.

"I hope to expand the menu to include gluten-free options. What do you think?" he asked.

Lucy cocked her head to the side and regarded him. "I think that's a great idea." Lucy knew that more and more people were trying a gluten-free diet, whether it was due to having food allergies or wanting a healthier lifestyle. Many restaurants were offering gluten-free dishes.

"And Raffi?" Azad asked.

She tapped her foot on the barstool as she considered her father's opinion on the matter. "We have to get it past him, but I'm the new manager now, remember?"

Azad just smiled. "I know, but does he?"

Lucy rolled her eyes. Her father was stubborn, but this was different. How could he complain about expanding the menu with Azad as the head chef? It's not like they were asking him to install new, stainless-steel shelving in the storage room or changing their inventory process from manual to electronic. The only possible cost would be to print new menus to include a gluten-free section. No biggie in Lucy's opinion.

"I'll talk to him." She gifted him with a big smile. "My dad shouldn't complain. Customers love your food. I get compliments for the chef all the time."

Azad grinned. "Just don't tell your mother."

Angela was even more stubborn, and sensitive when it came to her cooking. She loved Azad like a son, something she kept reminding Lucy of at every chance, but she was territorial about her cooking. It was like insulting her firstborn, only worse.

As the night progressed, Lucy enjoyed her drinks and the company even more. They had a long history together and they reminisced about their teenage and college years. They were both careful not to mention their breakup after college. Back then, she'd thought they were headed toward marriage, but Azad wasn't ready. He'd broken her heart, but now that she'd returned home and was older and wiser, she knew it had been for the best. If she'd followed her parents' wishes and married Azad straight out of college, she wouldn't have graduated from law school, wouldn't have worked in a Philadelphia firm for eight years, and wouldn't have gained the education or experience to know what she really wanted out of life. She would have stayed home, had children, and worked in the restaurant. She may or may not have been fulfilled. But she certainly wouldn't have the wisdom to solve murders.

Now, she truly knew what she wanted out of life. She was happy here and fulfilled as the manager of Kebab Kitchen. And most surprising of all, she was excited to be back with Azad.

Life had gone full circle, but not without a few bumps in the road along the way.

These thoughts led Lucy to thinking about the other reason she was here tonight: to confirm Sophia's alibi the night of Gilbert's murder.

Candace showed up just in time, and they ordered two more beers on tap. Lucy ran her finger down the frosty mug. "Hey, Candace, is Mac around tonight?"

Candace popped a bubble. "Sure thing. Give me a minute and I'll fetch him for you." She sidled down the bar to serve another customer.

Azad gave her a curious look. "Why do you want to know if Mac MacCabe's in the house?"

Lucy experienced a moment of trepidation. "No reason."

"Hmm. I know that expression. You and Katie have decided to fully embrace this murder investigation, haven't you?"

Her stomach tightened at his serious expression. Azad had said he'd understood her inquisitive nature, but she knew he worried about her, too. She could lie and dismiss his concerns. It would be a lot easier. But lying was no basis for a relationship, and they *were* in a relationship.

"Spill it," he said.

Still, she hesitated, not sure how he would respond. She stiffened her spine and her resolve. If he cared for her—truly cared—he would understand. "I'm helping out a friend."

"When you say 'friend,' do you mean Melanie Haven?"

She sighed. He was much more perceptive than she thought. "How do you know?"

"It was her taffy, wasn't it? The way Gilbert was killed was explained in the paper in detail."

No doubt. As soon as the police made an official statement, Stan Slade would report it in the *Town News*.

"You're right. Katie and I want to help Melanie," Lucy admitted. "But she's not who I want to ask Mac about. I want to ask him about the victim's wife, Sophia Lubinski."

Azad's brow furrowed. "What does Gilbert's wife have to do with Mac MacCabe?"

"Sophia claims she was at the pub the night of the bonfire and has an alibi for the murder. I want to know if Mac remembers seeing Sophia that night."

Azad tapped his fingers on the bar. "Why didn't you just say so?"

She looked down. "Because I know how you feel about me and Katie asking questions. You worry."

Azad placed a finger beneath her chin and raised her eyes to his. "Like I said before, I also know you, and that's why I like you. Let me help out."

Could he surprise her any more? He was turning out to be a considerate and supportive boyfriend. He'd helped her by picking up a screwdriver and installing the stainless-steel shelving in the storage room when she'd thought it would take months. He'd helped her by quitting his fancy Atlantic City *sous* chef job and taking on the position of full-time chef at Kebab Kitchen. He'd helped her by showing her people can change when they wanted to.

Now he was helping her question someone who might have important information about Gilbert's murder.

She wanted to kiss him.

He lowered his hand and winked at her. "If you keep looking at me that way, I'll forget about talking to Mac and pick you up and carry you out of here."

Oh my. That didn't sound so bad.

"I hear you're asking for me?"

Lucy dragged her gaze away from Azad's to find Mac McCabe standing behind the bar. Tall and well-built, his brown hair was pulled back in a ponytail and held by a leather string.

"Hey, Mac," Azad said. "We wanted to ask you something. Do you remember the night Gilbert Lubinski was killed?"

"I do. It was a busy night here. I was shocked to learn of it the next day. Poor guy was killed right on the beach. Bad for business."

"Do you know Gilbert's wife, Sophia?" Lucy asked.

"Yup. Strange thing is, she was here that night. I'll never forget it. It was the first time we had a long chat. She was talking to me about weird stuff."

"What do you mean by weird stuff?" Lucy asked.

"Stuff I don't normally talk about with my customers, and that's saying something, because I talk a lot behind this bar. At first, I thought she must have been drunk, but she was nursing her Jack and Coke. No, she was just in the mood to talk about her dreams of moving away from the Jersey shore to pursue a modeling career in New York City."

"She never mentioned her husband?" Azad asked.

"Only that she was going through a nasty divorce," Mac said.

Sophia wanted to be a model. Was there a chance Gilbert had vetoed her dreams and she longed to get rid of him? "Do you know what time she was here?" Lucy asked.

"All night. She walked in here around seven o'clock and stayed until closing at two in the morning," Mac said. "Come to think of it, she sat on the same barstool you're sitting on now."

Disappointment felt like a heavy anchor in Lucy's stomach. If Sophia was here all night bemoaning her modeling dreams to Mac, she couldn't have killed Gilbert. Sophia's alibi was airtight.

"Thanks," Lucy said.

Mac wiped down the bar, then walked away to talk with another customer a few stools away.

"Did you get what you needed?" Azad asked.

"I did, but it doesn't help. I really thought Sophia was responsible for Gilbert's murder, but her alibi is solid."

Sadly, everything kept leading back to Melanie. Melanie and her saltwater taffy.

* * *

After another beer, Lucy needed to make a quick trip to the ladies' room.

"I'll be right back," she told Azad as she slipped off her barstool.

As she waded through the crowded bar toward her destination, she passed a group at the pool table in the rear of the bar. Others gathered around tables or stood talking and laughing with friends.

The restrooms were located just outside the back storage room. Lucy had once glimpsed inside the room to see cases of beer and alcohol and wine bottles. She spotted the sign for the ladies' room— a female stick figure with a skirt—when a voice called out.

"Lucy, wait!"

Lucy spun around to see Candace rushing forward, her face red.

"There's something I want to tell you and I couldn't do it out there," Candace said, breathing heavily and glancing back to the pub room.

Lucy's heart raced. "What's wrong?"

Candace shook her head. "Nothing serious. I heard you asking Mac about Sophia."

Lucy's pulse started to pound a bit more, this time with excitement rather than fear. "What about her?"

Candace brushed her hands on her apron pockets. "Sophia was at the bar the night of Gilbert's murder."

Lucy listened with rising dismay. Had Candace chased her down only to confirm Sophia's alibi?

"But not for the entire night," Candace added.

"What do you mean?" Lucy asked. "Mac said he saw her and spoke with her."

"He did. But Mac didn't tend the bar the entire night. I did. At one point, I was in the storage room fetching a case of beer when I saw Sophia scoot out the back door. She never saw me. Sophia was gone for about thirty minutes, then returned and stayed until closing at two in the morning."

Thirty minutes.

Mac's Irish Pub was only a two-block walk to the beach. It was enough time to leave the pub, rush to the beach, lure Gilbert aside, and kill him.

Mac had said that Sophia had talked about "weird stuff" and mentioned her dreams of pursuing modeling. It all made sense. She had purposely chatted with the bar owner in order to be memorable to him, to create her alibi. All the while, she'd planned to slip away through the back door for a short window of time, then had returned to the bar until closing.

It was brilliant.

Maybe Sophia thought that striking Gilbert on the head was enough to rid herself of an unwanted husband, but at the sight of the saltwater taffy, she knew she could put the blame on someone else—specifically, Melanie.

Lucy's attention focused on Candace. "You sure it was Sophia?"

"Positive."

"Why didn't you say so earlier? Even tell the police?"

"I didn't think it was relevant until you came in here asking Mac about it today. I just thought Sophia was leaving through the back door to meet a lover or a boyfriend." A momentary look of discomfort crossed Candace's face. "I know all about a woman making bad choices from my high school years. Who am I to judge?"

Lucy knew Candace was talking about her deadbeat boyfriend from high school, who failed to pay child support for her son.

"Thanks for telling me, Candace. I'm not blaming you for anything."

"I also know you've become a resident sleuth. If you can help figure out who killed that sleazy landlord, we can all go about preparing for the upcoming summer season."

If there was anyone who knew about Lucy's exploits, it was Candace. A manager in a popular Ocean Crest tavern was as good as the high-speed internet in the small town.

"Thanks again for the info, Candace. It helps more than you know."

"I had a great time tonight." Azad slid his arm around Lucy's waist as they stood outside his truck. He'd dropped her off in front of Eloisa's home and escorted her to the porch.

"I had a good time, too." She had fun simply talking with Azad, listening to the bar's music, and sharing a few drinks.

Then there was the unexpected news from Candace outside the ladies' room—information that blew a gaping hole in Sophia Lubinski's alibi.

"I hope what you learned helps." Azad's breath ruffled her hair.

Lucy had informed Azad of Candace's shocking news. Once again, she'd debated keeping it to herself. For all his good intentions and words at the bar, she didn't want to worry him. But she could do both, couldn't she? Keep Azad in the loop, but put his mind at ease at the same time?

Lucy toyed with the top button of his shirt. "I'm going to tell Bill what I learned."

"Good idea. I hope the police wrap up this murder business soon. The summer isn't the only thing that's around the corner. Easter is, too. It would be nice to have a worry-free holiday."

Lucy leaned into his embrace. His cologne smelled wonderful, a mix of spice and male. Azad always smelled good, whether it was from his tantalizing cooking at the restaurant or when they were on a date.

He smiled down at her. Acting on impulse, she stood on tiptoe and touched her lips to his. Azad's arms tightened around her waist as he kissed her back, slowly and leisurely. Her heart slammed against her ribs as his kiss sang through her veins. She pressed her palms against his solid chest and could feel his heart pounding beneath the cotton in a rhythm that matched her own. They kept kissing, lips and tongue melding together in a delicious sensation. His lips were more persuasive than she cared to admit. She wanted him to come inside and climb the steps to her upstairs apartment, but he'd made his intentions clear. He wanted to take it slow.

But at the same time, he wasn't acting like he would resist.

A light flicked on inside the house. Out of the corner of her eye, she spotted the curtains of the bay window flutter. Had Cupid jumped up on the couch and ruffled the curtains, or was Eloisa watching them?

Gah.

Lucy felt like a horny teenager on a date whose parents were waiting up for her.

Azad broke the kiss and smiled down at her. "I have a feeling we're being watched."

"You too? We are going to have to start sneaking around the back, trekking through the sand, and entering my apartment from the deck stairs."

He arched a dark eyebrow. "Why didn't I think of that?"

"You'd like to come inside?"

Did her voice sound too hopeful?

He brushed a loose curl from her cheek and tucked it around her ear. His coffee-brown eyes appeared darker, more intense. The clouds shifted and a shaft of moonlight illuminated his handsome face, the clear-cut lines of his profile.

"Soon. But not tonight," he said. "It's not that I don't want to, but I meant it when I said that we shouldn't rush into things. I know I messed up in the past. I also know you were hesitant to start dating me again, and that you had serious doubts about having a relationship with your head chef. I'm interested in a serious, long-term relationship with you, Lucy Berberian. I need you to be certain."

She looked up at him in surprise and adoration.

He'd been right about her doubts. So much was at stake with them working together. Parts of her, the deepest parts, were still uncertain.

His words *serious* and *long-term* rattled in her head.

Did he have to be so considerate? And why did that make him even more attractive?

Chapter Eighteen

"Sophia lied about her alibi? Good work, Lucy!"
Katie said over the phone.

"I really didn't do anything. I asked Mac McCabe
and he said she was there all night. I was lucky Candace overheard and sought me out by the ladies'
room to tell me." Lucy had called Katie after Azad
left. Eloisa had mysteriously disappeared as soon as
Lucy had opened the front door and headed upstairs to her apartment. Even Cupid was quiet.

"Still, good work. We can add Sophia back to
the suspect list," Katie said.

Lucy held her cell phone as she made sure the
door that led to the downstairs was firmly closed.
"She was only gone half an hour."

Gadoo came forward in a blur and started to do
figure eights between her legs. She reached down
to scratch beneath the orange and black cat's silky
chin, and he purred.

"It's enough time. She's fit enough to make that
run. We saw her in yoga, remember?" Katie asked.

"How can I forget?"

"By the way, how was your date with Azad? You're calling me so I know he didn't come inside your apartment."

Damn. She didn't want to go into details. "Yeah, well, he wants to take it slow, remember?

"He wants you to be sure."

Double damn. Katie knew her so well.

"What's it gonna take for you to be sure?" Katie asked.

She didn't want to talk about it. Not when her own feelings were confusing. She liked Azad. A lot. When she was with him, it felt right. But she hadn't even been back in Ocean Crest for a year and everything was changing day by day. Kebab Kitchen was a big part of her life. She needed that stability, and the restaurant needed Azad.

"It's not that easy. He works for me now."

"Get over it, Lucy. Your working relationship won't get in the way. Next time we get together, we need to talk about *your* issues."

The following morning, Lucy's running shoes pounded on the boards. She breathed in the fresh ocean air and the scent of frying bacon from one of the boardwalk restaurants that served breakfast. She spotted several bicycles and surreys with signs that read "CITTERONI'S BICYCLE RENTAL" on the back and knew Michael's bicycle shop was picking up business as the weather grew warmer every day and it came closer to the summer season. Joggers and walkers jostled for space and maneuvered around the bicycles.

She passed a four-person surrey and smiled at the sight of a three-year-old girl sitting in the front basket. Lucy waved, and the little girl rang the surrey bell and waved back. Lucy kept going and spotted a few of the motorcycle riders jogging. Even without their Harley-Davidson leather jackets, she recognized their faces, some bearded with long hair and others smoothly shaven with trimmed cuts. Many of the women bikers ran with tank tops and capris. Many had colorful ink on their arms and legs, and Lucy suspected the tattoo parlor on the boardwalk would do a brisk business this week.

She passed the Sun and Surf Shop owned by Harold Harper, which sold beach clothing, and Gray's Novelty Shop. She spotted the owners, elderly sisters Edna and Edith Gray inside. Shelves were crowded with sunscreen, boogie boards, beach toys, and an array of local jewelry made of shells. A large glass tank sat in the front of the store and contained a dozen or so hermit crabs, their shells painted different colors and designs.

A seagull squawked and drew her attention to where the bird circled a toddler with blond ponytails beside her parents. She began walking with her mother, a breakfast bagel in her outstretched hand. Just as Lucy was about to shout out a warning, the seagull swooped down and plucked the bagel out of the child's hand.

Wailing immediately ensued.

Lucy had seen it coming, but hadn't been fast enough to prevent disaster. But that was the way nature—or Jersey shore seagulls—worked around here. The mother whipped out a banana from her purse, peeled it, and handed it to the child. The little girl stopped crying as soon as she took a bite of the fruit.

Crises contained.

"Lucy!"

Lucy swiveled to see Madame Vega waving from outside her psychic salon. She snuffed out her cigarette in the lower half of a plastic soda bottle that had been cut to serve as a makeshift ashtray.

"Time for a reading today?" Madame asked.

Not really. Lucy needed to shower and return to the restaurant to finish payroll before the lunch shift, but she was torn between duty and fortune-telling. Plus, Madame Vega was a boardwalk fixture. She'd been a presence here since Lucy had been in pigtails, riding on her father's shoulders as he strolled the boardwalk with Emma by his side. Not much happened around here that Madame Vega didn't know about—or predict. She'd even unwittingly helped Lucy solve a crime in the past.

That was another reason Lucy felt she should take the time to have her cards read. She could ask Madame what she'd seen or heard, if anything, the evening of the bonfire. The woman spent hours in her psychic salon, and there was a good chance she'd been here the evening Gilbert was killed.

"Sure, I have time," Lucy said. "It's been a while since you've read my cards."

Madame smiled and waved Lucy inside. "Hurry up, then. The spirits are strong today."

Lucy hadn't believed in tarot cards. It was like hocus-pocus to her. But then Madame Vega had been surprisingly accurate, especially about Azad, and Lucy had turned from a nonbeliever to an occasional skeptic.

She walked into the room and sat at a red-velvet-draped table. Madame Vega adjusted her flowing blue robe and sat across from her. Reaching for a matching blue turban with a fake blue jewel in the center, she placed it on her gray curls and rested her hands on the table.

"No tarot today. The cards do not have the answers you're looking for," Madame said.

"They don't? Why not?" Lucy frowned. She hadn't expected this from the psychic. She'd come to look forward to having her cards read. It was like going to the casino: You never knew what cards you'd draw or if you'd be lucky or not, but you still wanted to take a chance.

Madame adjusted her voluminous sleeves. "The spirits, just like the ocean winds, are blowing a different direction." Her voice was calm, her gaze steady.

Lucy suppressed the urge to roll her eyes. "I didn't notice."

"The spirits don't talk to you."

Lucy was returning to being a complete unbeliever, and fast. First, she hadn't felt an ocean breeze this morning. She would have loved to feel one as she'd jogged. And second, what did an ocean breeze have to do with reading tarot cards?

Madame turned her hand over on the table. "Relax and give me your hand."

"You plan on reading my palm?"

"Yes. Stop talking."

Lucy let out a breath and placed her hand, palm up, on the red-velvet tablecloth. She'd much rather have her cards read. It had been somewhat fun to pick the cards and then turn them over to discover which ones she'd selected. Each tarot card was different and had pictures that Lucy couldn't make sense of, but Madame excelled at interpreting them.

Madame Vega's hand was cool as she held Lucy's. "Your heart line curves upward, which means you are outwardly affectionate to those in your inner circle."

Lucy liked to think so. She grew up with loving parents who'd often told her and Emma that they loved them. Their affectionate nature used to annoy Lucy as a teenager, but as she grew older, she also grew to appreciate Angela and Raffi. When Lucy was a kid and went to Katie's house, the differences between their upbringings was stark. Katie's parents rarely told her that they loved her. Katie knew she was loved, but it wasn't until she was grown and married to Bill that she'd confessed to Lucy that she'd felt like something was missing in her childhood. She made up for it by telling Bill she loved him every day.

Madame's wrinkled brow creased a bit more as she stared at Lucy's palm. "You also have gaps on your heart line, which indicate that you have known heartbreak."

She had. Azad had broken her heart after college. Would that show in her palm? Lucy leaned forward to see what Madame was pointing to. "What gaps?"

"Right here. And here."

Lucy saw them, then. Tiny little breaks in the line. Other than Azad, Lucy had experienced one or two failed romantic episodes when she'd worked in Philadelphia, but no one had captured her interest or her heart. She guessed that each of those doomed relationships could have led to a broken line on her palm.

Was that why she was hesitant to fully embrace love? Because of the gaps on her heart line? Was there a gap in her future with Azad?

Her stomach tightened and she stared at her palm with renewed interest. There was something about Madame Vega that was compelling. Maybe all those years passing her psychic salon as a kid had captivated Lucy more than she'd realized.

Madame turned her hand this way and that to see better in the candlelight. "Do not let the past interfere with your future. You must work hard to overcome your doubts. The gaps are early on and do not continue."

Thank goodness. That meant her relationship with Azad would stay on track. She hoped the woman's prediction was spot on. Once more, Lucy looked down to be sure she was seeing the same thing Madame Vega was.

"Are you sure about this stuff?" Lucy asked.

"*Shh.* I said no chitchat," Madame admonished. "Now, your head line is the second line. It curves downward toward the wrist."

"Is that bad?" She was beginning to believe more and more.

"It means you are creative and trusting."

She didn't think of herself as overly creative, especially in the kitchen. Her mother's cooking lessons were still a struggle, even though she'd improved. Her dishes were edible and tasted better with each attempt. But was she creative in other ways?

Madame looked at her with curiosity. "You did

attend law school, didn't you? Don't you have to
be a creative thinker for that?"

Lucy shrugged. "I suppose." Three years of law
school had taught her to think outside the box, and
to analyze every aspect of a case in order to represent a client zealously. Certainly, that counted as
creative. It also came in handy when solving a puzzle such as *who killed Gilbert?*

"As for trusting," Lucy said. "I'm not so sure."

"You trust your friends."

It wasn't a question, but a statement. How did
Madame know this?

"Yes, but that's different," Lucy said.

Madame ignored her argument and continued.
"Now, your life line is strong and deep. It means
you are enthusiastic about your life here."

She may not have wanted to stay in Ocean Crest
months ago, when she left the firm, but she was
glad she had. She never would have been with her
best friend on a daily basis, never would have prevented her parents from selling Kebab Kitchen
and discovered the joy and satisfaction of managing the place.

"What about how long I'll live and that stuff?"

Madame tsked. "What everyone thinks is wrong.
The lifeline does not represent longevity."

Too bad. Lucy had always thought longevity ran
in her family. Her grandmother had lived into her
nineties. She'd always hoped stubbornness had
something to do with it, and both Angela and Raffi
Berberian had boatloads of that trait.

"Your faint line, the vertical line in the center of
your palm, is both weak and strong. I haven't seen
that before."

Lucy felt a moment of trepidation. Madame Vega had been doing this for years and had probably seen a thousand palms. What could be so different about hers?

"You attract loyalty, but also trouble."

"What does that mean?"

Madame looked up and met Lucy's eyes. "You have a knack for finding bodies."

Lucy drew in her breath. "I wouldn't call it a knack. That sounds like a good trait."

Madame shrugged a skinny shoulder and adjusted her turban. "You unearth answers, but need help along the way."

Lucy immediately thought of Katie. No doubt her friend had aided her in the past. It also helped that Katie had an obsession for crime-fighting television shows. Madame Vega had also said that Lucy was good at getting answers. Maybe it was time to ask her what she knew about Gilbert's murder.

"There is another mystery in Ocean Crest. If you're right about my palm, I need some help unearthing answers," Lucy said.

Madame Vega set down Lucy's palm and leaned back in her seat. "I assume you're speaking of Mr. Lubinski's murder at the bonfire?"

"The bonfire took place on the beach, not far from your salon. Did you happen to be here that night?" Lucy asked.

"Until the summer season starts, I usually close early. But I was here that night, writing bills."

Lucy knew the psychic must have electric and heating bills to pay, but for some reason it seemed strange to imagine her writing a check. "Did you see anything that night?"

"I saw only one person—Eloisa Lubinski. She was walking on the beach. I assumed she was heading home from somewhere."

Eloisa had already confessed she'd walked home from one of her ladies' nights out. It didn't help her case that she'd told Detective Clemmons as well. But the detective couldn't seriously consider the eightysomething woman a serious suspect, could he? Gilbert may have wanted to evict his aunt from her home, but Eloisa wouldn't have killed him because of that.

"Not less than half an hour after I saw Eloisa," Madame Vega continued. "I heard the sirens and came outside to see the police Jeeps as they drove across the sand and stopped by the bonfire."

Lucy sat back, a bit disappointed. She'd been sure Madame would have seen something or someone other than Eloisa that night. "That's all you saw?"

"Yes," she said, then hesitated as she played with the voluminous sleeves of her robe. "But there is another person who may have the information you seek," Madame said.

"Who?"

"You should check out Tessa's Tattoo Parlor. She was open late that night. A lot of bikers want body ink, and Tessa's parlor has been a whirlwind."

"Good idea." Lucy had already suspected the tattoo parlor would be busy. She'd lost count of how many tattooed motorcycle tourists she'd seen during her morning run. And Tessa had been working on the boardwalk for a long time. Not as long as Madame Vega had been reading palms and tarot cards, but the tattoo artist was renowned at the Jersey shore for her intricate skin artwork. If Lucy had known Tessa was open late the night of the bonfire, she would have spoken to her sooner.

Suddenly anxious to follow up on this lead, Lucy stood and pulled a ten from the zippered pocket of her running shorts.

Madame Vega held up a hand. "No payment for today."

"You sure?"

"I didn't summon you here for payment." The woman's mouth dipped into a frown, and the wrinkles around her eyes deepened. Pressing both palms on the velvet-draped table, she leaned forward. "There's one more thing you must know. The murderer remains in town."

Lucy's gaze snapped to hers. "How do you know that?"

"I can sense it. There is an evil presence in Ocean Crest."

What the heck did that mean? A shiver of trepidation traveled down Lucy's spine as she held the psychic's stare. "How does that work exactly?"

Madame shrugged again. "I cannot explain it, I just know. You be careful, Lucy. Your palm says you are good at unearthing answers, but you may not be so lucky to escape unscathed this time."

Chapter Nineteen

Lucy's eyes adjusted to the morning sunlight from the dim psychic salon as she continued on her run. Madame's warning kept slipping through her thoughts.

There is an evil presence in Ocean Crest.

Her warning had merit. There *was* a good chance the murderer remained in town.

But how was Lucy to ferret him or her out?

At least the psychic had given Lucy a lead. Tessa's Tattoos was a short jog from Madame Vega's. As soon as Lucy stepped inside the parlor, the loud buzzing of a tattoo machine sounded. Tessa was hard at work inking a middle-aged man with thinning brown hair. He had numerous tattoos on his arms and a snake that wound around his neck like a boa constrictor.

Tessa wore blue gloves, the same kind a doctor might use while examining a patient. The man reclined in a black leather chair, and Tessa sat in a

backless, wheeled chair that allowed her to easily
access her clients from any angle. Lucy watched, fascinated, as the needles of the tattoo gun pierced the
man's skin at a superfast pace, and Tessa traced a design of a Celtic cross she'd drawn on the man's
chest.

"Be right with you," Tessa said without looking
up or stopping her work.

Lucy felt a bit queasy watching. She'd never had
a high tolerance for pain and couldn't imagine
getting a tattoo. She dreaded the flu shot every
year and squeezed her eyes shut until the nurse
had finished. The first time she'd had her eyebrows waxed, she'd squirmed like a baby. When
the cosmetologist suggested waxing her legs, or
heaven help her, a Brazilian bikini wax, Lucy had
sped from the beauty salon.

Lucy turned away from the scene to scan the
room. Pictures of Tessa's artwork covered the
walls—everything imaginable, from birds of prey,
eagles with roses, skulls, and dragons and serpents.
All the pictures were intricate works of varying colors that could be permanently tattooed on any
body part.

Tessa stood and snapped off her gloves. "You'll
have to come back to finish," she instructed the
man.

The middle-aged man stood, his face a bit pale.
Lucy wondered if he would pass out, but he made
it out of the parlor on his own two feet.

Tessa came over to Lucy. "Hello."

A slim, short woman in her early fifties, Tessa
had shoulder-length blue hair and wore black
army boots. She was dressed in a tank top and

short skirt that showed off her tattooed arms and legs. A tongue-piercing was visible when she smiled.

"Hi. My name is Lucy Berberian."

"I know who you are. You're the owner of that Mediterranean restaurant. I ate there a couple of weeks ago and saw you."

"I'm not the owner. Just the manager."

"Hmm. You have the best hummus around. I've wanted to go back to your hummus bar ever since."

"Thanks."

She arched a brow, and Lucy noticed it was pierced as well. "Want a tattoo of hummus? I can draw whatever you like."

"No, I'm not here for a tattoo. I was wondering if you were open the night Gilbert Lubinski was killed on the beach, and if you saw anything."

"I was. I've been superbusy here since the first day the Bikers on the Beach festival began."

Lucy knew Tessa's time was in high demand. Stan Slade had written an article about her. For all of Tessa's appearance—blue hair, inked arms and legs, and piercings—she was a skilled artist and a master with the ink gun. People came from all over South Jersey for Tessa's unique designs, or for one of her premade creations from her wall of ink, or to transform a bad tattoo with a new one. With all the bikers in town, Lucy imagined Tessa was in even higher demand.

"Did you happen to hear anything?" Lucy asked.

"The machines are loud, especially when you're crouched over someone, working. Why are you asking?"

"I was on the beach that night. I'm looking into a few things."

A sharp gleam lit her dark eyes. "I get it. Are you being accused? No, wait. It has to be a friend. Am I close?"

Lucy stared. How could she tell?

"I don't just tattoo," Tessa said. "I have to read people's minds when they walk in here. Most have a vague idea of what they want, but rely on me to dig deep and really figure it out. At times, I feel like a shrink. Too bad I can't bill myself out as one."

Lucy could see it. If she were going to get a tattoo, she'd have somewhat of an idea, but would have to rely on Tessa's expertise to flesh out her design. It must be a very personal experience. Tessa wouldn't only have to be a great artist, but a bit of a psychic as well. Madame Vega would have stiff competition.

Just then, another man strolled in. A tall, blond man with a tattoo of barbed wire around his large biceps. In Lucy's opinion, it was ugly and discolored, and Lucy wondered if he was here to have Tessa cover it up with a better tattoo.

"Take a seat," Tessa said. "I'll be right with you." She steered Lucy to the back of the parlor and away from her newest customer. Lucy spotted bottles of ink of varying colors and another tattoo gun on a table.

"Do the police have any suspects?" Tessa asked.

"They do, but I think they have the wrong people in mind," Lucy said.

"Ah, it is a friend, then."

Tessa was more perceptive than most people, probably more than the police. Before she could respond, another male voice sounded from the front of the parlor.

"You got to be kidding me! You have nerve," an angry male shouted.

"Get over yourself."

"Shove it."

"Make me."

Lucy looked at Tessa, wide-eyed. "What's going on?"

Without answering, Tessa sprinted to the front to investigate. Lucy, hot on her heels, was shocked to discover one of the angry voices belonged to Pumpkin. His slightly long, dark hair was tied back, and a shadow of a beard darkened his square chin.

"Pumpkin? What are you doing here?" Lucy asked.

"Hey, Lucy. Getting a tattoo." Pumpkin's gaze traveled down Lucy's arms and legs. "What about you? Are you getting your first one?"

"What's going on here?" Tessa demanded.

"He has my appointment time." Pumpkin's brows slashed down and his jaw hardened as he pointed to the blond man he'd been fighting.

The large, blond man's face screwed into an identical angry expression, and he stood to face Pumpkin, his fists clenched at his sides. "Like hell. He has mine."

Truly? Lucy couldn't fathom physically fighting

over an appointment. The two men looked ready
to tear each other apart. Their argument showed
just how much Tessa's time was valued.

Tessa bravely stepped between the giants, rolling
her eyes as if she were dealing with two oversize
toddlers. She looked tiny and fierce as she glowered at both of them. "We'll settle this nice, boys,
or I won't tattoo either of you. There's been an obvious mix-up."

"Seriously, Tessa? You're hard to get an appointment with and I made this one a long time ago,"
the blond man said.

"Me too," Pumpkin countered.

"One of you has to go, but I promise to squeeze
you in later and spend extra time on your tattoo.
I'll give you a fifty-percent discount, too," Tessa
said.

"Fine. I'll go," Pumpkin said.

"Good boy. How about same time next Tues-
day?"

"I'll be here." Pumpkin left, and the blond man
returned to the leather chair and sat.

Once again, Tessa steered Lucy out of earshot
of her customer.

"I can't believe they almost came to a fistfight
over an appointment with you," Lucy said.

Tessa smirked. "Those two don't like each other;
something about a bar brawl years ago."

"I've only recently gotten to know Pumpkin, but
I never imagined him losing his temper like that,"
Lucy said.

"They are both serious hotheads."

Lucy may not have learned about Gilbert's murder, but Tessa's statement reminded Lucy how little she knew about Pumpkin. He'd had a beef with Gilbert for unpaid landscaping bills and dug-up flowers, but a serious hothead? And over a tattoo appointment?

"They both acted like asses, but you handled it well," Lucy said.

"What can I say? Tattoos can bring out high emotions."

Chapter Twenty

Lucy thought about all she'd discovered as she left the tattoo parlor and started jogging the boardwalk. Madame Vega and Tessa hadn't seen or heard anything from the bonfire, but Lucy had learned something from each visit. She was still surprised at Pumpkin's display of temper from a double-booked tattoo appointment. He wasn't the only suspect, though, and others had stronger motives to want Gilbert dead, but it would take a while for Lucy to forget his anger.

She needed to head to her jetty to think about what she knew so far and run through the list of suspects and their motives.

She reached the middle of the boardwalk, and the blacklight minigolf came into view. Craig Smith stood outside. Dressed in a button-downed, short-sleeved shirt and khakis, he looked ready for a day in the office. He checked his watch, then walked inside. Lucy knew he wanted to buy the business and that he'd hired Max as his real estate broker. Maybe he was meeting Max this morning.

Max hadn't been pleased to find her in the minigolf last time, and he didn't want her to interfere with a sale. She would keep going this time. She'd had her fill of boardwalk adventure already today.

She was several yards away when she spotted Sophia Lubinski rush up the boardwalk ramp in four-inch heels and make a beeline for the entrance to the blacklight minigolf as fast as she could.

Sophia's appearance was so unexpected that Lucy tripped over the raised edge of a board and barely caught herself before falling flat on her face.

What the heck was Sophia doing meeting with Craig in the minigolf?

Curiosity rose hot within Lucy. Something not quite kosher was happening, and she wanted to find out what was going on. She made it to the minigolf entrance and glanced inside, but didn't see either Craig or Sophia. It was too early; the minigolf didn't open until eleven o'clock. No one was manning the front desk. Taking advantage of the situation, Lucy darted inside.

Like the first time she'd been here, everything was cast in an eerie neon glow. She was grateful for her gray T-shirt and black shorts. Like the last time she was here, nothing glowed except for her shoelaces. She heard voices and headed deeper into the place.

She spotted the two of them all the way in the back by the last display, the clown.

She froze, her heart pumping at the sight of the pasty-white face and red hair. Why did they have to meet by the scary clown?

Lucy ducked behind the sandcastle display and listened.

"How fast can you get me the cash?" Sophia asked.

Sophia's white sundress glowed under the ultraviolet lights. Her pale blond hair was pulled back in a high ponytail. And even though the lighting made it impossible to tell, Lucy would bet every dollar in her running shorts that Sophia had a full face of makeup.

Craig folded his arms across his chest and leaned on the clown. "Fast. I want those condos."

"I can't believe Gilbert didn't sell his share to you if the price was right," Sophia said.

"Oh, he planned to sell his share, just not to me. Gilbert wanted to screw me over and sell his half of the units to another investor. He knew how badly I wanted them."

Sophia scoffed. "Gilbert was cruel. He knew how badly I wanted a divorce and he was dragging it out so I would run out of money to pay my lawyer, and he hoped I would give in to his demands of measly alimony. That's just the way he worked."

"Well, he won't be getting his way now, will he?" Craig said.

Lucy's foot was growing numb, but she dared not move. A partnership between Craig and Sophia? Who would have suspected? Did she kill him to inherit her share of the condos and sell them to Craig for quick cash? Or did Craig kill his partner, knowing Sophia would sell Gilbert's share of the condos to him? Craig had admitted to desperately wanting them.

Sophia tapped her high heel. "I'll sign the sale documents tomorrow if you have the money."

Craig shook his head and held up a hand. "Not so fast."

"Why not?" Sophia demanded.

"As much as I want to say yes, we should wait at least a month. We can't arouse suspicion."

Sophia's face screwed into a disgusted expression. "Fine. I've waited years. One more month won't kill me."

Sophia started to turn away when Craig placed a hand on her arm. "Wait a minute. I want to know something. What do you plan to do with the money?"

"Ditch this little beach town. I'm headed for New York City. It's where all the big modeling agencies are located. I plan to land a modeling deal."

Mac McCabe had said Sophia had talked about her modeling ambitions in New York. Had she taken it one step too far and killed her husband to pursue her dreams? Had Gilbert mocked her dreams and stood in her way? Had he held the purse strings and prevented Sophia from going to the city?

Or had Craig killed his business partner over some condominiums?

Or had they done it together?

Either way, it was looking more and more like either Sophia or Craig were murderers.

Chapter Twenty-One

❦

Lucy never made it to the jetty. By the time she'd updated Katie on all her boardwalk jogging adventures for the day, she'd had to work the rest of the evening.

The following morning, Lucy had a different destination in mind, and she headed to Emma and Max's home.

Her ten-year-old niece, Niari, opened the door before Lucy had a chance to knock.

"Hi, Mokour Lucy!"

Lucy gave Niari a big hug. "Mokour" translated into "mother's sister" in Armenian. Her niece was dressed in a red soccer jersey, black soccer shorts, and cleats. Her light brown hair was in a ponytail and she wore a red, glitter headband that read, "Strikers."

"Are you coming to my soccer game?" Niari asked.

"I wouldn't miss it," Lucy said. "Where's your mom?"

"She's getting ready. Sally is also meeting us at the game. My dad can't come because he's showing a house to a buyer."

"That's okay. With the three of us cheering you on, you have to score," Lucy said.

"You bet!"

A quick ride later in separate cars, Lucy, Emma, and Sally were standing on the town's soccer field waiting for Niari's team to warm up. The coach called out, and the girls began running around the field. Niari gave a jaunty wave on her way by.

Sally smiled and waved at Niari's coach.

"Nice of you to come, too, Sally," Lucy said.

Sally pushed a wayward lock of hair behind her ear as she gazed out onto the field. "I wouldn't miss it. I try to come to a few of her games. I dated Coach Randal back in high school."

"Don't distract the coach," Emma admonished. "We need to win this game to advance to the next flight."

Lucy chuckled, but Sally ignored Emma. "I know a few people on the other team, too," Sally said as she grinned at parents standing on the sidelines.

Sally knew more than just a few. She was a local encyclopedia of townsfolk, and locals loved her at the restaurant. Sally would stroll around as she took orders, served meals, and talked up a storm with her customers. It was no wonder she knew parents from the opposing team, who'd traveled from a few towns over.

Niari's team began to line up and shoot balls into the net. Soon after, the referees arrived, a man and a woman dressed in striped yellow tops, black shorts, and cleats. With a blast of the whistle, the game started, and players from both teams ran up and down the field. For the first half they battled it out, both teams a good match. No one scored, but Niari played well in midfield.

"Go, Niari!" Lucy shouted, when her niece had an opportunity to score. Niari shot, but the goalie stopped the ball from flying into the net.

"Keep up the pressure!" Sally and Emma both yelled.

At halftime, Emma went to talk with fellow parents from Niari's team, and Lucy was left alone with Sally.

"How's Melanie?" Sally asked.

"Not great."

"We all know she didn't do it. She's a candy maker, for heaven's sake, not a killer." Sally eyed Lucy. "Have you or Katie found any leads?"

Lucy's hands were jammed into her jacket pockets. "What makes you think we're digging into things?"

"Oh, please. I know you too well, Lucy. I've been with your family for years, and just because your mom and Azad want you to stay out of things doesn't mean you should. You want to help others. It's part of your personality." Sally leaned close and whispered, "And I think it's great."

Lucy was grateful and relieved for Sally's support. She wasn't just a longtime waitress, but a good friend. "Okay. I confess. Katie and I have been asking some questions, but we haven't had much luck. I'm afraid I won't be able to help my friend."

Sally squeezed her arm. "I don't believe that. Keep digging. Melanie needs you. Meanwhile, I'll keep my ears open at the restaurant. People talk about all sorts of things after a satisfying meal."

"Thanks, Sally."

Another blast of the whistle and the second half of the game began. As time ticked by, both sides tried to score, but with no luck. Then, Niari passed the ball to a teammate who took a shot and scored.

"Great assist!" Emma yelled out.

A few minutes later, Niari had a breakaway of her own, took the shot, and the ball flew into the corner of the net.

The three women cheered and clapped. "I knew my niece could do it!" Lucy said.

"You must be good luck," Emma said. "Niari will want you at all her games."

Lucy wouldn't mind. Another benefit of returning home was spending time with her niece. The game ended with a two-zero win. The players made their way to their parents and Lucy gave Niari a big hug.

"Winner's choice. Ice cream or funnel cake on the boardwalk?" Lucy said.

"What about both?" Niari asked.

"It's fine by me if it's okay with your mom."

Emma nodded. "I did promise her something special if she scored. We'll meet you on the board-walk."

Lucy nodded. She needed to use the ladies' room before leaving the soccer field. "I'll meet you by the Freezy Cone." She waved and headed for a redbrick building near the parking lot.

Thank God, the town had real bathrooms, no porta-potties. On her way back out, she spotted a man with a hoodie pulled over his baseball cap that shadowed his face. He pushed away from the brick wall just as she stepped outside and made her way to the parking lot.

Footsteps scraped on the blacktop behind her. She glimpsed back to see he was about ten feet away.

An unbidden image of the dark figure on the beach sprang to mind. She couldn't confirm it, but she could have sworn that the figure had turned to look at her while she had been sitting on her patio with Gadoo.

She had a strange feeling the same man was following her now.

Most of the players and their families had already left the field; only a few remained in the parking lot. She spotted a couple of teenagers playing with a ball in a far field.

She picked up her pace. The unmistakable sound of footsteps told her he had as well.

Her Toyota came into view. Pressing the fob, she unlocked her car and quickly slid inside. She shut the door and immediately locked it. The man walked right by.

A glance in her rearview mirror revealed he was gone.

He must have cut through the parked cars to find his own.

She released a held-in breath. She was being paranoid. It was bright daylight. One shout and *someone* would have come running.

No one was following her.

* * *

As soon as Lucy parked by the boardwalk, she pulled out her cell and dialed Katie.

"Ocean Crest Town Hall."

"It's me. Did Bill mention any unsavory men lingering around town?"

"No, why?" Katie asked.

"I had the weird feeling I was being followed to my car by a man leaving Niari's soccer game today," Lucy said.

Katie's tone was serious over the phone. "Following you? Did you recognize him?"

"No. He wore a baseball cap and a hoodie. I couldn't see his face clearly." She bit her lower lip. "I know it sounds silly."

"It doesn't sound silly at all. Our instincts exist to protect us. You should have called Bill."

"I will next time. But it turned out to be nothing. I got in my car and the guy walked right by." Lucy hesitated, then decided to tell Katie her other story. "I also spotted a dark figure on the beach a couple of evenings ago. He was walking on the dunes and stopped to look up to where I was sitting on my patio. He didn't linger; it was only a couple of seconds, and then he just turned around and disappeared on the beach."

"Now you're starting to sound a bit paranoid," Katie said.

"I know, right?"

"Bill hasn't mentioned anyone loitering around town. The bikers have been a pretty calm bunch. They ride in the day, and most go to Mac's Pub at night or walk on the boardwalk. But I'll ask him."

"Thanks." It put Lucy's mind at ease knowing

that Bill was always there for both of them. He was still a beat cop who patrolled the town. If something was amiss, he would know it. Meanwhile, Niari was waiting to celebrate her winning goal.

Lucy hung up the phone and headed to the boardwalk for ice cream.

Chapter Twenty-Two

Bright and early the next morning, Lucy arrived at the restaurant to find her mother already stirring a large pot on the stove. Her signature beehive was perfectly arranged and the gold cross she always wore gleamed in the fluorescent lighting. Lucy knew better than to ask why her semiretired parent was here at five forty in the morning. For thirty years, Angela had risen early and arrived in the kitchen to prep for the upcoming day. Angela was an exceptional cook, taught by her own mother and mother-in-law. For years, her Armenian, Lebanese, and Greek dishes drew patrons from Ocean Crest and out of town. Like Madame Vega, her mother was a fixture in the town, not on the boardwalk, but in the restaurant.

Old habits die hard.

Her father, Raffi, didn't have this problem and had slipped into retirement a bit more easily. He often spent his mornings at Lola's Coffee Shop, drinking coffee with friends.

"You're late," her mother said as she cast Lucy a look over her shoulder.

Lucy glanced at the clock on the kitchen wall. "By ten minutes."

"It's still late."

Lucy knew better than to argue with her mother, especially this early. Lucy eyed the empty coffee urn. She needed caffeine if she was going to make it through the morning. She turned her attention back to the stove. "What's on the menu?"

"*Kebab yepvatz lolig.*"

Lamb kebabs with tomato sauce.

"Just like my mother-in-law prepared it. It's practice for when you host Easter.

It went without saying that Lucy needed the practice.

Lucy took a deep breath. The dishes were growing more and more complicated. She'd recently "mastered" hummus, baklava made with phyllo dough that was as thin as sheets of newspaper, and stuffed grape leaves with meat and rice. She knew the lamb kebabs with tomato sauce were delicious, but tricky. If you didn't season the lamb and prepare the sauce correctly, or if you overcooked the lamb, it would be dry and tough to chew. It didn't help that Angela was a perfectionist.

"Don't have that look on your face. I already marinated the lamb. We need to do the rest." Lucy's relief was short-lived. When she followed her mother into the walk-in refrigerator she found four large, stainless-steel bowls of marinated lamb.

This will take forever!

She knew shish kebab night was the most popular at the restaurant, but she'd never had to prepare *all* the food.

Back in the kitchen, Lucy slipped on plastic gloves and began the tedious task of threading the marinated, cubed lamb onto skewers. By the time Lucy's bowl was half-full, her mother had threaded twice as many skewers.

"How do you do it so fast, Mom?"

"Experience. You'll get better."

Lucy didn't necessarily want to get *that* much better. She just wanted to know how to make the dishes. As the manager, she felt she should know how each dish on the menu was made, but she didn't want to take Azad's job. He was the head chef now and could prepare anything much better than she could—some would say even better than Angela.

But that wasn't something she'd ever discuss with her mother.

"Next, we have to prepare the sauce that we'll pour over the meat once it's grilled. Sauté the onions, but don't burn them," her mother warned.

Lucy followed instructions and began heating the onions, then added diced and seeded tomatoes and spices. Delicious smells soon filled the kitchen.

Angela glanced over her shoulder as she worked. "How are you and Azad?"

Lucy stiffened, and the spoon clattered against the side of the pot. She warily glanced at her mom. Her parents both adored Azad and had wanted her to reconcile with him the day she set foot in Ocean Crest. Her mother especially liked him, and had once commented that if Lucy married him it would keep the business in the family. The manager and the cook—it was just like her parents' roles. The idea was enough to make her run for the hills.

Her relationship with Azad was not something she was willing to talk about with her mother. Other things, like cooking and her fascination with Cooking Kurt from the food channel were, but not Azad.

"Well?" Angela asked, her voice impatient.

"Azad is fine. We both are."

"Hmm. Your father said you went on a date. I'm happy. He is good for you, Lucy." Her mother must have sensed that the topic of conversation wouldn't go much farther. "Well, what have you and Katie been up to?"

This was a better topic, but it also came with pitfalls.

"We are the same," Lucy said, evading the question her mother was really asking.

But her mother would not be put off. "Are you and Katie still worried about your friend, Melanie Haven?"

Her mother understood that both Katie and Lucy had a hard time staying out of things, especially when one of their friends was in trouble. She also knew her mother had been vocal about not wanting Lucy to put herself in danger by investigating the recent crime. Lucy hesitated, then decided to be honest. "Who wouldn't be?"

Her mother sighed as she continued to watch Lucy stir the pot. "Melanie is a good girl. I don't know why that detective thinks she killed Gilbert Lubinski."

Her mother's words captured her attention, and Lucy turned to look her in the eye. "What do you mean?"

"Detective Clemmons came here yesterday to ask me questions about Melanie."

Lucy took a quick, sharp breath. "What? Why would he do that?"

"I thought it was unusual at first myself, then guessed he was simply asking townsfolk about her." Angela waved her hand. "You know, about Melanie's character."

Her mother may have rationalized the detective's behavior, but Lucy wasn't convinced. "I haven't heard of him speaking with any other townsfolk. What else did he ask you?"

"He wanted to know more about the Haven family. I told him I didn't know much. Only that the father opened the candy shop on the boardwalk around the same time we opened Kebab Kitchen. I mentioned that Melanie had a sister, but I haven't seen much of her over the years."

Lucy's mind kicked into overdrive. Why would Clemmons come here to ask her mother questions? What could he possibly have been thinking? That Lucy had held something back when he'd questioned her at the bonfire?

She could ask Bill, but she doubted he would know the answer. Bill hadn't yet been promoted to detective and he wasn't on the case.

"He would have asked Raffi, too, if he was here." Her mother's lips thinned with irritation. "Your father was at Lola's Coffee Shop, which is where he'll go this morning."

"Is that a problem?"

"It is. I want you to go there this morning and fetch him for me."

Really? She had no desire to get involved in her parents' quarrel over her father's coffee and social habits. But she wanted to know if Clemmons had found her father and questioned him as well. "I'm supposed to meet Katie there this morning. If I see Dad, I'll tell him you're asking for him," Lucy said.

"One more thing. I asked your father to take me to Cooking Kurt's book signing in Philadelphia."

"He has another cookbook out already?" Lucy asked.

Her mother pierced her with an annoyed stare. "He's a chef, Lucy. But that's not the point. Your father refuses to take me. Talk to him."

Her father disliked the celebrity chef and had often commented that Cooking Kurt was a fraud. Because of how quickly he kept pumping out cookbooks, Lucy wondered if her dad's bias had merit.

"Mom, I'll try to—"

A loud pounding like cannonballs striking the front door made Lucy jump.

"Who's that this early in the morning?" Angela asked.

"I'll go check." Lucy washed her hands, removed her apron, and hurried through the swinging doors that led from the kitchen into the dining room. The restaurant wouldn't open until nearly eleven, and the front door remained locked.

Out the large bay window, she spotted the *Ocean Crest Town News* van parked in the handicapped spot, then noticed Stan Slade, the head reporter, standing outside the front door. He pounded on the door once more.

Lucy slid the dead bolt and cracked open the door. "Hello. The restaurant doesn't open for another couple of hours."

"I'm aware," Slade said. "But the news business starts at the crack of dawn."

Lucy's gut tightened. Clearly, he wasn't here to eat. That meant he was here to interview her or ask her probing questions. Neither possibility sat well with her. They didn't have a great past relationship.

"What do you want?" she asked.

Stan pushed his black-rimmed glasses up the bridge of his nose. "Is that any way to greet a friend?"

Lucy shot him a look of disbelief. Stan Slade had left a high-paying New York City reporting job to relocate to Ocean Crest and take the position of head reporter of the *Town News*. No one knew why Slade had done it. Had he hated the big city, or had something happened there to force him to come live in the small shore town?

Either way, his past articles had not put Lucy or the restaurant in a positive light, and he'd caused nothing but trouble for her. She didn't trust him one bit.

At Lucy's silence, a corner of his mouth twisted upward. "All right," he grumbled, "maybe not good friends, but allies."

When she tapped her foot, he tried again. "Acquaintances," he muttered.

Lucy opened the door wide, and Stan strode inside, halting by the hostess stand. He wasn't that much taller than she was, maybe five foot five, but he always seemed to peer down at her through his dark-rimmed glasses.

"Why exactly are you here, Mr. Slade?" Lucy asked.

"To interview you about the circumstances of Gilbert Lubinski's death."

Well, talk about abrupt. The man always got straight to the point. His brash manner put her on guard. "Why me? There were plenty of other people at the bonfire."

"None of them found the body."

"I didn't find the body," she countered.

"Ah, but your friend Melanie Haven did. But she refuses to talk about it and slammed her candy-shop door in my face."

Smart girl. Lucy was beginning to wonder why she'd unlocked her front door.

"You're the second one to find the body," he said. "My readers want details."

Her agitation grew. She was getting nowhere arguing with the stubborn reporter. She needed to make him leave, the faster the better. "You should ask the police. Maybe even ask to see the coroner's report. It would be much more accurate than whatever I can tell you."

"Readers want juicy details. Not some clinical report."

She dug her fingernails into her palms in frustration. She needed to stay in control, calm and collected. If he thought he would get nowhere, he would leave on his own. "I'm sorry, I don't have anything for you."

"I also know you can't resist sticking your nose in other people's business."

So much for control! Her frustration veered into anger in a heartbeat. "What the heck does that mean?"

He stepped away from the hostess stand and came close, his dark eyes focused on her behind his glasses. "I meant it as a compliment. Your track record's better than the police's."

"It didn't sound like a compliment."

Slade flashed a crooked smile. "How about a truce? If you ever need to make something publicly known, promise me you'll come to me first."

She eyed him warily. It was a strange request. He'd never asked her to do something like this before. He'd mentioned allies, and Lucy couldn't help but wonder if this was what he'd meant. She also couldn't imagine an instance when she'd need him to print something, other than a paid advertisement for the restaurant and a coupon for ten percent off a customer's bill during the summer season.

Were newspaper sales slagging, or was there more to his offer? She could never tell with Stan Slade.

She became aware that he was waiting for her response. "Fine. If there's something I want to put out there, I'll come to you first. Now, would you please leave? I have a lot to do before the lunch hour."

Chapter Twenty-Three

By the time Lucy and her mother finished, it was around eight o'clock in the morning. Lucy headed straight for Lola's Coffee shop. As soon as she opened the door, the heavenly scent of freshly ground coffee beans drifted to her.

Lola Stewart was behind the counter serving a line of caffeine-deprived-looking customers. A tall, thin woman, Lola's steel-gray hair was styled in her customary low bun. A tower of chunky white mugs was stacked behind the counter, and a refrigerated case displayed tempting Danishes, muffins, and assorted pastries from Cutie's Cupcakes. The sound of the hissing espresso machine as it turned milk into a frothy foam, combined with the chattering of customers sitting at colorful bistro tables, was as comforting as the smell.

Katie was already seated at a cozy table for two tucked away in the corner. She waved when she saw Lucy and pointed to a takeout cup with a cardboard sleeve and a muffin on a plate. Lucy hurried over and sat in a wire-backed chair across from her.

"A cappuccino and a banana nut muffin for you," Katie said.

Lucy reached for the cup. "You're the best."

"I know. But be careful! It's steaming hot."

Lucy removed the lid and blew on the steaming cappuccino. She reached for a sugar stick—one of her favorite things at the coffee shop—and stirred the crystal sugar into her cappuccino.

Katie stirred milk into her coffee and took a small sip. "I still can't believe it. First, Sophia lies about her alibi. Then, she secretly meets Craig and offers to sell him her inherited half of the Seagull Condos."

Lucy had already updated Katie on what she'd discovered at Mac's Pub and the blacklight minigolf. "Both Sophia and Craig had strong motive and opportunity to want Gilbert dead. Craig was already at the bonfire. Sophia had a half-hour window to get to the beach and kill her husband."

Katie leaned forward and lowered her voice. "What if they both had a hand in the murder?"

"You think they were in it together?" Lucy's brow furrowed as she considered the scenario. It was a good theory. "It's entirely possible. Maybe one of them struck Gilbert from behind with the driftwood and the other suffocated him. It was pretty convenient that the saltwater taffy was there. Melanie is the perfect scapegoat, especially after everyone witnessed her fight with Gilbert on the beach."

Katie set down her cup. "Maybe they thought they'd killed him by striking him senseless. Only when they noticed him still breathing did they think to suffocate him. It would have been easy to shove a wad of saltwater taffy down Gilbert's throat if he was already unconscious. Like you said, framing Melanie was a bonus."

This was an even better theory. "So far, it's working. Detective Clemmons has his eye on Melanie. He came to the restaurant to ask my mom what she knew about Melanie and her family."

"He did? Bill didn't mention anything about that. I would have told you if he had. But it doesn't surprise me. Bill isn't working the case and he's not a detective yet. He wouldn't be privy to Clemmons's thinking."

"I fear Detective Clemmons will be arresting Melanie soon. How do we tell Clemmons what we've learned without getting into trouble ourselves?"

"You didn't do anything wrong," Katie said. "You were at the pub and Candace tracked you down to tell you that Sophia lied about spending the entire night at the bar."

"True. But that's not what I'm worried about."

"Then what?"

"What about my eavesdropping on Craig and Sophia at the blacklight minigolf? Last time I checked, sneaking into a business before it's open isn't legal."

Katie wrinkled her nose. "Yeah, well . . . forget about telling Clemmons right now. It's too soon anyway. And we still have other suspects to consider. Melanie's sister, Rhonda, had an online gambling problem and borrowed cash from Gilbert."

"That doesn't exactly look good for Melanie either. She tried to help her sister out when she couldn't make Gilbert's high-interest payments. Gilbert started going after Melanie when she fell behind on her own rent. Melanie had just as strong a motive as Rhonda to want Gilbert dead. The police will consider it additional motive."

Katie sighed. "Gilbert didn't have a shortage of people who disliked him. He wasn't well-liked by many of his tenants either. Plus, he was a town loan shark. But before we delve into that mess, I think we should look into Pumpkin O'Connor."

Lucy pulled her sugar stick out of her coffee. All the sugar had melted. She thought about the scene at the tattoo parlor, and Pumpkin's anger over a mixed-up appointment. He may have acted like a jerk, but it didn't add up to why he'd want to murder Gilbert. "Pumpkin doesn't have a strong-enough motive. All he did was dig up a few flower beds because Gilbert didn't pay for his landscaping services."

"That's not the entire reason," Katie said. "I asked my coworkers at the town hall, and some said that Pumpkin has quite a temper. He came in a couple of times ranting and raving about Gilbert not paying him and wanted to know how the township could help. When someone told him the township couldn't intervene in private matters and told him to file a small claims lawsuit with the county, Pumpkin hollered something fierce and said he'd take care of Gilbert himself. I remembered what you said about Pumpkin picking a fight at Tessa's Tattoo Parlor. If he gets that angry over a tattoo appointment and unpaid landscaping, maybe he lost it and killed Gilbert."

"Wow!" So they didn't have just one example of Pumpkin's temper, but two. And he'd gone so far as to publicly threaten to take care of Gilbert himself. Lucy wondered if Michael knew about his friend's anger issues. Or if he knew about Craig's business ambitions.

Michael had told her he'd met both men at a motorcycle club three years ago and they had enjoyed riding together ever since. How well did he know either Pumpkin or Craig? It wasn't as if you could talk when you rode side by side. Did they meet at bars beforehand and talk about things other than motorcycles?

"Another coworker told me that Pumpkin owns a large greenhouse in town. It's where he parks his trucks at the end of the day. I figure we can find him there when he's not landscaping. We should check it out today after I get off work. I get off early on Fridays."

"What about Bill?" Lucy asked.

Katie looked down at her coffee. "What about him?"

"You know what I mean," Lucy said. "He wouldn't be okay with us snooping around."

Katie shook her head. "Don't worry about Bill. We aren't doing anything wrong. It's not like we're breaking and entering into someone's business in the middle of the night."

"God only knows, we've done that before," Lucy muttered.

Katie wasn't just talking about Lucy's escapade into the minigolf on the boardwalk in the morning. They'd done worse together in the past. They'd also been caught in the act and dodged a bullet as they'd fled.

Lucy suppressed a shiver just recalling the memory.

Katie settled back in her chair. "What I meant to say is that we're just going to a landscaper's greenhouse to talk with the owner. For all anyone knows, I want to buy mulch and flowers for my flower bed. If we happen to learn something, we can spill it all to Bill."

Lucy let out a held-in breath. "I guess you're right."

Katie stood and gathered her purse and coffee. "I get off at three. I'll pick you up after work."

Lucy pushed back her chair. "Sounds good." She reached for her purse and froze. The door opened and her father stepped inside the coffee shop. She nearly dropped her bag. "Oh brother, there's my dad."

"Is that a problem?" Katie asked.

After meeting Katie, Lucy had forgotten that Raffi liked to frequent Lola's Coffee Shop to see friends. An image of her mother flashed before her—her short stature and military bearing, the signature beehive, the stern expression when she'd brought up her father, and suddenly, Lucy didn't want to get involved. If her mother had an issue with her father, she could march down here herself and confront him.

"My mom hates that he comes here every morning. She told me to fetch my dad if I saw him."

Katie shot her an incredulous look. "Seriously? Why'd you agree? Getting involved in your parent's marital disputes may be more dangerous than confronting Clemmons."

"Thanks for the encouragement. I had another reason for agreeing. I want to see if Clemmons asked my dad questions."

Katie waggled her fingers at Lucy. "Good luck with that."

"You're not going to stay to help?"

"Nope. I have more common sense than interfering with my own parents' quarrels. See you later."

Lucy waited until her father got in line for coffee before approaching him. "Hi, Dad."

"Lucy! What are you doing here?" His dark brows drew together like a hairy caterpillar. "Did your mother send you?"

How much to admit? She forced a smile and kept his gaze. "Yes and no. It's true that Mom doesn't like your coffee-shop habit, but I came here this morning to meet Katie before she had to go to work."

"Where's Katie?" He looked beyond her shoulder.

"She left already, but I want to talk with you about something else."

He eyed her curiously. "Oh? It sounds serious. Is it about the inventory? You want more time to go out with Azad Saturday nights? I've been looking at the estimates you set out for me in the office."

"No, it's not about Azad or inventory." She heard the frustration in her voice. She wanted a computerized inventory system, had nagged him for one for months. And now he was considering it because he thought she needed more time to go out with Azad? Really? Is that what it took? She would have pulled strings and used that excuse a long time ago if she'd thought of it.

Her father made it up to the counter and placed his order. Lucy followed him to a table that seated six and he pulled out a chair for her.

"My friends should be here soon," Raffi said. "Now, what did you want to talk about?"

Lucy leveled her gaze at her father. "Detective Clemmons came to the restaurant and asked Mom questions about Melanie Haven and her family. She said you weren't there."

"I heard about the detective's visit."

"Did he track you down, too?" Lucy asked.

He opened the coffee lid and added cream. "No. At least, not yet."

"Will you promise to tell me if he does?"

A probing look came into his eyes. "I'll promise if you tell me the truth. Did your mother send you here this morning?"

She eyed him warily. "Mom told me to find you, but like I said, I was meeting Katie here anyway."

He let out a long sigh. "Your mother hates that I come here. Now that we're retired, she wants me to spend mornings with her."

"Is that so bad?"

"No, but I have friends here. Friends that I used to see on a regular basis at the restaurant. We talk sports and politics. Your mother should understand. I don't keep her from her church friends every Sunday."

When her parents ran the restaurant full-time, they both had an abundance of acquaintances. Running the business was like running an active social calendar. Certain friends came to eat on certain days. There was always plenty of chatting with people who liked to share stories. Then there was the waitstaff, Sally and Emma, and cooks, Butch and Azad, and others who had worked at Kebab Kitchen throughout the thirty years—all of whom were like one big, extended family. Her father simply missed the social interaction.

So did her mother in her own way.

For the first time, Lucy realized retirement—even semiretirement—had been a hard adjustment for her parents.

She touched his hand. "You should explain it to Mom. She'd understand. She's probably feeling the same way and misses talking with the customers. She probably thinks you can fill the void by staying home in the mornings."

Surprise flashed across her father's face. "You think so? I never thought she felt the same."

Lucy was amazed that two people who had been married for over forty years could still have communication problems and have difficulty sharing their current feelings. Marriage took work, her mother often said.

"I think Mom does feel the same way. Meanwhile, she mentioned an outing in Philadelphia for Cooking Kurt's newest cookbook signing. You should take Mom and spend time together. It will be good for you both."

At the mention of Cooking Kurt, her father's jaw tensed, displaying his deep frustration. "That man is a fraud. It's his second cookbook in less than six months. You don't actually believe he wrote either book, do you?"

Lucy had her own doubts about the handsome celebrity chef. "Maybe he's like Martha Stewart and has his own staff. You should still take Mom."

"I hate going into the city," he grumbled.

She knew that for a fact about her father. When Lucy worked in Philadelphia, her parents never visited. She had to travel to see them for the holidays. Even though the city was only an hour and a half drive—ninety miles from Ocean Crest—crossing the Ben Franklin Bridge into the city was like traveling to a foreign country for her father.

"You don't have to drive," Lucy said. "Take the bus. It will please Mom, and you can spend quality time together."

Raffi cradled his cup in silence, a brooding expression on his face. "All right. I'll do it for her. I'll also cut it short today, before your mother comes down here and drags me back home by my hair." He ran his hand over his balding pate. "God only knows, I have little left as it is."

Chapter Twenty-Four

Lucy was waiting for Katie in the restaurant's parking lot when Katie pulled up in her Jeep.

"I looked up the address for Pumpkin's greenhouse on my cell phone," Katie said.

Lucy sat in the passenger seat and reached for her seat belt. "Good. I have about two hours." Azad and Butch were handling the kitchen and Sally and Emma could hold down the fort in the dining room so that Lucy could escape.

Katie started the engine and they drove down Ocean Avenue and passed the boardwalk ramp. Lucy glimpsed the ocean between buildings, a brilliant blue line on the horizon, as Katie continued driving. They made it to the end of town, and rather than leave Ocean Crest, Katie turned left. Houses blurred by, until they came to a bumpy dirt road. The Jeep's suspension bounced, and Lucy jostled in her seat.

Lucy pulled her seat belt tight. "You might want

to slow down on this back road. It's not the Indy 500."

"Don't be a back-seat driver. Besides, we're here."

Lucy looked up to see a large glass and steel greenhouse come into view. A handmade sign, "PUMPKIN'S LANDSCAPING," was written in big, black letters attached to a wooden stake. Pumpkin's landscaping pickup truck was parked on the side of the greenhouse.

Katie parked next to the truck, and they stepped outside. The late afternoon sun shone brightly, and Lucy cupped a hand over her eyes as she peered inside the greenhouse. Tables holding rows and rows of plants ran down the length of the interior. "I don't see anyone. Do you?"

Katie shook her head, then knocked on the glass door. No answer.

There was no lock on the door. She reached for the handle and cracked open the door. "Pumpkin? Are you in there?"

No answer.

"Maybe he's all the way in the back and can't hear us," Lucy said. "Let's go inside."

A worried expression flashed across Katie's face. "Maybe we shouldn't. Remember what happened when we snuck into Kevin Crowley's boardwalk trailer?"

"This is different. It's a greenhouse, not an office, and there's no lock," Lucy said. She opened the door wide and stepped inside. Katie was right behind her.

Humid warmth enveloped them in a wave. The

space was crowded down its center with four long worktables, holding gardening tools, bags of potting soil, and pots in every size imaginable. The scent of flowers, plants, and moist soil hung in the air like a heady perfume. Lucy walked down an aisle and recognized pots of colorful daffodils, hydrangeas, and tulips ready to be sold for Easter. Other plants and shrubs would brighten flower beds all over town, including Kebab Kitchen's flower boxes and landscaping.

"Pumpkin!" Lucy called out.

Katie walked ahead of her. "No one's here. Pumpkin must have more than one truck if he left one behind. I have paper in my purse. Should we leave a note for him?"

Lucy contemplated the idea, then shook her head. "No. Now that we know where this place is, we can catch up with him later. I really don't think Pumpkin is our strongest suspect anyway. He may have a temper, but do you really think he murdered Gilbert for unpaid landscaping bills?"

"Nah, I guess not and—" Katie stiffened, her eyes widening at something she spotted over Lucy's shoulder. "We may not have to wait. He just pulled up out front."

Lucy spun around and followed Katie's gaze to see a second pickup truck park by the greenhouse door. "Let's go. We can talk to him now."

As she watched, Pumpkin walked around the truck to open the passenger-side door. Sophia Lubinski stepped out. Dressed in a short red dress and high-heeled sandals, she smoothed down her skirt. A second later, she reached up to kiss Pumpkin fully on the mouth.

Lucy stiffened in shock as she watched the scene unfold. "Oh my God. Do you see—"

Katie's gaze was riveted. "I see. What are Pumpkin and Sophia doing together?"

"I don't know, but clearly they haven't spotted your Jeep parked on the side behind his spare truck."

The couple broke apart, and Lucy grabbed Katie's arm. "They're headed here. We have to hide."

Katie's blue eyes grew wide. "Hide? Where?"

Lucy scanned the rows of tables until her gaze landed on the last one. "Over here. Quick!" She pulled Katie with her and they scrambled beneath the table. At the last second, Lucy moved two potted urns of ferns in front of them to conceal their hiding place.

The door to the greenhouse opened and footsteps scraped the concrete floor.

"I've missed you so much, baby," Pumpkin said.

"Me too," Sophia purred. "I could barely wait for us to be together."

Through a crack between the ferns, Lucy spied the couple. Sophia's long, blond hair was loose and cascaded down her back in a way that would make most women envious. Pumpkin held her around her waist with one arm; then, with an impatient sweep of his free hand, he pushed aside the table's contents, picked Sophia up, and placed her on the edge of the table. Heated kissing ensued.

"I can't believe it! That woman works every angle," Katie whispered.

Lucy was just as surprised. First Sophia made a

deal with Craig, and all along she was sleeping with Pumpkin. "She does get around."

It was looking more and more as if Sophia Lubinski had murdered her husband.

She wanted cash for Gilbert's half of the Seagull Condos.

She wanted to end her contested divorce proceedings and go to New York and get a modeling contract.

She wanted her lover, Pumpkin.

Two questions remained: were Craig or Pumpkin involved, too?

"Oh, no. My leg is falling asleep and my nose is itching from all these flowering plants." Katie sniffled, then rubbed her nose. "Are we going to have to witness their entire amorous encounter?"

The thought made Lucy's stomach tilt. "I hope not."

A moan sounded, followed by a groan. Lucy wanted to shut out what she was seeing and hearing. She wanted out of this greenhouse and fast. But how?

Lucy's head started to ache. The humidity, along with the cramped position, made her feel lightheaded. Katie looked even worse. Her nose was red and running, her eyes puffy. If she sneezed, all would be lost.

"My foot is numb. I have to move," Katie said.

"Wait. Don't!"

Too late. Katie shifted, and her shoulder bumped the table and upended a potted plant. To Lucy's horror, the plant teetered on the edge of the table. She tried to reach out and steady it, but the large urns she'd moved to hide their position slowed her down. Gravity won, and the pot smashed to the ground in a mess of broken pottery and dirt.

Oh no!

Lucy's stomach dropped into her shoes. She whirled to Katie, who had a panicked look in her eyes. She mouthed the word *Sorry.*

"What was that?" Sophia asked.

"Stay here. I'll check."

Fear knotted inside Lucy as the scrape of boots imminently approached. It was only a matter of time before they would be discovered. Rather than wait for the inevitable, she pushed the urns aside and crawled out from under the table. Katie followed.

"It's just us," Lucy said.

Pumpkin stopped short, his eyes sharp and assessing as he saw them. "Lucy!" His gaze flew to Katie. "Katie?"

"What are you two doing here?" Sophia said as she approached, her pretty face screwed into a scowl.

"We came to talk to Pumpkin, but when we saw you two get out of the truck . . . well . . . we didn't want to intrude." Lucy wasn't sure how Pumpkin or Sophia would respond, but it was the truth.

Pumpkin's hard features softened and he looked to Sophia. "We know this looks bad."

"It does," Katie said. She sneezed and then stomped her foot to get feeling to return to it after their cramped position. "It looks really bad if you ask me."

Leave it to Katie to be forthright. For someone

who never wanted to sneak into places, her accusatory nature came out when they were cornered. The problem was, they could be facing stone-cold killers.

Sophia clasped Pumpkin's hand and her blue eyes filled with tears. "I know what you're thinking, but we didn't do it. We didn't kill Gilbert."

Lucy was surprised at Sophia's unexpected show of emotion. Was she for real or putting on a fabulous show? "We aren't the police, but they are going to want to know about your relationship."

Whatever type of relationship they were involved in. Sex? Or was there an emotional attachment and commitment?

"It's none of their business," Pumpkin said.

Katie's mouth dipped into a frown. "Are you kidding? The victim's wife is having an affair with a person of interest, who also happened to be at the bonfire. My husband is a cop and he'd want to know."

Lucy was torn between carefully watching Pumpkin for his response and slapping a hand over Katie's mouth. *They could be killers!*

What they needed to do was escape and fast, then worry about telling Bill. She eyed Pumpkin's muscles and broad shoulders. He could easily overpower two women, and the man had a temper. The last thing they needed was to provoke him.

Lucy didn't want to mention that she'd learned about Sophia selling her share of the condos to Craig. That just might set the woman off . . . or worse, Pumpkin.

Sophia calmed Pumpkin with a hand on his arm. "We didn't do it. I know what it looks like. I was the cheating spouse, and along with Pumpkin, my lover, we killed my husband. But that didn't happen."

"Sophia wasn't even at the bonfire. She has an alibi for that night," Pumpkin said.

Lucy spoke up then. "Your so-called alibi isn't as solid as you'd like us to believe. There's a half-hour window of unaccountability. It's enough time for you to leave the pub and make it to the beach." So much for not prodding a guilty couple.

"How do you know about that?" Sophia asked.

Katie gave her a pointed stare. "It doesn't matter how Lucy knows, only that she does."

"You're right," Sophia conceded. "I stepped outside the back door of Mac's Pub that night so I could sit in my car and call Pumpkin. It's the only time I had all day to talk with him. I didn't kill Gilbert."

It was a good excuse, but certainly not a solid alibi if Pumpkin was involved in the murder. They could have scheduled a phone call as Sophia made her way to the bonfire in case the police looked into her phone records. "If not you, then who?" Lucy asked.

Sophia and Pumpkin exchanged a look that led Lucy to believe they were debating whether to share something with them. A moment later, they must have agreed, because Sophia nodded.

"Gilbert wasn't just a landlord. He had another side business—a small but profitable one."

"Okay." Although Sophia was vague, Lucy suspected she knew what the woman was referring to. "Do you mean his moneylending activities?"

"You know about that, too?" Pumpkin asked, clearly surprised.

"We've heard. Gilbert loaned money to town residents who didn't qualify for bank loans. I wasn't sure *you* knew," Lucy said.

Sophia's fingers twisted her skirt. "I recently learned about it by eavesdropping on Gilbert's phone calls. I thought he was having an affair and I could somehow use infidelity against him in the divorce proceedings. It turned out he had a side business, which was worse. He'd been hiding money from me and didn't report the extra income to my divorce lawyer," she said, bitterness lacing her tone.

Sophia didn't sound as if she'd be bothered by her husband's possible infidelity. But hiding cash took Gilbert's betrayal to a much higher level. In Sophia's mind, it was more motive to want to kill her husband than cheating.

"Gilbert wasn't very nice about how he handled the loans. From what I've heard, there are other people who had reason to want my husband dead. One such person was at the bonfire," Sophia said.

"You mean Melanie Haven?" Lucy's tone was harsher than she would have liked.

Sophia's eyes were no longer tearing when she met Lucy's gaze. "Her taffy was found in his throat."

Lucy was growing tired of people bringing up that fact. "It doesn't mean Melanie killed him."

"Well, we didn't either," Pumpkin said.

"If you think others had motive, why didn't you tell the police about Gilbert's moneylending practices?" Lucy asked.

"I don't have proof. I heard him mention that he required signed loan papers from one of his borrowers over the phone, but I never found any record of them. I searched everywhere, but no luck. Gilbert was a slippery bastard," Sophia said.

Lucy recalled Azad mentioning that he'd signed loan documents when he'd borrowed from Gilbert, and he hadn't received the papers back until he'd made his last payment. "Again, you could have mentioned this to the police and they could have issued search warrants."

Sophia moistened her lips. "I don't trust the police."

"And you trust us? Why?" Lucy asked.

Sophia looked from Katie to Lucy. "You already learned about the gap in time in my alibi and Gilbert's moneylending. That takes a good amount of sleuthing. And from what I've heard, you have a better history of finding out the truth around here. My bet is on you."

Chapter Twenty-Five

"That was a close one," Katie said as they drove on the dirt road leading back to Ocean Avenue.

"For someone who's afraid of entering businesses uninvited, you certainly have no fear when it comes to confronting possible murderers," Lucy said.

"You were worried in there?" Katie asked.

"You bet. Sophia's alibi is a bust. She claims she sat in her car and called Pumpkin, but she could have just as easily met him on the beach to dispose of her unwanted husband. If either of them thought we were a real threat, we could have been in big trouble. Who would think to look for us in a greenhouse off the beaten path? We could probably outrun Sophia, but not Pumpkin."

Katie's fingers tightened on the steering wheel. "You're right! I guess I lost more than feeling in my leg, but my head. I couldn't help myself."

"Thankfully, it worked out okay." Lucy turned to

look at Katie. "Do you believe their claims of innocence?"

Katie hesitated. "It wouldn't be the first time passion led to murder."

"What about Sophia's tears?"

"I'm not sure I buy her performance."

"Me either. Sophia could be a fabulous actress. I purposely didn't mention that I overheard her conversation with Craig Smith. She wants the cash from her inherited share of the Seagull Condos to go to New York City and pursue a modeling career."

"Did she mention Pumpkin when she was talking with Craig?" Katie asked.

"Nope."

"You think she'd take the cash and leave Pumpkin behind?" Katie asked.

"It sure sounded like Sophia wants a modeling career more than a boyfriend. I wonder if Pumpkin knows about her dealings with Craig or her ambitions?"

"This is turning into a bad love triangle. Everything points back to Sophia. She even knew about Gilbert's moneylending," Katie said.

"If only she knew where Gilbert kept his papers. We could learn the names of others who owed Gilbert cash," Lucy said.

"We know one already—Rhonda, Melanie's sister," Katie said.

"Rhonda and who else?" Lucy said. "We have to tell Bill what we know so far."

"I'll take care of it," Katie said. "He may not like us getting involved, but it's not like we planned on hiding in a greenhouse or watching those two make out. Ugh!"

Lucy was about to respond when her cell phone rang. She rummaged through her purse and recognized her father's cell phone number on her screen.

"Hi, Dad."

"You made me promise to tell you if the detective came around asking me questions. He did," Raffi said.

Lucy's heart pounded in her chest. What on earth did Clemmons think her parents knew? Some hidden secret about Melanie, her family, or Haven Candies?

Clemmons might be doing his job, but it felt like he was harassing her parents. She also needed a way to convey the information she'd learned with Katie about Sophia and Craig—and Sophia and Pumpkin. But how?

Lucy bit her bottom lip. Katie said she'd tell Bill, but Lucy didn't want Bill to suffer any consequences from their investigation either. The one common denominator in all this mess was Sophia.

But how could she tell Clemmons without getting in trouble?

"I didn't tell him anything your mother hadn't already," Raffi said.

Lucy still didn't like the fact that Clemmons was sniffing around her family. He was also offtrack in finding the real killer. "Thanks for calling me, Dad. I have one more errand to run, then I'll see you at the restaurant." She ended the call and shoved the phone back into her purse.

"I take it Clemmons asked your dad about Melanie," Katie said.

Katie's Jeep pulled into the restaurant's parking lot. "Clemmons has it all wrong. Drop me off by my car. It's time I paid the detective a visit."

Lucy pulled into the last visitors' spot of the Ocean Crest Police Station. A middle-aged police officer with dark, curly hair and a goatee sat behind the reception desk.

"My name is Lucy Berberian and I'm here to see Detective Clemmons."

"Is he expecting you?"

"No, but he will want to see me."

The officer eyed her curiously before picking up a phone and speaking quietly to someone. "He does want to see you." He buzzed her inside. "I'll show you to the detective's office."

Lucy flashed a smile. "Oh, I know where it is."

The officer shot her a sharp look. "Still, I'll walk you inside."

She supposed she shouldn't have admitted to knowing where Clemmons's office was located. It made her sound like she'd been in trouble in the past.

If only he knew.

The main room was crowded with desks, most of them occupied by police officers who were busy typing reports on their computers. Bill Watson's desk was empty. Lucy suspected he was on patrol.

"Ms. Berberian, how nice of you to visit." Detective Clemmons appeared and extended his hand.

Tall and thin, his straw-colored hair was parted on the side and his mustache twitched when he shook her hand. He wore a jacket and a wrinkled white shirt, and tie.

She forced a smile. "Is this a bad time?"

"Not at all. It's a perfect time."

Lucy turned at the second voice, a female one, to see Prosecutor Marsha Walsh approach from behind a desk. Lucy breathed in a shallow, quick gasp.

Of all the rotten luck!

Prosecutor Walsh looked the same as the last few times Lucy had seen her. The woman was slender and meticulously dressed in a pantsuit and respectable heels. Her short brown hair was styled in a bob—not a hair out of place. But it was her sharp brown eyes that shone with intelligence that put Lucy on edge.

Lucy had wanted to ask Clemmons why he was questioning her parents. She hoped to lead him away from Melanie and in the direction of Sophia without revealing how she'd obtained her knowledge. But things were complicated now. She had to choose her words very carefully.

"Sit with us for a minute, Ms. Berberian," the prosecutor said.

Did she have a choice? "Okay."

Clemmons led her not into his office but into a room down the hall. He opened the door and motioned for her to enter. It was a sparsely furnished room, containing only a table, a single chair on one side, and two chairs on the opposite side. It was painted a blinding white, and she blinked beneath bright fluorescent lights. Her anxiety ratcheted a notch. Clearly, this was where the police questioned suspects or persons of interest.

Clemmons motioned for her to sit. The detective and the prosecutor sat across from her.

Lucy shifted in the metal chair. If there ever was a hot seat, this was it.

"To what do we owe the pleasure?" Clemmons asked.

Lucy swallowed. She struggled to remember her planned speech. "Why are you harassing my parents?" She blurted out the question, then inwardly cringed. That wasn't how she'd planned to broach the subject.

Clemmons leaned back in his seat. "I visited Kebab Kitchen to ask your mother routine questions. I followed up with your father later."

"What routine questions? My parents weren't at the scene of the crime."

"No. But your parents are long-term residents. I wanted to know what they knew about Haven Candies."

"You mean about Melanie Haven in particular," Lucy said.

"Perhaps. Either way, I don't have to justify police investigation to you, Ms. Berberian."

Lucy's fingers curled on her lap beneath the table. "I know you do not have to justify yourself to me. But you're wrong about Melanie Haven. She is not a killer."

"How do you know that?" Prosecutor Walsh spoke for the first time since they entered the room.

Lucy met her gaze. "I just know. We've been friends for a long time. Melanie Haven is not the type of person who could kill someone in cold blood."

"Well, if you came here to express your instincts based on your friendship, this is going to be a very short talk. Let us do our jobs," Clemmons said.

"But you are overlooking other suspects." Lucy regretted the statement as soon as it left her lips. She needed to watch what she said, but the presence of the two made her feel outnumbered and unsure of herself.

The detective's eyes narrowed. "What else do you know?"

"What do you mean?"

"No need to play dumb on my behalf, Ms. Berberian. I know you and your sidekick, Katie Watson, can't help but stick your noses in crime around here," Walsh said.

Stan Slade had accused her of the same thing. Coming from the prosecutor, it sounded much worse.

"Katie and I are not nosy, and I'm not playing dumb." Lucy hoped her voice sounded firm. Something about the wily prosecutor always put her on edge. Perhaps it was because she was whip smart and rarely lost a case. Lucy had looked into her professional achievements a while back. She was a shark in the courtroom. As a fellow lawyer, Lucy couldn't help but admire Walsh, but that didn't make her feel any more comfortable around her.

"I've reminded you before that your actions have consequences. Not just for yourself, but for Mrs. Watson's husband. You wouldn't want to unwittingly involve Bill Watson in covering up for you and his wife, would you?"

Lucy sat up straight. "Excuse me? What exactly are you threatening?"

"Mr. Watson is in the final stages of being promoted to detective himself. How would it look if his wife and her best friend were found meddling in police matters?" Walsh leaned forward and held Lucy's gaze. "So, if you know something, it would be best if you tell us."

All bravado left Lucy. She struggled to breathe, as if an invisible hand tightened on her throat. How to tell Walsh and Clemmons what she'd learned without getting herself or Katie in trouble and, most importantly, without putting Bill's promotion in jeopardy?

The silence lengthened between them, making Lucy even more uncomfortable.

Surprisingly, it was Clemmons who came to her aid.

"Relax, Lucy. No one is accusing you of anything at this point. Prosecutor Walsh is simply interested in your knowledge. We have your statement from the bonfire. But we also know that as the manager of Kebab Kitchen, you may hear things from customers that as police we may not learn," Clemmons said.

Lucy blinked in surprise. She'd never thought Detective Calvin Clemmons would come to her defense. They'd had a rocky relationship in the past, but things had improved between them. Her mother had welcomed Clemmons to celebratory family gatherings, and Lucy had felt that his grudge had softened against her family. He'd even been amicable around Emma at the restaurant.

Angela's baklava and shish kebab had a certain way of getting to a man's stomach . . . and heart.

But Prosecutor Walsh was an entirely different entity.

"He's right. We just want to know what you know." Walsh's pointed glare seemed to pierce right through Lucy.

"Fine. I only meant that, other than Melanie Haven, shouldn't you be looking into other suspects?"

"Such as?"

How exactly could she tip them off? She couldn't confess she'd broken into the blacklight minigolf and eavesdropped on Craig and Sophia as they'd struck a deal. She could start with information that was public knowledge—knowledge any investigator worth his salt should have discovered.

"Gilbert didn't get along with a lot of people. I've heard he was in a fight outside the Seagull Condominiums in Bayville," Lucy said. She knew the police already knew that information from Bill.

"Are you talking about the filed Bayville police report about a disturbance between the victim, Gilbert Lubinski, and his business partner, Craig Smith?" Walsh asked.

Lucy feigned surprise. "You know about that?"

Walsh tapped the table. "Believe it or not, we're not incompetent, Ms. Berberian."

"I didn't suggest you were, but if you know about the police report, why aren't you looking into Craig?" Lucy asked.

Clemmons glared. "Who says we're not?"

"Because you are interrogating my parents about

Melanie Haven." Lucy took a deep breath and decided to just go for it. It wasn't as if investigators did not know to suspect a victim's spouse. "Did you confirm Mrs. Lubinski's alibi?"

Walsh arched a perfectly plucked brow. "Which one? Your landlady or the victim's wife?"

Lucy sat up straight, all her apprehension leaving her in a swoosh. "You can't be serious? My elderly landlady could not have killed her nephew."

"Why not? One minute you're accusing us of overlooking suspects and now you're saying we shouldn't consider certain ones," Walsh said.

Lucy's frustration grew, but she held her tongue from spitting out a scathing retort.

She's baiting you.

Lucy knew all about this tactic from law school. *Don't let a smart adversary provoke you into saying something you'll regret later.* And Walsh was one smart cookie.

Keep calm, Lucy. Stay focused on the goal.

Lucy met the prosecutor's gaze straight on. "I think we are on the same page, Ms. Walsh. If you want to waste your resources investigating my landlady, that is your call. But we both know I meant Gilbert's *wife*, Sophia. Have you looked into her whereabouts that day?"

Walsh's lips curled in a smile that did not reach her eyes. "Rest assured, we are doing our jobs. Anything else you want to share? Anything about your *friend*, Melanie Haven?" Walsh asked.

An image of Rhonda rose in Lucy's mind. Rhonda, who'd gotten in over her head with online gambling debts and went to Gilbert for a loan rather than confess all to her husband. When she couldn't make the payments, she'd gone to Melanie for help. Melanie had done what she could until she'd put herself at risk. Another reason Melanie had wanted Gilbert dead. Lucy dared not mention what she knew. It would point them directly back to Melanie.

Lucy met the prosecutor's probing stare. "No."

Walsh reached into her leather briefcase and handed Lucy a card embossed with the State of New Jersey logo. "Call me when you change your mind, Ms. Berberian."

Not bloody likely.

Not until she had solid proof of Melanie's innocence.

Chapter Twenty-Six

Sand sprayed the backs of Lucy's calves as she ran on the beach. The sun was strong this afternoon and sweat beaded on her brow. Recent events had confused matters, and there was one place where she could always sort things out. The beach jetty came into view. Lucy sprinted the remaining distance, then made her way to the end of the jetty. Drinking from her water bottle, she sat and scanned the horizon.

The Atlantic Ocean stretched out before her in a dazzling display of Mother Nature. Seagulls soared above, and a sailboat with a colorful sail drifted by. A refreshing gust of ocean air cooled her overheated skin.

Lucy's thoughts sharpened as she contemplated the puzzle of Gilbert's murder. There was no lack of suspects, but some had more motive than others.

The first that came to mind was Gilbert's wife, Sophia. Despite her claims of innocence—and her tears—she had the strongest motive. She also had opportunity—the half-hour window of time when she'd left the bar. Sophia could have arrived at the beach bonfire and killed a hated husband. Then there was the fact that Sophia inherited half of the lucrative Seagull Condominiums and planned to sell her share to Gilbert's business partner, Craig. Her affair with Pumpkin added another layer of intrigue.

That led to another suspect. Craig Smith had motive and opportunity and had been at the bonfire. He also hated his business partner. Craig had previously fought with Gilbert, and a Bayville police report had resulted from the incident. With a bit of sleuthing, Lucy had learned that Craig wanted to buy out Gilbert's share of the Seagull Condominiums, and Gilbert had planned to sell his share to anyone—but Craig. But Craig had found another way to get his hands on what he wanted by buying the condos from Gilbert's widow.

Pumpkin was at the bonfire as well. Lucy had never believed unpaid landscaping bills were reason enough to kill, but then, she'd never imagined he was sleeping with Sophia. And Pumpkin was a hothead. Whether Sophia was manipulating Pumpkin, or Pumpkin had killed Gilbert at her urging, the result was the same. Gilbert was dead.

Katie's words returned to her:

It wouldn't be the first time passion resulted in murder.

Rhonda could not be dismissed as a suspect. She was a casualty of Gilbert's lending practices. Unbeknownst to her husband, she'd borrowed cash to pay off online gambling debts. When she couldn't make the payments plus the high-interest rates, she'd gone to her sister, Melanie, for help. When Melanie ran out of cash and couldn't pay her own rent, Gilbert had threatened to go to Rhonda's husband. Rhonda had been desperate to keep her gambling problem secret from her husband. Had Gilbert's threat pushed her over the edge and forced her to take matters into her own hands?

It was all so confusing. Too many people had strong motives and opportunity and were capable of doing the foul deed.

If only all the available evidence didn't point to Melanie. Everyone had witnessed her fight with Gilbert, and when the police dug into her history with her landlord, they'd found even more evidence against her, including numerous fights over raised rent. The fact that Melanie's saltwater taffy was used to choke Gilbert only added to the suspicions of her guilt.

Lucy stood and brushed sand from her legs. She couldn't help but think that she was missing a key piece of evidence—something she could hand over to Clemmons and Prosecutor Walsh that would point them in the right direction.

If she could locate and peek into Gilbert's safe or whatever place he kept his important papers, maybe she would find something important. Something that would exonerate Melanie and point to the real killer. Maybe Eloisa could help. She hadn't been particularly close with her nephew, but maybe she'd seen or heard something useful from one of her conversations with Gilbert.

Lucy drained her water bottle. She may not

have cracked the case, but she had a plan and she felt better. Her jetty always seemed to help.

Lucy jogged back to the boardwalk ramp and ran down the boards when she heard a shout, quickly followed by another. Spotting a crowd gathered on the boards, she picked up her pace. As she got closer, she realized the crowd was outside Haven Candies.

Madame Vega's blue turban stood above the mass of people. The psychic must have just stepped outside her salon at the noise.

Lucy went straight to her side. "What's going on?"

"The cops just showed up and stormed the candy store," Madame Vega said.

"Why?" Lucy craned to look inside. Her height always put her at a disadvantage in crowds and she had to shift from side to side to see between bodies.

"I saw it in my cards, remember? An evil presence remains in Ocean Crest."

Lucy shot a sidelong look at the woman before her attention returned to the crowd.

Melanie wasn't evil, but maybe someone else here was.

Two policemen, including Bill, stepped out of the store and began ushering the crowd aside.

"Bill!" Lucy shouted as she pushed her way through the gawking throng.

Bill stopped short in dismay when he saw her. "Lucy, you should go home."

"Why? What's going on inside?"

His blue eyes met hers and he shook his head. "I'm sorry. There's nothing I could do."

"What do you mean?"

Just then, Detective Clemmons emerged from

the candy store escorting Melanie Haven in handcuffs.

"Melanie!" Lucy cried out.

Melanie's pale face was streaked with tears. "They think I killed Gilbert. Lucy, you have to help!"

Lucy reached for Melanie, but Clemmons pulled her away.

Lucy followed and spoke fast. "Don't say anything, Melanie. Do you hear me? Not a word. I'll call an attorney, Clyde Winters."

Clemmons shot Lucy a dark glare. "Get out of our way and stop interfering, Ms. Berberian."

Lucy refused to back down. "I'm not interfering, but you have this all wrong, Detective."

Clemmons loomed above Lucy, his mouth set in a grim line. "Do I need to have you handcuffed for interfering with an arrest?"

Bill placed a hand on Lucy's arm and stopped her from delivering a scathing response. "Not now," he said in her ear.

Lucy backed down, allowing Bill to lead her aside. She knew he was right. No sense provoking Clemmons, not when he had her friend arrested. Lucy watched helplessly as Melanie was led down the boardwalk ramp and placed in a police car.

Her stomach knotted like a tangled fishing line. Time had run out. "She didn't do it. She didn't kill Gilbert."

Bill sighed and pushed back his officer's hat. "You may be right, but Prosecutor Walsh wouldn't have approved the arrest if there wasn't strong evidence against her. If you ask me, Melanie Haven is in a lot of trouble."

* * *

Lucy had once joked that Clyde Winters was the oldest practicing attorney she knew. That was saying a lot, because Lucy had worked with lawyers of all ages during her eight years at the Philadelphia firm. But Clyde was still sharp, and Lucy had called him to help with Azad in the past. Tall, rail-thin, and bald, he had an abundance of age spots on his neck and hands. He was also quick to smile.

Lucy met Clyde in the lobby of the police station. "Thanks for coming, Mr. Winters."

"It's Clyde, and I'm happy to do it. Sounds like your friend is in a bit of a bind."

"More than a bit. She's just been arrested for murder." She'd filled Clyde in on the phone, and his calm manner was reassuring.

"Let's go see her, shall we?" Clyde said.

They were buzzed into the station. Bill greeted them and led them down a long hall and stopped by a closed door. Bill removed a key ring that was clipped to his waist, selected a key, and unlocked the door. Lucy and Clyde stepped inside.

Lucy had been here once before and hated it even more than the interrogation room she'd been questioned in days ago. It was a barely furnished, dingy white room in need of a fresh coat of paint. A table with a hand-printing station and ink pads sat in the corner. A duct-tape line on the cracked linoleum floor indicated where a prisoner should stand to have their mug shots taken. A pair of sliding, outer jail doors were at the end of the room. A glance inside revealed four cells.

One was occupied. Melanie, her fingers wrapped around the bars of her cell, looked sickly.

Lucy knew prisoners were only temporarily held in Ocean Crest's police station until they were processed, then taken to the larger county jail to await arraignment. Melanie would only spend a couple of days here, then be carted off to the county jail and exposed to all types of hardened criminals.

Bill selected another key from the ring and slid open the outer jail doors. "Give me a minute to get her settled."

Through the bars, they could see Bill lead Melanie to a chair at a metal desk, then lock her handcuffs to a thick, metal ring on the table.

Bill opened the outer doors, and Lucy and Clyde stepped inside.

"Is it really necessary to cuff her hands to the table?" Lucy asked Bill.

Bill avoided eye contact. "Sorry, but it's standard procedure. Give a shout when you're done, and I'll come get you both." He left and shut the outer doors on his way out. The loud sound of the bars locking into place made Lucy jump, and gooseflesh rise on her arms.

They pulled out chairs and sat across from Melanie. Lucy took a breath and focused on her incarcerated friend. "This is Clyde Winters, the attorney I spoke with you about."

"Hello, Mr. Winters. I'm grateful for your presence, but I don't know how I'm going to pay for your services." Melanie spoke calmly, but with no light in her eyes, no smile of greeting.

Clyde placed a reassuring hand over hers chained to the table. "Don't worry about that right now, Melanie. We're here because we believe you didn't kill Gilbert."

Lucy wasn't as circumspect. Melanie's arrest was like a ticking bomb in Lucy's mind. They were running out of time. "Mr. Winters is right, Melanie. But if there's something you are not telling us, now is the time."

"I've told you everything. You believe me, don't you, Lucy?" Pain flickered in Melanie's eyes.

Lucy forced aside any feelings of sorrow or sympathy for Melanie's current incarceration. Instead, she kicked into legal mode. From the first day, Lucy had sensed that Melanie wasn't being entirely truthful, and that she was withholding information. Now, Melanie was behind bars and handcuffed to a table. That meant the police would stop searching for the real killer.

They desperately needed a lead, and fast.

"What about your sister, Rhonda?" Lucy asked.

Melanie's expression shuttered. "What about her?"

"She has an online gambling habit, and instead of telling her husband, she borrowed money from Gilbert. When she couldn't make the payments plus his high interest, she went to you. Because of your good heart, you tried to help your sister."

Melanie's mouth fell open. "How did you—"

"It doesn't matter how I know," Lucy said. "What matters is that I'm right. As a result of you helping out your sister, you put yourself in a bad position and you fell behind on your own rent. Then Gilbert started harassing you. Am I right?"

Melanie's lips thinned. "Okay, fine. I helped my

sister with her payments and fell a little behind on my own. So what?"

"You didn't think to tell me?" Lucy said.

"I didn't think it was relevant."

"Ms. Berberian is right. It is very relevant. A jury will find this unfavorable for you," Clyde said. "You should have informed us."

"Did you happen to see where Gilbert kept his papers?"

"What papers?" Melanie asked.

"Your apartment lease. Or, even more important, Rhonda's loan paperwork," Lucy said.

Melanie shook her head. "No, he never confided in me. Gilbert hand-delivered my lease."

Lucy suspected as much. "Is there anything else we should know?" Lucy asked.

Melanie shook her head. "No."

Lucy wanted to believe her. Melanie had everything to lose by withholding information from her attorney.

"If convicted of Gilbert Lubinski's murder, you could spend thirty years in state prison," Clyde said. "But we will do everything in our power to prevent that outcome."

The last traces of Melanie's resistance vanished and she sagged in her seat. Her voice broke miserably, and she lowered her head. Lucy suspected if her hands weren't handcuffed to the table, she would have sobbed into them.

"There is one thing. But it looks even worse for me." A tear trickled down Melanie's cheek.

What could look worse?

Lucy pressed her hands on the table and leaned forward. "This is your last chance to tell us."

Melanie's voice broke. "Gilbert took things too far."

"Too far, how?" Clyde's voice was gentler than Lucy's would have been.

"Gilbert said he suspected his wife of cheating and he wanted to get back at her any way he could. He cornered me in my apartment and tried to kiss me. He said he'd forget about my past rent if I slept with him."

What a sleazeball! Lucy's already poor opinion of Gilbert slid farther into the toilet.

"What did you do?" Lucy asked.

A fire lit Melanie's gaze. "I slapped him and told him I wouldn't sleep with him if he was the last man alive, and that I'd kill him if he ever tried to touch me again."

"Did anyone hear you?" Clyde asked.

"I don't think so. I never told a soul. Only Rhonda knew."

"Did Rhonda try to help you?" Lucy asked.

"No. She was petrified that Gilbert would make good on his threat and tell her husband about her online gambling debts."

Rhonda knew and didn't try to help her sister? If anyone sexually harassed Emma, Lucy would stand up for her sister in a heartbeat. Was Rhonda that selfish? Or had Rhonda, unbeknownst to Melanie, taken matters into her own hands?

Chapter Twenty-Seven

Lucy strode into the offices of the *Town News* with one purpose in mind. Stan Slade was in his office typing on a computer keyboard with his right hand, a cigarette dangling from his left.

"I thought most offices were smoke-free these days," Lucy said.

Stan looked up, a bright mockery invading his stare. "I made an exception for myself. Are you here to harass me for smoking and to warn me about the risks of cancer?"

"Neither. But it's not a bad idea. It's like a cloud in here, and secondhand smoke is just as dangerous for your coworkers and visitors."

He ground his cigarette into an ashtray and then opened the window. "Better?"

"Yes, thank you."

He pushed away from his desk and shot her a penetrating glare. "Okay. You have my curiosity. What's with the visit?"

"You told me to come to you if I want to break a story."

"Is this about Gilbert Lubinski's murder?"

"It is."

His eyes lit up like a drooling dog that just heard Pavlov's bell. He flipped open a notepad and whipped out a pencil that had been tucked behind his ear. "I'm listening."

She kept all inflection from her voice. "Gilbert wasn't just a Jersey shore landlord. He was a loan shark."

Stan lowered his pencil. "Who'd he loan cash to?"

"Ocean Crest residents who didn't qualify for bank loans for whatever reason. He wasn't nice about his high-interest rates or collection tactics."

She didn't think it was possible for Slade's eyes to light up even more behind his dark-rimmed glasses. "By tactics do you mean the strong-arm methods that rival Atlantic City mob bosses?"

"I didn't say that."

"You didn't have to. I'm good at reading between the lines."

He was also good at printing half-truths that led readers to draw their own conclusions—mostly wrong ones that had harmed Kebab Kitchen's reputation in the past.

"Gilbert didn't beat anyone," Lucy said. "He was just persistent." He'd threatened to tell Rhonda's husband about her gambling addiction. Most shockingly, he'd sexually harassed Melanie.

Rhonda knew everything. Rhonda—who had just as much motive as Melanie to kill Gilbert—but that wasn't something she'd share with the reporter.

Lucy's motives for visiting the reporter were clear. She wanted Stan's future article on Detective Clemmons's desk and on Prosecutor Walsh's radar. If they started looking into Gilbert's side money-lending business, they would expand their police efforts and look past Melanie. They could find the loan documents and learn who else owed Gilbert cash and who stood to gain from his murder. Other than Rhonda, who else was out there?

Who owed even more?

Sophia didn't know where Gilbert kept his papers. Lucy and Katie were at a dead end. Only the police had the resources and abilities to search the town. With Melanie behind bars, Lucy didn't think the police would continue to investigate the murder.

Worse, if Melanie spilled her entire story to the prosecutor, it would tighten the noose around her neck. Gilbert had been a sleazeball who tried to kiss her and blackmail her with sex in exchange for past rent. It added to her motive to want Gilbert dead.

That's where Stan Slade and the *Town News* came into play. It was the perfect way to tip off the police without getting herself or Katie in trouble or, even worse, harming Bill Watson's future career as an Ocean Crest detective.

Lucy placed her palms on Stan's desk and leaned forward. "I must be an anonymous source."

For once Stan Slade didn't argue. "You got it. It will be printed tomorrow morning. Now, tell me everything about Gilbert's dark, moneylending side."

* * *

"Where's my hummus!" Sally said. "We need more jalapeño and white bean hummus for the hummus bar."

"Coming right up," Butch said behind the cook's counter.

It was two days after her jail visit with Melanie and her stop by Stan Slade's office, and the lunch shift was in full swing. Shish kebab was on the menu and customers were pouring in faster than Lucy's father could seat them. Lucy rushed around helping Emma and Sally serve platters of hot shish kebab, potato and cheese bake, and string beans sautéed in a tomato sauce to tables before the hot food could cool.

"Hey, Lucy," Butch called out. "Azad made the hummus. Can you save me a trip by fetching it and delivering it to the hummus bar?"

"Sure thing." Lucy passed through the swinging kitchen doors that led into the kitchen. Warm air from the stoves and grills blasted her already over-heated cheeks. She'd learned long ago that running a restaurant was hard work. It took stamina, patience, and endurance, but was the most rewarding job she'd ever held.

She headed straight for the back of the kitchen where Azad was stirring a tall pot of rice pilaf.

"Butch said you made extra hummus. We need jalapeño and white bean."

Azad set down his spoon. "It's on a high shelf in the walk-in refrigerator. I'll get it for you."

Lucy didn't need a reminder that she was short and Azad was over six feet tall. She made a mental note to purchase another step stool.

She followed him into the walk-in refrigerator. The cool air felt refreshing and she took a deep breath. The space was larger than the tiny office in the corner of the storage room. Steel shelving held everything from fresh seafood from the fish market to raw meat from the butcher to vegetables from the farmers market to her mother's cooked rice pudding. The heavy, insulated door closed behind them, but never locked—a safety feature—and could be pushed open with a hip or a foot by workers carrying armfuls of food.

Azad reached up high on the top shelf and took down two containers of hummus. "I just made them this morning," he said as he handed them to her.

The containers were cool as she cradled them in her arms. Rather than leave the walk-in, Lucy hesitated as a thought crossed her mind. The walk-in refrigerator was the only place that guaranteed privacy in the busy kitchen, and she could ask the question that had come to mind.

"Hey, Azad. You said you borrowed money from Gilbert to pay for culinary school. Did you ever sign loan papers?" Lucy asked.

"I did. He brought them to my house."

"Your house? You never went to his home or anything?"

"No. I remember because I needed to pay my tuition bill and he came over with a check and paperwork. Why? Is that important?"

"I'm trying to find out if Gilbert had an office in town where he stored all his papers."

"Beats me. I was lucky enough to get my *sous* chef job in Atlantic City and pay off my loan soon after graduating. Gilbert gave me a copy of my loan papers and signed them as paid in full."

Disappointment settled in her stomach. Other than Rhonda, Azad was the only person she knew who had borrowed money from Gilbert. She'd really thought Azad might know. She glanced at the bin of hummus in her arms. "The hummus looks great."

"Sorry I wasn't able to help with Gilbert, but I have a feeling you'll figure this all out soon."

"Thanks for believing in me." She was still a little surprised that Azad was being supportive of her sleuthing efforts. It wasn't that he didn't want her to help a friend, but that he didn't want her to be in harm's way.

"Before I forget, I saw the article in the *Town News* this morning about Gilbert's moneylending business. You were Stan Slade's anonymous source, weren't you?" he asked.

Her lips curved in a smile. "I'll never tell."

"Your smile says it all. Plus, there's that nervous tic by your eye when you fib." He stepped close to touch her temple with a forefinger.

"You know me too well." She wasn't upset by his keen perception this time. Rather, her smile widened.

His stare was bold as he assessed her frankly. "Like I said, your need to help others is a part of your personality and one of the reasons I like you so much."

Wow. Her heart did a little dance as she gazed up at him.

His finger traced a path by her eye to her cheek, and two deep lines of worry appeared between his eyes. "Just promise me you'll stay safe."

"I promise."

She had no intention of getting into danger. Stan Slade had printed the article. If all worked as planned, Detective Clemmons should soon find where Gilbert kept his loan papers and start looking into suspects other than Melanie.

Azad leaned down to give her a brief kiss. His lips were whisper soft and set off a wild swirl in the pit of her stomach. She clutched the bins of hummus, afraid she would drop them. She wished they weren't in the way and she could press against his muscular chest and deepen the kiss.

Who would have thought hummus would prevent a heated encounter?

Azad pulled back and looked into her eyes. "Too bad we have a full dining room out there."

"Oh, right."

Too bad indeed.

Lucy felt her face grow warm again. She must look a mess—curly hair frizzing from the humidity in the kitchen and red cheeks. Why did she lose her head so easily around him? Azad looked cool, composed, and handsome.

"How about we go out tonight? I'd like to take you to dinner," Azad said.

"What about the dinner shift here?"

"I already asked your parents. They said they're happy to cover."

Of course they did. They adored Azad, and if he'd asked her parents to work at the restaurant so that he could take Lucy out for the evening, Raffi and Angela would be more than happy to agree.

She was no longer surprised that it didn't bother her one bit.

She grinned like a simpleton. "Dinner sounds great."

"I'll pick you up at five." He opened the refrigerator door for her and she traipsed back through the swinging doors into the dining room.

Once she was back at work, her thoughts returned to her problems. Azad's lack of knowledge regarding Gilbert was a setback for sure, but she had to figure things out soon or Melanie would be—

"Lucy! A customer at table six is asking for you," Emma said.

Lucy jumped, then quickened her pace. "I'll be right there."

She headed for the hummus bar, which happened to be near table number six. She could restock the hummus and then see to the customer who had asked for—

Lucy rounded the corner and nearly tripped and dropped both tubs when she spotted who was waiting for her.

Rhonda.

She sat alone at a table set for two. A menu was spread open before her, but Rhonda wasn't looking at it. Instead, she was gazing unseeing out the bay window.

What on earth was Rhonda doing here, asking for her?

Rhonda gave her a bland smile when she spotted Lucy. "Hi, Lucy. You don't know me, but my name is Rhonda Stevens. I'm Melanie Haven's sister."

Lucy may not have officially been introduced to Rhonda, but she knew quite a bit about the woman. Most wasn't favorable.

Lucy came close and set the hummus bins on the table, curious to hear why Rhonda had come to the restaurant and asked to see her.

"Hello, Rhonda. Would you like to hear our specials?" Lucy started to pull a waitress pad from her back pocket.

"No, that's not why I'm here."

"You're not here to eat?"

Rhonda's fingers curled around the edges of the menu. "I heard about Melanie's arrest, and that you are helping my sister."

"I'm not representing her as her lawyer, just doing all I can for her as a friend. Mr. Winters is her defense attorney."

"Thank you for that. I haven't seen her since the arrest."

"Is that why you're here? To ask about your sister's well-being? She's not doing great." Lucy spoke calmly, but didn't smile.

"What can I do to help my sister?"

"You really want to help?"

Rhonda sat up like she had been jolted with an electric wire. "Yes!"

Lucy pulled out the chair opposite Rhonda and sat. "You can start by telling me about your loan with Gilbert Lubinski."

Rhonda's face clouded with uneasiness. "How do you know about that?"

"It doesn't matter now, does it? You were right about my wanting to help Melanie. Your sister is sitting in a jail cell accused of murdering the man you borrowed money from to pay off your gambling debts."

Awkwardly, Rhonda cleared her throat. "It sounds awful when you sum it up like that."

"It is. I may not know you personally, but I was familiar with your moneylender's reputation. Why on earth would you ever borrow cash from the likes of Gilbert?"

Rhonda's fingers continued working the edges of the laminated menu. "Melanie asked me the same thing. I knew about Gilbert's reputation, but I was desperate."

Lucy's lips thinned with irritation. "You didn't have to involve your sister. You knew Melanie has a soft heart and would sacrifice to help you. Maybe if you confessed all to your husband, Melanie wouldn't be sitting in a jail cell."

Rhonda succeeded in peeling away the plastic layer of the menu. "You don't understand. My husband's father was a gambler. If Noah found out that I'd been secretly gambling online, he would have thrown a fit and filed for divorce. I heard that Gilbert helped Ocean Crest residents when they were in a financial bind, and I went to him. I signed the papers even though I understood that the cash came with a ridiculously high-interest rate. I thought I could win it all back gambling online. I was so sure, but then I only got more into debt."

Lucy snatched the menu from Rhonda before it was completely destroyed. "So, you went to your sister rather than tell your husband, Noah?"

"Melanie was furious at first. She couldn't believe I'd borrowed from Gilbert. She warned me about her landlord, but it was too late. I was in too deep. She helped as best she could, but she fell behind on her own rent."

"It wasn't just her rent, was it?"

"I don't know what—"

"Cut the lies. Melanie had to fight off Gilbert's unwanted sexual advances, so much so that she slapped him and threatened to kill him."

"I never meant for it to go that far."

"You did nothing to help your sister."

Rhonda's face took on a green tint. "You don't understand. Gilbert threatened to tell my husband about my problems. I couldn't let that happen!"

Did Rhonda realize she was admitting motive for murder? Was she desperate enough to have her sister take the fall? Or worse, set Melanie up by shoving taffy down Gilbert's throat?

"I know what you're thinking," Rhonda said.

Lucy hoped not.

"That I'm a selfish person, and that I would let my sister go to jail to save my own hide." Rhonda bit her lower lip.

"Well . . . it does seem that way."

Her eyes flew to Lucy's. "It's not true. I love Melanie!"

As she sat across from Rhonda, Lucy thought the woman was telling the truth. She may have had a strong motive to kill Gilbert to protect her own marriage, but Lucy wasn't convinced Rhonda would set her sister up to take the fall for the crime.

Lucy thought about all she'd learned. Maybe Rhonda could be of use after all.

"You said you signed loan papers? Where did you meet Gilbert to sign them?" Lucy asked.

Rhonda regarded her quizzically for a moment, then answered. "At his office."

"His office? Where?"

"I thought it was strange at first, but Gilbert met me at the Seagull Condominiums in Bayville. It was condo number nine on the first floor behind the parking garage. He told me to knock twice, then he opened the door."

Lucy's pulse thrummed in her veins. Gilbert kept an office in the condominiums out of town? In a perverse way, it all made sense. He kept his side business secret from his wife and the income hidden.

Lucy needed to search his office, but assumed it would be locked. Katie would be in full agreement regarding the search. Lucy thought about telling Clemmons or Prosecutor Walsh what she'd learned, but she pushed the thought aside. She'd gone to Stan Slade to put the police on notice of other suspects. But that was when she didn't know where Gilbert kept his papers. Now she knew. And if she tipped off the prosecutor that she—along with Katie—were "sticking their noses" where they shouldn't, they would put Bill's promotion in jeopardy. No, she had to obtain concrete evidence. If not, Melanie would remain incarcerated.

Lucy needed the key to condo number nine. She also needed to run everything she'd learned by Katie.

She stood and reached for the hummus. "Thanks, Rhonda. You should visit Melanie. If you apologize, I think she may forgive you."

An eager look flashed across Rhonda's face. "You think so? We haven't been getting along lately, but I truly am sorry. I also want to help any way I can."

"You already have."

"I wish I could have been there when Rhonda paid you a surprise visit," Katie told Lucy over the phone.

"She seems genuine about wanting to help her sister. And she gave us a big lead." Lucy had called Katie and updated her as soon as Rhonda left the restaurant.

"Gilbert was smart to keep an out-of-town office. He kept everything secret from his wife. Sophia's divorce attorney would be all over those records, searching for more income for alimony. And I still can't believe he thought Melanie was fair game for sex just because she owed him money," Katie said.

"We need solid evidence that Melanie didn't kill Gilbert," Lucy said. "But the condo has to be locked."

"Can we pick the lock?" Katie asked.

Lucy pursed her lips. "That's not exactly my area of expertise."

"Mine either," Katie said.

"You mean you never learned from all the TV detective and crime shows you've watched over the years?" Lucy asked.

"Ha! But no. Watching and doing are two entirely different things. What about your landlady?"

"What about her?"

"Other than Sophia, she was Gilbert's closest living relative. I doubt Gilbert would have left the key for his wife. Maybe Eloisa Lubinski knows where it is," Katie said.

Why hadn't Lucy thought of that? "Good idea. I'll ask her before I go out with Azad tonight."

"I want to search the place with you, but tonight is our bowling league with Bill and friends. If I cancel, he'll know something's up," Katie said.

"Go bowling. If I find that key, I'll text you. Otherwise, we're breaking in."

Chapter Twenty-Eight

As soon as Lucy came home that afternoon after work, she went in search of her landlady. Eloisa wasn't home. Lucy didn't like waiting, but what choice did she have? Katie's suggestion was a good one. If Gilbert had left anyone the key to condo number nine, it would be Eloisa. Meanwhile, Lucy had a date night to dress for.

"I have somewhere special in mind for dinner, Lucy," Azad said as he opened the door of his truck for her.

"Where? Or are you going to leave me in suspense?" She smoothed her skirt and carefully got in the truck with her wedge sandals.

"It's a surprise."

She smiled. "I like a little bit of excitement."

"You mean more than crime solving?"

She eyed him, but his tone was light and the corners of his eyes crinkled in humor. He was teasing her about sleuthing, and a warm glow flowed through her.

She settled on the bench and attached the seat belt. Unsure of where they were headed on their date, she'd chosen a purple sheath dress. Azad looked great in a light blue, button-down shirt, navy jacket, and gray slacks, and Lucy tried not to stare.

She mentally shook her head. She was no longer a starry-eyed teenager, but a grown woman in an adult relationship. It was okay to find him attractive, just not *too* attractive. His intelligence and consideration were what really mattered.

They passed the two stop lights in town and left Ocean Crest. Azad had taken her to Le Gabriel, a fancy French restaurant in the past, and she wondered if that's where they were headed tonight. But they soon passed Le Gabriel and kept going. When he turned onto the Atlantic City expressway, she grew suspicious.

"You're taking me to Atlantic City?"

"Okay. You guessed the location, but not the restaurant."

Her curiosity grew. Azad had worked in a fancy Atlantic City casino restaurant, and he was well-acquainted with all the fine restaurants in the city.

The bright lights of the casinos came into view. They were big buildings with tall, lit signs. Some were on the Atlantic City boardwalk, others by the marina. There weren't as many casinos as there had been in the glory days of the city, but still enough to lure gamblers and tourists from all over the state.

He pulled into a multistory concrete parking garage and took a ticket to pay on his way out. He helped her out of the truck and took her hand in his. An elevator placed them on the casino floor—a cavernous, noisy room full of slot machines, blackjack, craps, roulette tables, and gamblers.

Azad's hand was warm as it held hers and he steered her through the floor. Wide-eyed, Lucy watched the scene unfold. A group of senior citizens were busy at the quarter slot machines, some preferring to push a button to spin the wheel rather than pulling the lever. Others sat at blackjack tables with their chips, intense looks on their faces as they studied their cards. A craps table had a boisterous crowd as a woman blew on the dice for a friend before she rolled the dice across the green baize. The roulette tables were also busy, and a group watched, mesmerized, as the little white balls spun and spun.

"I'm taking you to where I used to work," Azad said.

Lucy's looked up at him with surprised pleasure. "Chef Henry's."

Chef Henry Wu was a famous Japanese chef who had opened pricey Asian/Hawaiian fusion restaurants in cities across the country—one in Atlantic City.

She spotted the entrance to the restaurant. A menu behind glass was mounted on the wall outside for hungry patrons to peruse.

A maître d' dressed in a black suit seated them and handed them menus. Lucy was hungry and all the selections looked delicious. "You worked here. What do you suggest?"

"The tempura-crusted ahi roll appetizer. Macadamia nut mahi-mahi and braised short ribs for the main course. And you have to try the pineapple upside-down cake for dessert. We'll be sure to order an extra one for Katie."

Lucy peered at him above her menu. "She'll be raving jealous when she finds out we came here."

Azad's lips twitched with humor. "Bill will have to step up his game when he gets promoted."

"I'll let him know."

The waiter took their orders and delivered the bottle of merlot Azad had requested. Together, they enjoyed the wine until dinner was served. Lucy nearly swooned at the first taste of the ahi roll appetizer. The tuna was of such high quality that it nearly melted on her tongue. The short ribs were tender and flavorful, and Azad's mahi-mahi was light and flaky.

"You were right. This is sooo good."

Azad studied her. "Watching you eat is one of the things I like about you."

Lucy lowered her fork. "You make a girl self-conscious. Should I be daintier and have ordered a simple salad?"

"Could you have survived seeing me eat this?" He motioned to his own plate.

Her response was unhesitant. "Never."

"That's what I mean. I'm a chef. I appreciate a woman who's not afraid to enjoy her food." He smiled, and the sight sent her stomach into a delicious swirl.

The rest of dinner was just as good, but the pineapple cake was fabulous. True to his word, Azad ordered an extra dessert, and the waiter delivered it with a takeout box tied with a red bow.

On the way home, Azad stopped at the Ocean Crest beach. Lucy took off her sandals. and hand in hand, they walked by the surf. The sun was setting, and a gentle breeze blew from the ocean. She shivered at the cool air, and Azad removed his jacket and put it around her shoulders.

His heat and cologne wrapped around her and heightened her awareness of the man. They left the surf and he led her to one of the benches by the sand dunes.

"Let's stop here," he said.

"Are we stopping for a kiss?" she teased.

"After."

He gazed down at her, his look intense, and her body felt heavy and warm. She swallowed tightly. "After what?"

Then he did something that was completely unexpected. He sank to one knee and reached in his coat pocket, which was still draped around her shoulders, to withdraw a small, black box. He opened the lid to reveal a brilliant diamond nestled in black velvet. "Will you marry me, Lucy Berberian?"

Her heart beat rapidly in her chest, and her mouth fell open. She looked from the ring to the man. Azad's eyes were full of hope and vulnerability. Thoughts flitted through her mind like dry leaves in a blast of wind.

He was proposing. Marriage. To her.

One more glance in his eyes and she knew. Knew that she loved him, had loved him for a long, long time. Soon after he walked into Kebab Kitchen as a teenager, looking for a summer job.

"Yes," she said, her voice sounding breathless. "Yes, I'll marry you."

He broke into a broad grin that set his dark eyes alight. She touched his cheek, and his hand covered hers and held it there.

He rose. "Now I'll kiss you."

And he did.

Chapter Twenty-Nine

Later that evening, Lucy returned home with a diamond ring on her finger. She couldn't stop staring at it. It looked like someone else's hand.

I can't believe I'm engaged.

After a heated kiss in his truck, Azad had seen her to the door and left. She wasn't worried. She knew next time he would come inside and stay the night.

She planned on calling Katie on her cell at the bowling alley and sharing her news with her friend, but when she opened the front door and stepped inside, a whirring sound caught her attention. She was reminded of something else, something she'd planned to do tonight before going out with Azad. Rather than climb the stairs to her second-floor apartment, she went in search of her landlady.

She found Eloisa in her kitchen using a noisy hand mixer. The whirring sounded louder and filled the kitchen as she mixed batter in a stainless-steel bowl. Cupid lounged in his dog bed in the corner.

Lucy inhaled the scent of something delicious baking in the oven. "It smells great in here."

Caught off guard, Eloisa lifted the mixer from the bowl without turning it off. Batter flew at Lucy like buckshot.

"Oh!"

Eloisa turned off the mixer and scowled at Lucy. "What the heck were you thinking, sneaking up on me like that? You caught me by surprise." She handed Lucy a kitchen towel.

Lucy wiped her face and proceeded to smear the batter on her dress. Thank goodness she'd already gone on her date. "I wasn't sneaking up on you," she argued. "Did you think I was a criminal?"

"Who knew? I figured this mixer made a pretty good weapon."

"You don't need that. You have Cupid." Lucy warily eyed the shih tzu in the corner. The little dog yawned. Of all the times for him not to start yapping at the sight of her. Either he set her up or he was getting used to seeing her. Too bad Gadoo was upstairs. The cat would have set him off for sure.

The timer dinged, and Eloisa slipped on an oven mitt and opened the lime-green oven to pull out a batch of large muffins. Despite the batter all over her, Lucy inhaled the delicious smell. Even though she'd had dinner at a fabulous restaurant and enjoyed dessert, she had a sweet tooth and was still tempted.

"What are those?" Lucy asked.

"Blueberry muffins for the ladies after swim aerobics tomorrow." She set the muffins on the stove to cool and eyed Lucy up and down. "I feel bad for messing up your pretty dress. Want a muffin?"

"I ate tonight, but that looks good. I'll have a taste."

A plate with a muffin and a cup of tea was set before her. Lucy got the feeling that her landlady was happy for the company despite her not-so-friendly greeting.

Lucy bit into the muffin and her taste buds tingled in delight. "Wow! These are great. I didn't know you baked."

"There're a lot of things you don't know about me."

"I'm learning." Lucy took another bite and eyed her landlady with renewed interest.

"Wait one minute! Is that a rock on your finger?" Eloisa snatched Lucy's hand and examined the diamond.

"It is. Azad proposed tonight."

Eloisa whistled through her teeth. "Nice ring. That explains the fancy dress. I'm jealous, but I suppose that means your hottie will be coming around a lot more now."

"I suppose."

"Did you fire him? Or does he keep his job and the boss?"

"He keeps his job. Can I have my hand back now?"

Eloisa let go of her death grip, and Lucy promptly took another bite of muffin. That's when she spotted a cane resting on the side of the kitchen table that she hadn't noticed during the batter explosion. Had Eloisa hurt herself? "When did you start using a cane?"

Eloisa reached for it, then set it back against the table. "Do you like it? My friend, Rose, left it here. She doesn't need it back right away and has several. I'm thinking of using it so I can get a handicapped parking spot."

Lucy gaped. "That's just wrong."

Her reactions seemed to amuse Eloisa. "When you reach my age, nothing is wrong. Keep eating."

Lucy chewed and swallowed. "Can I ask you something?"

"About your chef fiancé?"

"No, about Gilbert."

Eloisa lowered her mug. "I knew burying him would only lead to more questions."

Lucy ignored her tone. There was much more to her landlady than social activities, sarcasm, and an unexpected ability to bake. "Did you know that Gilbert had a side business and the he loaned money to town residents?" She watched Eloisa for her reaction.

"I'm not surprised. I told you that Gilbert was trouble. His success was never enough for him. He always wanted more and more money."

"Well, he had his borrowers sign loan papers and stowed them in a secret office in the Seagull Condos in Bayville. Do you know where he kept the key?"

Eloisa tapped the side of her mug. "No . . . but . . ."

"But what?"

"The lawyer who read the will gave me a box that Gilbert had left for me. I haven't had the heart to open it." Eloisa stood and opened one of the kitchen cabinets. She returned with a small box and placed it on the kitchen table. She sank into her chair, a sorrowful expression on her face. "If it's cash, I don't want his blood money."

Lucy's gaze was glued to the small box. "Open it and see."

Eloisa lifted the lid. Inside were pictures of Gilbert as a young boy and a teenager, some with a younger Eloisa. Her face softened as she traced an image on one of the pictures. "Gilbert used to be a friendly, curious boy."

Eloisa flipped through the pictures. "Gilbert started to change during his high school years. After college, he became greedy, and it got worse from then on. But I never would have thought he'd call me crazy in order to evict me from my own home." One by one, she placed the pictures on the kitchen table.

Lucy's heart ached for the woman. Whatever Gilbert had become, he'd clearly meant something to her at one time. His betrayal must have been all the more painful.

When Eloisa came to the bottom of the box, she reached inside to withdraw a key. "You just may be in luck." She handed the key to Lucy.

Lucy raised the key to the kitchen light and read the small engraving etched on its surface. "Seagull Condominiums." She looked up. "Oh my gosh! This must be it. Can I have it?"

"It's yours."

Lucy stood. "I'm going tonight. No sense wasting time when Melanie is sitting in a cold jail cell."

"You're right." Eloisa reached for the cane. "But I'm going with you."

After a heated argument, Lucy gave up trying to convince Mrs. Lubinski to stay behind. Her land-lady had insisted on accompanying her and had grabbed her cane in case, she'd said, Lucy couldn't find parking. Lucy felt an urgency to get to the Seagull Condominiums and find Gilbert's office. Melanie's fate just might rest in her hands.

She would have called Katie, but her friend was out with her husband. Plus, Lucy didn't want to tip off Bill. Not until she had something worth telling him about.

"This is it," Lucy said as they stood outside condo number nine. Before Lucy could reach for the doorknob Eloisa stepped forward to rap her cane on the door.

Not surprisingly, no one answered.

"Go ahead. Use the key. I haven't got all night," Eloisa instructed.

Lucy bit her cheek. This was going to be a test of her patience, but she wouldn't have gotten this far if it wasn't for Eloisa finding the key. Lucy inserted the key into the lock. She felt a click, then the door swung wide open. For a second, she could only stare. "We did it."

"Did you doubt it?"

Frankly, yes.

Lucy felt a nudge in her lower back from the darned cane and stepped inside. Eloisa was right behind her and shut the door.

The place was sparely furnished with a desk, a

chair, and a computer and had an unpleasant, musky odor. The small kitchenette looked barren, not a plate on the granite counter. A glance in the bedroom revealed no bed or furniture.

"It wasn't a lover's nest. Whatever you could say about Gilbert, he wasn't a cheater," Eloisa said.

Not for lack of trying.

Poor Melanie had to deal with the pig's unwanted advances. Lucy would never tell Eloisa. The poor woman had enough bad memories to deal with regarding her nephew already.

"Where's the file cabinet or safe?" Lucy glanced around, but didn't see either a safe or a locked file cabinet by the computer.

Eloisa had disappeared into one of the rooms. "In here!" Her muffled voice sounded through the walls. Lucy opened a door to find a bathroom, her gaze drawn to a two-drawer file cabinet pushed against the wall opposite the toilet.

"Why on earth would he put a file cabinet in here?" Lucy said.

Eloisa shrugged a skinny shoulder. "Reading material?"

Ugh.

Lucy pushed the image aside and opened the first drawer. She realized Gilbert didn't need a safe if no one knew about his hidden condominium office. It really was the perfect hiding space. He owned half the building, so no one would question his coming and going. And if a false name was listed on the lease, not even his business partner, Craig Smith, would have known about the place.

She opened the top drawer and peered inside. One look at the file folders and Lucy knew she'd found gold. Five files were in a section marked, "Paid." She spotted Azad's file. As for the others, she was surprised at the names of local business owners. Either they hadn't qualified for a bank loan or hadn't wanted one. Beatrice Tretola, owner of the Big Tease Salon; Nola Devone, owner of the Freezy Cone. The names of other local business owners and town residents were on more files.

The next file folder contained the names of the outstanding borrowers: Rhonda Stevens; Ed Simmons, the Barbeque King; and Eric Scotch, a local bread baker.

The last name gave Lucy pause.

It was Kevin Crowley, the boardwalk tramcar owner.

She flipped through Kevin's file to discover he owed a whopping one hundred and fifty thousand dollars, the most by far of all the borrowers.

"Oh my gosh."

"What? I can't see without my reading glasses," Eloisa demanded as she hovered over Lucy's shoulder.

"Kevin Crowley borrowed one hundred and fifty thousand dollars from Gilbert. What on earth did he need that much money for?"

"His two new tramcars. Haven't you noticed?"

Lucy glanced over her shoulder. "No." She rarely rode the tramcar, only jogged out of the way when she heard the annoying speakers blaring.

Eloisa huffed. "You need to pay more attention to your surroundings."

Apparently, she did.

"Katie and I searched Mr. Crowley's trailer on the pier and didn't find anything," Lucy said. "He must keep his records elsewhere. That's a ton of cash to borrow from the likes of Gilbert. He must have had bad credit if he couldn't get a bank loan."

"It adds up to a big motive if you ask me."

Yes . . . yes, it did. Lucy's thoughts jumped into overdrive. "Gilbert did not file these loan documents with the county. The only evidence of this loan is sitting right here."

"How do you know that?"

"Because Gilbert was going through a contested divorce. If this loan was on file with the county, he'd have to report it to Sophia's lawyer. They'd learn of his interest income. He didn't. Sophia had no idea of his moneylending business. She only learned of it from eavesdropping on one of Gilbert's phone calls."

"I told you Gilbert was greedy. He was also sneaky."

"Both traits may have led to his death." Lucy clutched the file folder to her chest and reached for her purse to pull out her cell phone. "We need to get this to the police."

"I wouldn't do that if I were you."

Both women whirled at the dark voice to see Kevin Crowley standing in the bathroom doorway, a gun pointed at Lucy's chest.

Chapter Thirty

Sheer black fright went through Lucy as realization hit her like a sledgehammer.

Kevin Crowley had come for the last piece of evidence to link him to Gilbert's murder. But how had he known where to find them?

He extended his free hand. "Hand it over."

Lucy clutched the file tighter to her chest. "How did you know where to find this place?"

"I didn't. I've been following you."

"Since when?"

"Since you and your blonde friend showed up in my trailer on the boardwalk pier. Your excuse about an interview for a possible *Town News* article was pathetic. You didn't believe I actually bought that nonsense, did you?"

Instinct had told her that she was being watched, but she'd ignored it. First, on the deck of her condo. Then, at the soccer field. The man with the baseball cap and hoodie was the same height and build as Kevin.

Always go with your gut, Lucy!

"You also have a reputation around here for asking too many questions, Lucy. I couldn't take a chance. I hoped you'd leave it be with the arrest of Ms. Havens, but you can't seem to help yourself, can you? Now, hand over the file," Kevin said.

When she hesitated, he snatched it from her.

"You'd let an innocent woman take the fall for murder over two new tramcars?" Lucy asked.

A brief look of remorse flashed across his face, but it was gone in an instant, replaced with resolve. "I couldn't make the damned loan payments. Gilbert threated to file the documents with the court and proceed with collections. I couldn't allow that."

"So, you killed him?"

"Once I made the decision, I realized it was the only way. It was easy from then on."

He was cold and calculating—they were facing a madman. "How did you get to the bonfire?"

"I saw everything from my boardwalk pier. The bonfire was the perfect opportunity. It was already dark out. I slipped away and stalked Gilbert on the beach. I had planned to hit him on the head with my pistol, but I spotted the driftwood on the beach and snatched it on my way. Everyone was occupied making s'mores. Only Melanie Haven sat alone. I waited until Gilbert wandered away and struck him from behind."

"And the taffy?"

A twisted smile curved the left side of his lips. "He was still breathing. I was going to hit him again when I spotted pieces of taffy on the beach. It was a nice touch to finish the job, don't you think?"

"And to frame Melanie."

"From what I heard, there was no love lost between them."

Eloisa spoke up. "Now what? You can't shoot us here. People will hear gunshots and it will lead back to you."

Kevin's gaze swung to Eloisa and his eyes narrowed, as if he were noticing her for the first time. "You're right. Get moving. Both of you."

"Don't be an idiot. It's over," Eloisa said.

Kevin sneered. "Move it, old lady."

Eloisa's face hardened. "What did you call me?"

Lucy took her hand and lowered her voice. "He has the gun."

Next to her, Eloisa started to tremble with fear or outrage, or maybe both. Lucy glared at Kevin—tall and stocky—he was definitely strong enough to overpower Gilbert. He was also strong enough to take on two women. Lucy had to think fast. She captured Eloisa's gaze. They needed to come up with a plan without speaking.

Lucy still had her purse and cell phone. If he stayed distracted, maybe she could manage to reach her phone and call the police.

He led them outside and ushered them toward Lucy's Toyota. Lucy scanned the area for someone . . . anyone, but it was late and no one was in sight. Eloisa hurried along as best she could with her cane. Her landlady could be swift and Lucy knew she was acting.

Smart!

"You drive," Kevin instructed.

Lucy rummaged in her purse and pretended to search for her keys. Her fingers brushed her cell phone. If she could just dial 911 and leave the phone on . . .

Kevin grabbed the purse from her shoulder and pulled out her cell phone. "You don't think I'd let you have this, do you?"

She watched in dismay as he tossed her phone on the blacktop, then stomped on it with his construction boot until it made a loud crack. Then he picked up the destroyed phone and stuck it in his back pocket.

Crap.

Her plan to call for help had failed.

He tossed her car keys at her. "Open the passenger-side door and slide over to the driver's seat. You're driving."

She realized why he was making her enter the passenger side when he trained the gun on her as she struggled to climb over the gear shift.

Lucy slid behind the wheel and started the car. Kevin sat in the passenger seat, his gun never wavering as it aimed at her head. Eloisa sat in the back. Lucy slowly started to back up, then turn the car around.

"No funny business or the old lady dies first," he said to Lucy. "Drive back to Ocean Crest and park beneath the municipal pier."

He planned on taking them back to town and to his trailer on the municipal pier. Why? It was late and off-season. What was he thinking?

"What do you plan on doing?" Lucy asked.

"Taking you where your bodies won't be found."

Chapter Thirty-One

Lucy drove onto the main road leading back to Ocean Crest, her fingers gripping the steering wheel, trying to hold back panic. All the while she was highly aware of the gun aimed at her head. The car's headlights illuminated deserted streets. She contemplated purposely crashing the car, but one look in the rearview mirror revealed Eloisa wasn't wearing her seat belt. Her landlady looked ashen and vulnerable, and Lucy knew she couldn't take the risk; the car would stop suddenly and Eloisa could fly through the windshield and be killed.

No, she'd have to think of something else. She refused to allow this madman to kill them.

She passed the "WELCOME TO OCEAN CREST" sign and turned left toward the boardwalk. The municipal pier was only several blocks away, in a remote part of town. No one wanted to live by the trash and recycling containers, especially during the season when the stench could carry on the slightest sea breeze in the humid summer air.

She parked the car, and Kevin jabbed the pistol into her arm. "Out. Both of you. Head toward the pier."

They trudged along, Eloisa leaning heavily on her cane. If Lucy didn't know any better, she'd think the woman had always had a hard time walking. Slowly, they made it up the boardwalk ramp. All the neighboring stores were closed for the night, their rolling security gates down and locked. If Easter had passed and it was a month later, in May, the shops would still be open and a crowd of tourists would be on the boardwalk.

The tramcars were parked on the municipal pier for the night. A crescent moon illuminated the row of dumpsters and the tall, blue recycling containers. Kevin led them all the way to the front of the pier, closest to the ocean. One of the head tramcars had been disconnected from the passenger cars and was parked here.

"This is enough. You can't shoot us without anyone hearing," Lucy said.

"I don't plan to."

"Then what?"

"I plan on releasing the parking brake on this head tram and pushing it over the pier and into the ocean with you both trapped inside. Your bodies can be found during low tide."

Icy fear twisted around Lucy's heart. "You're crazy! Don't you think the police will suspect you if we're found in your tramcar?"

"No. There is no evidence connecting me to

Gilbert. Besides, why would I be stupid enough to murder two people in my own tramcar?"

His calm and logical reasoning was more frightening than the gun aimed at her chest. She thought of her friends. Katie would be devastated. And what about Azad? He'd proposed to her tonight. The moment he'd slipped the ring on her finger seemed like days ago, not hours. If something happened to her, he would blame himself for not protesting when he'd learned of her intentions to help Melanie by investigating Gilbert's murder. He'd be just as devastated as Katie.

"Get inside the tram."

Together, Lucy and Eloisa slid across the bench of the tramcar. The plastic felt as cold as a tomb.

Kevin tossed a pair of wire ties at Lucy. "Now, I only have one pair of these. I hadn't expected you to drag the old lady along. Wire tie her left hand to the tramcar frame first, then do your own."

The wire ties felt as sturdy as steel chains in Lucy's hands. Her mouth went dry as she turned toward Eloisa. They exchanged a look, and Lucy tried to communicate without words. Slowly, Eloisa raised her left arm to the steel frame. Her hand was shaking.

Lucy pulled the wire tie as loosely as she could.

"That's not tight enough," Kevin growled.

"I don't want to hurt her."

"I'll do it myself, dammit," he snapped.

Lucy shifted on the plastic bench as he came close. Eloisa's right hand tightened on her cane.

"Now!" Lucy whispered vehemently.

Quick as a rattlesnake, Eloisa struck out with her cane and struck Kevin hard on the head.

"Shit!" he howled out as he clutched his fore-head.

"Run!" Eloisa shouted.

Lucy didn't waste a second. She shot out of the tramcar and sprinted down the pier. She risked a glance back to see Kevin rise and take off after her in hot pursuit. Panic rioted within her, but she pushed it down. She needed all her wits about her to survive. At least Kevin hadn't bothered with Eloisa. The elderly woman was already tied to the tramcar and he wouldn't release the brake and push it into the ocean until he had both of them trapped inside.

But Lucy wasn't about to allow that.

She needed to get help. She ran as fast as she could. Heavy footsteps sounded off the boards, and she knew Kevin was not far behind. She flew down the boardwalk ramp and onto the sidewalk. Her daily jogs helped twofold now: she wasn't winded and she was familiar with the area. The road was wider here to allow for trash and recy-cling trucks to drive up the ramp and onto the mu-nicipal pier. The closest home was a few blocks away.

She could backtrack and hide in the sand dunes or beneath the boardwalk, but that would prevent her from calling for help. Without her cell phone, she needed to find a way to call the police.

Her mind spun and she made a snap decision. Haven Candies wasn't far on the boardwalk. The store was closed on the boardwalk front, but if she could make it to the back storage room, she knew how to get inside.

She sprinted down the back street, her legs pumping until she came to the back of Haven Candies. Glancing up at the flight of stairs that led to the storage room of the candy store, she risked another glance back. Kevin was closer than she'd thought. Rushing up the stairs, she lunged for the fake seagull, pressed the latch in the bird's belly, and withdrew the key to the back storage room.

Opening the door, she stepped inside, slammed the door shut, and turned the lock. Her heart pounded so loudly it felt like it would burst from her chest. An emergency light dimly lit the space and boxes lined the perimeter of the storage room. With renewed energy, she burst into the candy shop.

The shop was also dimly lit, and the spare light illuminated boxes of taffy, the candy behind the counter, and part of the back workroom where the fudge was stored. It was enough light. She knew the layout of the shop, and she reached for the landline telephone mounted on a wall behind the counter with sweaty hands. The keyboard lit up and she dialed 911.

"What's your emergency?"

"I need—"

A cacophony of noise made her jump. "Lucy! Where are you? No sense hiding from me."

Lucy dropped the phone.

Oh my God. Kevin had broken down the back door!

"Hello? What's your emergency?" the dispatcher's faint voice could be heard from the receiver on the floor.

Lucy fell silent as she ducked behind the candy

counter and crawled into the back workroom. A long worktable was cluttered with boxes and trays of fudge covered with plastic wrap. She needed to hide—fast. As long as the phone remained connected, the police would trace the call and arrive as standard procedure. She just needed to hide long enough for them to show up.

She searched for something to use as a weapon. More boxes of taffy and trays of candy cluttered the workspace. No knife or sharp tool. Her gaze landed on the copper pot used to make fudge. She knew how darned heavy it could be.

Grasping the copper pot, Lucy flattened her back against a shelf and hid.

"Once I find you, I won't wait to drag you back to the tramcar. I'll kill you here," Kevin said, his voice harsh.

The scrape of his shoes on the floor told her he was close. Her breathing was ragged, her fingers sweaty as she clutched the pot.

His shadow crossed the floor, then he took one more step. She lifted the pot as high as she could and swung it with all her might.

The crack as the pot hit him quivered through her arm. Kevin fell like a tall oak.

For a heart-pounding moment, she stared wide-eyed at his body. Then she sprinted out the back door and down the stairs. She needed to get out of the shop and search for help in case the police didn't arrive in time. Who knew how long Kevin would stay on the floor? Had she killed him? Or just stunned him?

Halfway down the storage room stairs, she hit a

solid wall and stumbled back. She cried out in alarm.

Strong arms grasped hers and steadied her. "Ms. Berberian! Are you all right?"

She looked up to see Detective Calvin Clemmons, his features shadowed by the moonlight. She could just make out his beard and straw-colored hair.

"Lucy!" Bill Watson was right behind him on the stairs. "Are you hurt?"

Her legs almost crumpled beneath her in relief. Thank goodness for the emergency dispatcher. "I'm fine. Kevin Crowley is up there!" She pointed to the candy store. "And Mrs. Lubinski is tied to a tramcar on the municipal pier."

Both men looked at each other. Bill wasted no time in speaking into the radio at his shoulder for officers to get to the pier ASAP.

"Stay down there," Bill said, pointing to the bottom of the staircase.

The two officers climbed the remaining stairs, and moments later, Bill came down with Kevin Crowley in handcuffs. Blood flowed from a gash in Kevin's forehead.

He took one look at Lucy and scowled. "You! You ruined everything!" Kevin jerked in Bill's grasp.

"Don't even try it," Clemmons growled.

Bill led Kevin away and placed him in the back of his patrol car.

Clemmons's lips thinned as he looked down at her. "I read the article in the *Town News* about Gilbert's moneylending. I have a feeling you were

Stan Slade's anonymous source, just as you're smack in the middle of this. Am I right?"

Lucy raised her chin a notch. She wouldn't confess to being Stan Slade's source behind the article. "I told you Melanie was innocent."

Clemmons nodded once, then his mouth curved in an uncharacteristic grin. "For once, I'm happy to agree with you."

Chapter Thirty-Two

❦

"Oh my gosh," Katie said as she looked at Lucy's ring. "I don't know what's more shocking: that Azad proposed or that you fled from a murderer on the boardwalk."

"I'm still trying to process it all myself," Lucy said.

They were sitting at Katie's kitchen counter. Lucy had arrived early the following morning with the box of pineapple cake from Chef Henry Wu's, along with news of her engagement. Bill had already told Katie what had happened the previous night. Eloisa had been released from the wire tie on the tramcar. Both Lucy and Eloisa had refused medical treatment and had been relieved to collapse into their own beds that night.

"Let me see the ring again." Katie rested her fork on the end of her plate, where she'd been indulging in the pineapple cake.

Lucy extended her hand, and the round diamond shimmered beneath Katie's kitchen lights.

Katie squealed in delight. She shot from her stool and hugged Lucy. "The ring is to die for! I'm so happy for you. It's about time he proposed."

"I wasn't sure myself about everything."

"And now?"

"I'm sure. Very sure. It feels right. It's always been Azad for me."

Lucy knew it deep in her bones. She was confident the boardwalk medium, Madame Vega, would agree with her.

"We have to check out all the reception sites. There's the Castle of the Sea, of course, but you may not want to be that formal. Plus, it's very pricey."

"And we found a body there, remember?" It would take a long while before she forgot the gruesome image. Kebab Kitchen had been catering a wedding then, but this time she would plan her own wedding.

Katie waved a hand, as if that fact was unimportant. "Whatever. I'm not superstitious. But there's also Catelli's Manor, Paoli's Catering, and The Sea View. We can also visit out-of-town reception halls. And it's never too early to start on the guest list."

Lucy's mind whirled at the speed in which Katie was spitting out plans. "Hold up! We just got engaged last night. You are putting me in a panic."

"As your matron of honor, it's my duty to give you a fabulous bachelorette party and help in any way I can."

There was no question that Katie would be her maid of honor. Emma would understand. But as for everything else—bachelorette parties, catering halls, and a guest list? Her mother would have a say in everything, especially a guest list, because Lucy had a large extended family. She wasn't ready.

"Have you told your parents?" Katie asked.

"No. You're the first."

"Your mom and dad are going to freak. They've wanted you two together since you graduated from college."

Lucy rubbed her temple. "Don't remind me." She knew Angela and Raffi would be beside themselves with happiness. For some reason, she felt like a rebellious teenager. Did she want to hear her mother's voice: "I told you so. If you weren't so stubborn, this would have happened a year ago."

Oh, brother.

"I only hope they take it in stride and don't start baking baklava for our wedding dessert just yet," Lucy said.

"Aw, let them have their happiness. I know I'm thrilled."

"What's all the squealing about?" Bill walked into the kitchen. He was in his uniform and ready to go to the station.

"Lucy and Azad got engaged! Isn't it exciting?" Katie said.

"Congratulations are definitely in order, Lucy." Bill hugged Lucy. "I always knew Azad was a good guy. But if he ever screws up, you come tell me, okay?"

Lucy smiled at Bill's protectiveness. "Thanks, I will."

"By the way, you should know that Kevin Crowley sang like a canary and admitted to Gilbert's murder. He's going to go to prison for a long time."

"Then last night's boardwalk mayhem was all worth it," Lucy said.

"How's your landlady faring?" Bill asked.

"She was up and about this morning as usual. She may not have had the best relationship with her nephew, but I think she's relieved Gilbert's murderer will be brought to justice," Lucy said. "Now, if you'll both excuse me, I better go tell my parents about the better part of last night."

Next on her stop was the restaurant. Azad was working, but he'd promised not to say a word to her parents. Lucy wanted to break the good news.

She found her parents hunched over the desk in the cramped storage room office. Time sheets were spread across the surface. No matter how often she'd told her father that she would completely take over the task, Raffi beat her to it. Lucy had finally come to the realization that her father needed something to do to keep himself occupied in semiretirement.

"Hi, Mom and Dad."

Angela removed her reading glasses, and they dangled from a decorative chain around her neck. "Hello, Lucy. We left a message on your cell phone not to come in to work today. We thought you'd need a day off after what happened last night."

"Your mother is right," Raffi said. Both her parents looked at her with concern.

Lucy took a breath and decided the best way to deliver her news was to announce it without preamble. "I'm fine. Truly, I am. But I'm not here to talk about Kevin Crowley's arrest. I have other news. Azad and I are engaged." She held out her left hand to show off her shiny bauble.

A deafening silence filled the space.

Lucy's eyes darted from her mother to her father, then back to her mother.

Her mother finally spoke up. "Is this a joke?"

"No. Azad proposed earlier last night, and I accepted. I thought you'd be happy."

Chaos took over in the blink of an eye. Her parents shot from their seats and started talking over each other. She found herself engulfed in her father's arms, his stubble tickling her cheek, and then thrust into her mother's arms. For a petite woman, her mother's arms embraced her surprisingly tightly.

"We are so happy for you both." Tears flowed down her mother's cheeks, and Lucy felt her own eyes well up. She hadn't seen her mother cry in years.

"Where's Azad? I need to congratulate my future son-in-law," Raffi said.

His words made her mother cry even more.

"I'm going to be a sappy mess at the wedding," Angela said, sniffling.

Lucy's worries about her mother's reaction and anticipated words, "I told you so," vanished. Angela's crying almost drowned out the thundering of Lucy's own heart, and tears began running down her own cheeks.

Not tears of sadness, but of happiness.

"It will be all right, Mom," Lucy said.

Her mother lifted her head and met Lucy's eyes. "This is going to be the best Easter."

* * *

After her parents insisted she take the day off, Lucy made a stop at Lola's Coffee Shop. She needed a special pick-me-up and a cappuccino was calling. She headed straight for the counter when she heard her name.

"Hey, Lucy!"

Three men were sitting at a table tucked in a corner—Michael, with Pumpkin and Craig.

She left the line and went over to their table. "Good morning." It was the first time she'd seen Pumpkin after she and Katie had found him in his greenhouse smooching with Sophia. It wasn't an image Lucy would be able to forget for a long while.

As for Craig, he'd never found out she'd eavesdropped on him in the blacklight minigolf. Or had he?

Pumpkin was wearing worn jeans and a tight T-shirt that revealed muscles and a new tattoo of a skull and crossbones on his forearm. Tessa had been busy at her boardwalk tattoo parlor.

Pumpkin reached for a newspaper on the table. "The whole town is abuzz with Kevin Crowley's arrest for Gilbert's murder. According to the local paper, you had a part in it," Pumpkin said.

Stan Slade must have been up all night if the details had been printed already. "I had a small part. The police were the real heroes," Lucy said.

In Lucy's opinion, they were. They'd arrived to drag Kevin out of the candy shop in handcuffs and free Mrs. Lubinski from the tramcar on the pier.

Pumpkin folded the paper and flashed a smile. "We've decided to forgive you for thinking we could have murdered Gilbert."

Lucy blinked, unsure how to respond to *that*.

"What he means," Craig said, "is that we don't blame you. Circumstances did look bad." In contrast to Pumpkin, he was dressed in a polo shirt and khakis.

"Thanks," Lucy said. What else was she to say?

"Despite your downplaying your role, we're happy to hear that you and Mrs. Lubinski weren't injured," Michael said.

Thanks to the newspaper article, Lucy would face questions from nosy townsfolk for weeks. Lucy cleared her throat as she turned back to Pumpkin. "How is Sophia?"

Pumpkin's grin widened. "I plan to follow her to New York City to support her aspiring modeling career."

Lucy was surprised. Sophia must have shared her modeling ambitions with him. Both Lucy and Katie had doubted that Sophia would be honest. "Really?" Lucy asked. "What about your landscaping business in town?"

"It will be a long-distance relationship. I'm only busy during the spring and summer and plan to stay with Sophia during my off-season. Meanwhile, we can visit each other. New York City is not that far away."

No, it wasn't. Public transportation via train or bus made it a manageable commute.

"Good luck to both of you, and I hope Sophia lands a modeling contract." Lucy turned her attention to Craig. "What about you, Craig?"

"I'm staying in Ocean Crest," Craig said. "Sophia sold me her share of the Seagull Condominiums. And thanks to your brother-in-law, Max, I now own the blacklight minigolf. You can golf any time for free, Lucy."

"I'll take you up on that offer."

"Now that the Bikers on the Beach Festival is nearly over, we can celebrate with another bonfire," Michael said.

At Lucy's horrified expression, all three men laughed.

"I'm just joking, Lucy. No bonfires for a while," Michael said.

With the festival winding down, many of the motorcycle enthusiasts had already headed home. The town would soon gear up for the summer season. Lucy would be sure Kebab Kitchen was ready for an influx of tourists.

Craig reached for his mug. "We have the summer to look forward to. How about windsurfing?"

"Windsurfing sounds good to me," Lucy said.

She waved and headed for the coffee line and her cappuccino. Michael pushed back his chair and followed her with his empty mug. Once they were away from the two other men, Michael nudged her shoulder. "Don't worry about harassing them a bit in the past. They both had pretty strong motives to get rid of Gilbert, and they know it. Besides, they still would ride their Harley-Davidsons with you any day. I know I haven't changed my opinion."

Gratitude welled in her chest. "Thanks, Michael."

"By the way, when were you going to tell me?"

"About what?"

His gaze darted to her hand, then returned to her face. "The rock on your finger."

She shifted uncomfortably on her feet. Although

there was nothing between them but friendship, she felt awkward telling Michael. "Azad proposed last night. I didn't purposely forget to tell you. I've just had a lot on my mind."

"Did this happen before you escaped a murderer on the boardwalk?"

"Thankfully, yes." He appeared calm, undisturbed, but she wasn't convinced. She studied his expression, searching for some reaction. "You okay with this news?"

"Are you happy?"

"Yes."

He nodded once. "Then I'm okay with it."

She let out a relieved breath. "You know you are one of my closest friends, right?"

Michael's face beamed in a dazzling smile. "Other than Katie?"

"You both rank pretty high."

He winked. "Good. How about a motorcycle ride next week after your Easter celebration?"

"I wouldn't miss it."

Lucy had one more stop to make. The boardwalk was a bit less busy since most of the bikers had left Ocean Crest. The candy shop was open, and Sarah was outside handing out fudge samples.

"Hi, Sarah," Lucy said as she took a sample of vanilla fudge from her tray. "I'm glad you're back."

"So am I. Thank goodness the police came to their senses and released Melanie. What were they thinking!"

"I have no idea. How is Melanie?" Lucy hadn't had a chance to see her friend since the day she had visited her in jail with Clyde Winters. She wondered how Melanie was handling things. A wrongful arrest and incarceration were not an experience a person could easily forget. She hoped Melanie didn't have nightmares.

"Melanie's better. Much better. She's inside getting ready to make a new batch of fudge. She'll be happy to see you," Sarah said.

Lucy found Melanie gathering ingredients on the worktable. A copper pot rested beside a bag of sugar. Lucy looked away from the pot. She didn't want to recall how she'd used it to defend herself against a murderous Kevin Crowley.

"Lucy!" Melanie cried out as soon as she saw her and hugged her.

"How are you?" Lucy asked.

"Good. Business has kept me busy and kept my mind off my time behind bars. I suppose I'll never entirely forget the experience, but I'm grateful to you and Katie for helping me. And to Mr. Winters for arranging my release with the police."

"I'm happy there will be fudge and taffy on the boardwalk again," Lucy said with a smile.

Melanie chuckled. "How can I ever thank you?"

Lucy cast a glance at the trays of fudge waiting to be cut and pieces placed into small cardboard boxes for the candy store's customers. "I love your chocolate nut fudge."

"I'll hand-deliver a box a week," Melanie promised.

Lucy's eyes widened. "Good heavens, no. I'll have to jog the boardwalk twice as often."

"Okay. How about a box a month? Share it with everyone at the restaurant."

Lucy nodded. "They'd love that. By the way, I never had the chance to tell you, but Rhonda came to visit me at the restaurant. She told me about her gambling problem and how you tried to help her and that it caused a rift between the two of you. How are you and Rhonda faring?"

Melanie wiped her hands on a towel, then leaned against the counter. "Rhonda visited me in jail and apologized. I forgave her, but only because she promised to start going to Gamblers Anonymous. I think she'll even tell her husband."

Lucy was surprised, but happy to hear this news. Rhonda had been sincere after all. "Good for her. I hope everything works out for Rhonda and Noah."

"Me too. She even invited me over for Easter dinner."

"Will you accept? If you're not comfortable, I'm hosting Easter at my new place this year and you are welcome to come," Lucy said.

"Thanks, but I accepted Rhonda's offer. It seems like things are going in the right direction with us." Melanie reached for a bag of sugar. "You want to help make fudge?"

Lucy warily eyed the copper pot. "Not today. I have to prepare for Easter."

Chapter Thirty-Three

❦

"Happy Easter!"

Lucy hugged her parents as they came inside her apartment. "Happy Easter, Mom and Dad."

"How is the lamb shish kebab?" Angela asked.

"It looks perfect," Lucy said.

Her mother eyed her suspiciously. "Oh? Where's Azad?"

"He's on the deck grilling."

"Then it will be perfect," Angela said.

Lucy rolled her eyes rather than argue with her mother. Lucy had marinated the lamb overnight and had prepared most of the side dishes herself, including the hummus. She'd even freshly baked *choereg* and would serve the sweetbread with cheese and baklava after dinner. She'd let her mother think Azad had done everything, then, after Angela had approved of each dish, she'd come clean and tell her the truth.

Deep down, Lucy knew her mother would be

proud of her. After all, her cooking lessons had taught Lucy everything she knew.

The entire town, including her family and friends, were relieved that Gilbert's murderer was in jail.

Her parents were also thrilled about the wedding. To Lucy's surprise, they hadn't brought up wedding plans or food for the reception and had been relatively quiet about the engagement at the restaurant. They'd told customers, but hadn't dragged Lucy from the kitchen to show off her diamond.

Katie, on the other hand, had been talking nonstop about the engagement. Her friend had even purchased wedding magazines showing glossy covers of ridiculously tall and rail-thin models in billowing gowns. Lucy was going to have to give up pastries, including her favorite, lemon meringue pie, from Cutie's bakery. She'd have to continue jogging the boardwalk and—heaven help her—maybe even take up yoga.

Next to arrive were Katie and Bill. Then Emma, Max, and Niari. And then Michael.

"Where's your feisty landlady?" Max asked.

"Mrs. Lubinski is outside, watching Azad cook."

"I do believe she has a crush on your fiancé," Max said.

"Ugh." It was probably true.

"Congrats again on the engagement," Michael said.

Michael and Azad may never be best friends, but the two men had come to tolerate each other.

"I really wasn't surprised when you told me the news," Michael said. "You and I may be good friends, but I've always thought of you as a great catch."

"Thanks, Michael."

"Still, he'd better treat you right. It's not just your father he'd have to answer to." The words were delivered lightly, but his smile didn't entirely reach his eyes. Michael would always have her back and be a good friend.

He handed her a bottle he was cradling under his arm. "I brought your father's favorite cognac from Armenia."

Raffi must have overheard. He was by their side in a flash, and Lucy passed him the bottle. Her father reverently turned it over in his hands and read the label, a satisfied expression on his face. "You did good, Michael."

"It isn't stocked everywhere. My father found it in an out-of-town liquor store."

Lucy knew Michael's father had his fingers in everything—legal and illegal. If Raffi knew this, he didn't bring it up. Her father's eyes shone with delight as he reached for glasses on the counter. "Thank Mr. Citteroni for me."

Azad opened the sliding glass door and came in with a tray of cooked lamb shish kebabs. The delicious aroma made everyone stop and stare at the platter. He placed it on a hot plate in the center of the table.

Lucy added chairs and everyone crowded together around the table. One look at Eloisa, and Lucy knew the woman was happy that she was not spending Easter alone with Cupid. Her landlady was growing on her, and fast. Maybe it was the near escape from a murderer, but they had bonded after that experience. Eloisa treated her almost . . . kindly.

Or maybe she just was on her best behavior around Azad. Lucy wondered how Eloisa would act at the wedding.

Either way, Lucy was happy she was here. She loved her apartment overlooking the ocean and needed to thank Max for the arrangement. Had he known she needed Eloisa as much as her landlady needed her?

One look at her brother-in-law seated across the table between Emma and Niari told her the answer. He was more observant than she'd given him credit for in the past.

Lucy brought out each of her dishes—pilaf, roasted eggplant and a vegetable platter, hummus, and Mediterranean couscous salad—and set everything on the table. Her nerves tightened as she watched everyone pass the dishes around. Would they approve of her cooking?

The food must have been good because for the next several minutes all she heard was the scrape of cutlery on the plates as people enjoyed the food. Her father helped himself to seconds.

"Azad, when did you make all this?" Angela asked.

Azad looked at Lucy with pride. "I didn't. Lucy did."

Everyone fell silent as Angela set down her fork and eyed her daughter. "It's delicious. You have been paying attention to my lessons."

Did Lucy imagine the sigh of relief from everyone present at her mother's praise?

"Thanks, Mom."

Azad kissed Lucy's cheek. "She's a quick learner."

Not really. But she would take the compliment.

Azad nudged her shoulder. "See? I told you not to worry. Everyone is getting along and enjoying the food."

"He's right. Look!" Niari said, pointing her fork to the corner of the room, where Gadoo and Cupid were lounging together on the pink couch.

"They've finally figured out how to cohabitate?" Katie asked.

Lucy was surprised to see the two pets sharing the same room, let alone the same couch cushion. Gadoo must have snuck inside when Azad had brought in the shish kebab from the deck. She hadn't spotted the cat. "I think they are both waiting for leftover lamb."

Niari lowered her fork. "Animals are always smarter than humans."

Lucy supposed her niece could be right more often than not.

"My Cupid is a lover, not a fighter," Eloisa said, her face beaming with pride as she looked at her pet.

Lucy *could* argue with that statement, but decided to keep eating instead.

"Bill also has good news to share," Katie said as she placed a hand on her husband's shoulder. "His promotion to detective has come through."

"Most surprising, Calvin Clemmons submitted a recommendation on my behalf," Bill said.

"I thought he'd opposed it?" Lucy said.

Bill shook his head. "He changed his mind."

Clemmons was changing. He hadn't given her a hard time when she'd literally run into him fleeing a murderous Kevin Crowley from the candy store. Clemmons could have complained about

Lucy's involvement to Prosecutor Walsh, and the prosecutor could have retaliated by dragging Lucy into the station for interfering with an active murder investigation. Instead, Clemmons had written a recommendation on Bill's behalf.

Lucy would thank the detective later by delivering a batch of baklava to the station.

"This is great news and more reason to celebrate," Lucy said.

Raffi raised a glass of cognac. "To Bill's promotion. To Azad and Lucy's engagement. And to a blessed Easter with family and friends."

Lucy looked to everyone present. Her life was changing with every season she spent at Ocean Crest. A flash of light caught on her engagement ring, and she marveled that she'd soon embark on a new journey. She cherished each person and relationship she had built during her return home.

Lucy raised her own glass. "To family, friends."

Katie leaned across the table. "Now we can talk about reception halls."

Author's Note

I grew up in the restaurant business, where my Armenian American parents owned a restaurant for almost thirty years in a small South Jersey town. I worked almost every job—from rolling silverware and wiping down tables as a tween, to hosting and waitressing as a teenager. My mother was a talented cook, and the grapevine in our backyard was more valued than any rosebush. I'd often come home from school to the delicious aromas of simmering grape leaves, stuffed peppers and tomatoes, and shish kebab.

But growing up in a family restaurant definitely had its pros and cons. As one of the owner's daughters, I'd often get last-minute calls from my father to waitress or hostess when another worker was sick. I used to grumble about it as a teenager, but I always showed up. Family came first. But there were plenty of great times, too, and my tips paid for my prom gown. Some of my favorite scenes in the book are straight from my memories—temperamental chefs, busy busboys, and gossipy waitstaff can be quite entertaining.

My *Kebab Kitchen Mystery* series also takes place at the Jersey shore. Ever since I was a little girl, my parents vacationed there. We now have two girls, and we still take them to the Jersey shore every

summer. As I wrote the books, I pictured my ficti-
tious small town of Ocean Crest at the Jersey
shore. I heard the seagulls squawking and pictured
them circling above the beach. I felt the lapping of
the ocean waves and the sand between my toes,
and imagined the brilliant Ferris wheel on the
boardwalk pier. I pictured myself in Ocean Crest—
minus the murders, of course.

I loved writing this book, and I'm happy to share
my own favorite family recipes with you. Enjoy the
food!

RECIPES

Lucy's Mediterranean Couscous Salad

¾ cup uncooked couscous
1 cup chicken broth
1½ cup cubed tomatoes
1½ cup peeled cucumber
½ cup halved pitted kalamata olives
¼ cup chopped sweet onions
2½ tablespoons lemon juice
2 tablespoons extra-virgin olive oil
Salt and pepper to taste

In saucepan, heat chicken broth to boiling. Stir in couscous. Remove from heat. Cover and let stand five minutes. Fluff with a fork.

In large bowl, place tomatoes, cucumber, olives, and onions. Stir in couscous.

Add lemon juice, oil, salt and pepper. Mix well. Cover and refrigerate for an hour. Enjoy!

Angela's Lamb Kebabs with Tomato Sauce

2 pounds leg of lamb or beef tenderloin, boned,
    with fat removed, and cut into 1-inch cubes
2½ tablespoons tomato paste
3 tablespoons extra-virgin olive oil
¼ teaspoon paprika
¼ teaspoon cayenne pepper to taste
2½ tablespoons lemon juice or red wine vinegar
1 onion sliced

Tomato Sauce
4 tablespoons butter
1 diced onion
2 beefsteak tomatoes, seeded and diced
¼ teaspoon paprika
Salt and pepper to taste

Place meat in bowl. Add tomato paste, oil, paprika, cayenne, lemon or vinegar, and onion. Mix well. Cover and refrigerate overnight.

To prepare the tomato sauce, heat butter in a skillet. Sauté onions till lightly golden. Add tomatoes. Cook for 10–15 minutes. Add paprika, salt and pepper.

Thread meat onto skewers. Grill the skewers over a charcoal fire. Turn the skewers until the meat is cooked on all sides. Pour warm tomato sauce onto a platter and place cooked kebabs on top. Best if served with rice pilaf. Enjoy!

Azad's Armenian Sweet Bread
(*Choereg*)

¼ ounce package of active dry yeast
¼ cup lukewarm water
¾ cup sugar
4 eggs
1 teaspoon salt
¾ cup melted butter
1 cup lukewarm whole milk
7 cups flour
Sesame seeds
3 Hershey chocolate bars (optional)

In a small bowl, combine yeast, water, teaspoon of sugar, and stir until mixture is dissolved. Set aside.

In large bowl, combine three of the eggs, salt, and remaining sugar. Add yeast mixture, butter, and milk. Mix with an electric mixer or by hand until blended. Add flour, a cup at a time, and mix with a dough hook of an electric mixer or by hand. Knead dough until it is smooth (about ten minutes). Cover bowl with a towel and set aside to rise for two hours. The dough should double in size.

Preheat oven to 375 degrees. Shape dough into small buns.

Optional: When shaping dough into small buns, insert two squares of chocolate into the bun, then seal the bun until it is closed.

Beat remaining egg and brush tops of buns with the egg wash. Sprinkle with sesame seeds. Bake for fifteen minutes until tops of buns are golden brown. Makes about three dozen buns.

Warm the buns in a toaster oven, oven, or microwave before serving for delicious, warm sweet bread.

ACKNOWLEDGMENTS

Writers create stories in solitude, but publishing a book is a team effort. I'm thankful for all the wonderful people who have helped me along the way. I will always be indebted to my parents, Anahid and Gabriel, and miss them every day. This series would never have been written if it wasn't for them. My life experiences growing up in the family restaurant were invaluable. They taught me to work hard and never stop believing in myself.

Thanks to my girls—Laura and Gabrielle—for believing in Mom. I'm eternally grateful to John for his never-ending support, encouragement, and love. I'm lucky we get to live this life together.

Thank you to my agent, Stephany Evans, for your guidance and for always believing in me.

And a special thank you to everyone at Kensington for believing in this series and all their work on my behalf.

Last, thanks to readers, booksellers, and librarians for reading my Kebab Kitchen Mystery series. I hope you enjoy the book as much as I loved writing it!

Be sure not to miss any
of Tina Kashian's
Kebab Kitchen Mystery series, including

ONE FETA IN THE GRAVE

As summer comes to an end in her Jersey shore
town, Lucy Berberian continues to manage her
family's Mediterranean restaurant. The Kebab
Kitchen also has a food tent at this year's beach
festival. But now a local businessman is under the
boardwalk—dead by the sea . . .

Keep reading for a special look!

CHAPTER 1

❧❧❧

"It looks like a giant nose."

Lucy Berberian's lips twitched at the words her longtime friend Katie Watson whispered into her ear.

"No. I think it's an oversized ear. Wait, it's a . . ." Lucy bit her lip, afraid to voice what other body part she thought was displayed, then suddenly realized the artist's true intent. "It's a big snail!"

Both women looked at each other, then burst out laughing, drawing the attention of a group of serious-looking men and women holding clipboards who were gathered around a sand sculpture a few yards away.

Lucy scanned the beach, noting the dozens of impressive sand sculptures. It was Sunday, the opening day of the Ocean Crest sand sculpture contest, the first event of many to celebrate the weeklong beach festival in the small Jersey shore town. The festival offered numerous activities on the boardwalk and on the beach. Surfing, beach

volleyball, and soccer competitions would thrill
tourists and beachgoers alike while a wine and
food tasting event would offer delicious morsels
from local restaurants to satisfy adventurous pal-
ates. Visitors would wander among the temporary
tents set up on the boardwalk while local musi-
cians performed beneath the bandstand. And all
during the week, shops would continue to sell beach
clothing, boogie boards, pails and shovels, hermit
crabs, and dozens of other summer-themed knick-
knacks. The amusement pier's old-fashioned wooden
roller coaster and Ferris wheel operated late into
the evening, and spectacular fireworks ended the
festivities Saturday night.

The festival was important for the local mer-
chants and the town. It was mid-August, and soon
after, the season would wind down and the small
town that could easily swell to triple its population
during the summer months would shrink to its
after-season size following Labor Day.

The sand sculpture contest kicked off the festival, and local artists had molded unique creations.
Mermaids, Greek and Roman gods and goddesses,
intricate castles, and a variety of marine life including sea turtles, horseshoe crabs, and fish fascinated onlookers. A lifelike sculpture of C-3PO
alongside R2-D2 from *Star Wars* drew kids of all
ages.

Clipboards in hand, Lucy and Katie walked
from creation to creation and marked their scores
on their judging sheets.

Katie chewed on her pencil as she stared at the
snail sculpture. "I'm not sure how to score this
one."

Lucy cocked her head to the side and squinted at the sculpture. "It's very detailed. I'm giving it a high score for creativity."

"I suppose." Katie didn't look convinced.

A flash of red on the beach caught Lucy's eye. A pretty, blond teenager in a fire-engine-red bikini flirted with a lifeguard sitting in his guard stand. Her brunette girlfriend stood next to her smiling.

"The one in the red looks like you did in high school," Lucy said. Katie was tall and slender with straight blond hair and blue eyes.

"You think so? I don't remember being that flirtatious, and the curvy brunette looks like you now."

Lucy rolled her eyes. "My bikini days are long over. And you always flirted with the lifeguards."

"The good old days," Katie said.

They burst out laughing. They'd been best friends since grade school, but were physical opposites. Lucy was shorter with dark, curly hair that never cooperated in the summer humidity, and her eyes were a deep brown. The two women came from different cultural backgrounds as well. Lucy was a first-generation American—a mix of Armenian, Greek, and Lebanese—and Katie had discovered, after recently putting together a family tree, that one of her ancestors fought under General Washington in the Revolutionary War.

Their differences never mattered. They were like sisters, and when Lucy had quit her job as a Philadelphia attorney and returned home, Katie had welcomed her back with open arms and offered Lucy her guest bedroom in the cozy rancher she shared with her husband, Bill, an Ocean Crest police officer.

They marked down their scores and turned to the next sculpture—an adorable sand snowman with shiny black shells for its eyes and a small conch shell for its nose—when angry voices drew their attention.

"You're biased and everyone knows it! How the hell did you get to be a judge?"

Lucy recognized the man as Harold Harper, a boardwalk business owner. Harold was stocky with reddish hair parted on one side and the beginnings of a goatee on his square chin. He wore a striped tank top, wrinkled khaki shorts, and sandals.

"What's it to you? Mind your own business."

Lucy didn't know the second man. Tall and thin, he had a shock of white hair, bushy eyebrows, and a tattoo of Wile E. Coyote on his right bicep. His untucked, white, T-shirt and army green shorts emphasized his height and lankiness.

"I'm also a judge. I'm making it my business," Harold said.

Lucy turned to Katie. "What's going on?"

"That's Harold Harper and Archie Kincaid," Katie said. "Archie came to town a year ago and opened Seaside Gifts, a store on the boardwalk. I issued his mercantile license at the town hall."

Katie worked at the Ocean Crest town hall and handled real estate taxes, zoning, pet licenses, and business licenses.

"Archie's going at it pretty good with Harold," Lucy said.

"They own shops next to each other on the

boardwalk. Sparks fly whenever they're within five feet of each other."

Their combative stances reminded Lucy of the TV commercials advertising a big mixed martial arts fight at one of the large Atlantic City casinos. Was it all bravado or could they really pack a punch?

Katie vigorously fanned her red cheeks with her clipboard. "If it has something to do with the judging, then I have to get involved."

Katie was the head judge on the judging committee for the sand sculpture contest. The committee appointed six additional judges and everyone's scores would be anonymously tallied. Lucy was one of the appointed judges.

Lucy had also been recruited to oversee the food and wine tasting event, which was part of the festival and would take place on the boardwalk. As the new manager of Kebab Kitchen, her family-owned Mediterranean restaurant, Lucy had been the perfect fit for the job. She'd also wanted to give back to the town who had warmly embraced her after she'd returned home months ago.

Harold and Archie glowered at each other and were starting to cause a scene. Several tourists had stopped on the beach to watch.

Lucy eyed them warily. "Maybe you should call Bill." A man in uniform carrying a gun could quickly calm down a fight between two idiots.

"I can handle it," Katie said, stiffening her spine as she approached the pair. "What's the problem, gentlemen?"

"He should be disqualified as a judge," Harold said, pointing his pen at Archie.

"Shut up, Harper! No one wants to hear your opinion," Archie countered.

This wasn't going well. If things escalated, then Lucy would call Bill on her cell phone.

"Why do you think he should be disqualified?" Katie asked.

"His nephew created that." Harold pointed to a sand sculpture of a sea serpent attacking a castle. "I glimpsed at his scores. He gave everyone lower scores and his nephew a ten. A ten! No one should get a perfect score."

Lucy had already judged the sculpture in question, and she tended to agree. The face of the serpent was not detailed, and one wall of the castle was starting to crumble. It was average, certainly not a ten—not when the competition was stiff and there were a lot of spectacular sculptures.

"Is this true about your nephew?" Katie asked.

Archie shrugged. "Neil is an aspiring artist and happened to enter this year."

Katie frowned. "Then as the head judge of the judging committee, I have to agree with Mr. Harper."

"What? Why?"

"The judging agreement you signed specifically says no family members are permitted to compete," Katie said.

"I didn't see that in the agreement," Archie protested.

"Maybe you should have read the fine print," Harold scoffed.

Archie whirled on Harold. "Maybe I should wallop you."

"You're nothing but a bully," Harold taunted.

"Mr. Harper, please." Katie said, holding up her hand. She turned to Archie. "Mr. Kincaid, I'm afraid you have to step down as a judge. There is a five-thousand-dollar prize at stake, and we can't afford an appearance of impropriety."

"You're kidding me, right?" Archie looked at her in disbelief.

"No. I'm quite serious."

Harold laughed, and a smug look crossed his face.

Rather than address his adversary, Archie stalked forward to stand toe to toe with Katie. "Are you accusing me of cheating?"

Katie was taken aback, but she didn't back down. She placed her hands on her hips. "I'm not accusing you of anything, just stating fact. The agreement was clear."

Archie jerked his head at Harold. "He put you up to this, didn't he?"

"Nope, but I sure am enjoying it," Harold drawled.

Archie ignored the barb and turned back to Katie. "What if I refuse to step down as a judge?"

Katie raised her chin. "Then your nephew's sculpture will have to be disqualified."

Archie's brows snapped downward like two angry caterpillars. "If you'd just keep your nose where it belongs instead of favoring Harold, lady, the rest of this judging would have gone without a hitch."

Katie's eyes narrowed. "What did you say to me?" Her fist clenched at her side, and Lucy feared her friend would be the one doing the walloping. Lucy was painfully aware that everyone's attention was focused on the pair.

"Just calm down, Katie." Lucy rushed forward to grab hold of her arm.

Lucy felt Katie's muscles tighten. "Like I said, either you step down or your nephew's sculpture will be eliminated from the competition."

"Let's move on," Lucy urged. "We can report everything to the festival committee and let them toss out his scores."

When neither seemed willing to break the standoff, Lucy tugged on Katie's arm. A group of children, dressed in bathing suits and holding pails and sand shovels, had gathered to stand behind the adults and stare, mouths agape.

Archie had enough sense to look contrite, and he backed up a step. "If those are my options, then I'll step down as judge." He extended his clipboard.

Lucy sprang forward and took the clipboard rather than risk Katie hitting him over the head with it. Together they watched as Archie stormed off the beach.

"You okay?" Lucy asked after they'd moved on.

Katie rubbed her temple. "Yeah. I just lost my temper."

"I don't blame you. Archie acted like a jerk. But Harold was no better in my opinion. He really pushed Archie's buttons. Why do they hate each other?"

"Like I said, they are boardwalk business neighbors. Harold called the township and complained that Archie's using cutthroat business tactics."

"How?"

"They both mostly sell T-shirts, boogie boards, bathing suits, all the other usual beach items. Harold claims Archie has slashed his prices below cost just to put Harold out of business. He claims Archie will turn around and raise his prices after Harold is forced to close his store."

Lucy knew boardwalk business owners had a little over three months—from Memorial Day to Labor Day—to earn their yearly living. The beach town was bursting at its seams with tourists during the season, and there was ample business to sell similar wares. But at the same time, it fed a competitive business nature.

"What can the town do?" Lucy asked.

"Nothing. It's a free economy."

Lucy shook her head. "Both men are stubborn as mules."

Katie let out a slow breath. "I'm just glad it ended before those two came to blows and one ended up dead."

The industrial KitchenAid mixer whirred and mixed the dough to a creamy smoothness. Inside the oven, the first trays of date cookies were almost finished, and they released their delicious smell into the restaurant's kitchen.

The oven timer dinged. "They look perfect," Lucy's mother, Angela Berberian, said.

"I need to make five more trays." Lucy wiped her hands on a clean dishcloth and peered into the oven.

Angela reached for a white apron emblazoned

with Kebab Kitchen's name in green letters. "I'll help."

The restaurant would serve cookies and baklava for dessert at the upcoming wine and food tasting event. Their head chef, Azad, would prepare his own savory dishes. Azad was creative, and Lucy couldn't wait to hear what he planned to serve.

The date cookies were a family favorite. Lucy's ten-year-old niece, Niari, was a typical picky tween eater. She wouldn't touch a date, let alone eat one. But the family recipe had fooled her. Niari had bitten into one of the soft cookies, mistakenly believed they were chocolate filled, and loved them. When Lucy had told her that they were stuffed with dates, not chocolate, Niari's eyes had widened like disks and her mouth had formed a perfect *O,* then she'd simply shrugged, and finished her cookie.

"Remove the trays before they overbake," her mother said.

Lucy reached for silicone mittens, pulled the trays out of the oven, and set them on the worktable to cool on racks. They smelled like heaven and her mouth watered at the sight. Each cookie was slightly brown and looked like a half-moon stuffed ravioli.

"Perfect," her mother said.

Lucy beamed. Angela Berberian didn't hand out praise easily. Her mother was the former chef of Kebab Kitchen and was a tyrant in the kitchen. At only five feet tall, she was tiny, but formidable. Anyone who'd ever worked with her knew better than to underestimate her culinary skill or to serve a dish that didn't meet her high standards. Angela wore her hair in her signature sixties beehive and the gold cross necklace she never removed.

Lucy had always believed life had played a cruel trick on her when she'd been born into her family. Her parents had opened Kebab Kitchen thirty years ago, and other than Lucy, every member of her family could cook. Her sister, Emma, could whip up a family meal for her husband, Max, and their daughter, Niari, in little time. Her father, Raffi, grew up knowing how to marinate and grill the perfect shish kebab.

Lucy had been the only one who couldn't boil water or scramble an egg, let alone prepare a tray of baklava. She'd gone to law school instead and had worked at a Philadelphia firm for eight years. But since returning home and taking over management of the restaurant, she'd been determined to learn.

It hadn't been easy. Lucy had spent hours in the kitchen with her mother learning how to make baklava, hummus, grape leaves stuffed with meat and rice, and other savory Mediterranean dishes. Frustrated and often overheated, there were times she wanted to quit, but she'd stuck with it, and she'd surprised everyone, mostly herself.

Her dishes came out not only edible, but good.

Not as good as her mother's or Azad's, but Lucy was more than pleased with her success. Plus, it wasn't as if she was taking over as head chef anytime soon. Lucy liked managing. Nothing was more satisfying than when the kitchen and dining room ran smoothly, and their customers enjoyed their meals.

The timer dinged again, and Lucy took out a

second batch of cookies. She'd had to make small batches by herself, but with her mother's help, they could roll, stuff, and bake much faster.

Her mother reached for a chunk of dough covered in plastic wrap. "Did you let this dough rest?" her mother asked.

"Thirty minutes."

"Good. You remembered."

Lucy reached for a rolling pin and joined her mother at the worktable. Adding a pinch of flour to her work surface so the dough wouldn't stick, Lucy started rolling. Once they rolled out the dough, they cut two-inch rounds with cookie cutters.

As they worked side by side, Lucy's mind turned back to the events of the morning. Angela had been in business in Ocean Crest for years and knew almost everyone in town. Maybe she'd have information on Archie or Harold.

"Hey, Mom, what do you know about Archie Kincaid?" Lucy asked.

"The owner of Seaside Gifts? He came to town about a year ago with his nephew and bought old man John's shop on the boardwalk. Why?" Angela continued cutting the dough with the cookie cutter as she spoke. She worked quickly, and Lucy had often admired her for her efficiency and endurance in the kitchen. Her mother never seemed to tire.

"Archie was a judge of the sand sculpture contest and never told the festival committee that his nephew was one of the sculptors. Archie gave Katie a hard time before he finally withdrew as a judge."

Her mother shrugged a slender shoulder. "I'm not surprised."

"You're not?"

Angela reached for a bowl of pitted and chopped dates that Lucy had prepared. She placed a tablespoon of filling in the center of each cut-out circle of dough. "Archie can be stubborn. His nephew, Neil, is a vagrant, and Archie tries to help the boy."

"Vagrant? What's that supposed to mean?" English was her mother's third language and sometimes she chose the wrong word to convey her meaning.

Angela waved a flour-coated hand. "You know. Wanderer. Bum. He says he's an artist, but never sells anything. He surfs all day and doesn't work. He needs a haircut and a shave."

Lucy chuckled as she finally got her mother's meaning. She thought negatively of any unshaved male with long hair. Old-school thinking for sure, but Lucy could almost picture Neil Kincaid based on her mother's description. "Mom, *bum* is not a politically correct term."

"Fine. Neil isn't homeless, he's lazy. He could get a job if he wanted. Instead, he spends his days on the beach. He lives with his uncle, Archie, above their store."

"Yes, well. Archie argued with Katie. But Harold Harper instigated it." After adding the filling, Lucy folded the dough to make a half-moon shape.

"It's no secret that the two dislike each other," her mother said.

"How do you know that?"

"Once, they happened to be in the restaurant at the same time. They started shouting across the dining room and drove poor Sally crazy. She threatened to kick them out if they didn't behave."

"Really? I can't picture Sally losing it." Sally was a longtime waitress at Kebab Kitchen. She had an easygoing personality and the locals loved her. As long as Lucy had known her, Sally had never lost her temper.

"Fortunately, both men have never been back to eat at the same time again." Angela set down her spoon and glanced at Lucy's workspace. "Be careful not to stuff the cookies too much."

Lucy immediately scraped some of the date filling back into the bowl. Once each cookie was filled, folded, and sealed, she placed it on a tray. Last, she brushed all the unbaked cookies with egg wash and slid the rack into the oven.

"What smells so good in here?"

Lucy turned to see Azad Zakarian walk in the kitchen. Tall, dark, and lean, the sight of the handsome head chef always made her pulse pound a bit too fast. His hair was wet, making it look almost black, and Lucy knew he'd gone home after the lunch shift to shower and return for the dinner shift. He hadn't yet put on his chef's coat, and he wore a tight white T-shirt that showed off muscled biceps and a lean stomach. She tore her gaze away.

Get a grip, Lucy.

She was his boss, and she needed better self-control if they were to continue to work together.

Not long ago, Azad had left his sous chef job at a fancy Atlantic City restaurant to become head chef of Kebab Kitchen. Her parents no longer worked full-time, and she couldn't have managed the place without him. It hadn't been the smoothest transition. Azad had broken her heart after college, and she'd sworn never to fall for that charming dimple ever again.

But since her return to Ocean Crest, Azad had expressed interest in resuming their romantic relationship.

Trouble.

Lucy was hesitant about any kind of relationship with him outside of the restaurant, but time and his steady pursuit—along with a bout of hormones—was wearing down her resistance.

Lucy cleared her throat. "We're making date cookies and baklava for the festival."

"They look great, too," he said.

Was that a compliment about just the cookies or was there more behind his words?

"What do you have planned for the festival menu?"

"I want samples that people can easily eat without utensils. I'm thinking of small wrapped gyros, bamboo skewers of lamb shish kebab, and grilled vegetable skewers of peppers, tomatoes, and onions. I also plan to make a meat bulgur sausage and falafel."

"Mmm. It all sounds delicious," Lucy said.

Azad flashed a grin, and the dimple in his cheek deepened. She was suddenly overly warm, and it had nothing to do with the heat from the ovens.

"Excuse me. We need more flour," she said. Grabbing the half-empty container, she left Azad with her mother and headed for the storage room. She didn't need more flour, she needed a break.

Shelves of dry items stacked the perimeter of the storage room. A tiny office was tucked away in the corner. She set the flour container on a shelf beside large bags of rice, bulgur, and spices—the essentials of Mediterranean cuisine.

Grabbing a bag of cat food on a far shelf, she headed out the back door to the rear parking lot. She shook the bag and seconds later, a patchy orange and black cat with yellow eyes sauntered from behind the Dumpster to wind around her feet.

"Hi, Gadoo. Where have you been?" She bent down to pet his soft fur and was rewarded with a rumbling purr.

Her mother had named the outdoor cat Gadoo which meant *cat* in Armenian. Not very original, but Lucy had taken a liking to the feisty feline and took over feeding him twice a day and making sure he always had enough water.

"I have your favorite." She opened the bag of kibbles and poured some into his bowl which she kept outside by the restaurant's back door. Gadoo looked up, blinked, then meowed.

"You want more?"

Another meow, louder this time.

"Spoiled kitty," she said, then added more food to his bowl. "If you keep eating like this, you'll have to watch your feline figure."

He responded with a twitch of his tail, and then began eating.

The back door opened, and Azad stepped out. "Hey. I was wondering where you went off to."

"I wanted to feed Gadoo." Obvious answer since the cat was chowing down at her feet. How long would it take for her to get over this nervousness around him when they were alone?

It didn't help that her parents had always wanted them to be together. "Keep the business in the family, Lucy," her mother had often said.

It had always been enough to make her run for the hills.

But now she was older and wiser. And Azad *had* changed. He was no longer the young, college boy who feared commitment. He'd stuck around and helped her by taking over as head chef.

Azad had put on his chef's coat, and he looked professional in the starched white jacket. Still, he shoved his hands into his pockets and a look of unease crossed his handsome features.

Maybe he was just as nervous as she was.

"Are you free Friday? There's a new French restaurant, Le Gabriel, that I think you'd like," he said. "Your mom is covering in the kitchen and your dad is managing then so it's not a problem."

He'd followed her outside to ask her on a date? "I've heard of Le Gabriel. It's received excellent reviews by the food critic in the *Ocean Crest Town News*."

"Are you free?" Azad's dark gaze met hers, and her heart skipped a beat.

Maybe it was time to take a leap. If a door of opportunity opened, shouldn't she step through it? "Yes," she said. "I'd like that."

Azad's mouth curved in a sensual smile. "Great. This time, I promise nothing will get in our way."

Connect with

U s

Visit us online at
KensingtonBooks.com
to read more from your favorite authors, see books
by series, view reading group guides, and more.

for sneak peeks, chances to win books and prize packs,
and to share your thoughts with other readers.

facebook.com/kensingtonpublishing
twitter.com/kensingtonbooks

Tell us what you think!

To share your thoughts, submit a review,
or sign up for our eNewsletters, please visit:
KensingtonBooks.com/TellUs.

Books by Bestselling Author
Fern Michaels

___**The Jury**	0-8217-7878-1	$6.99US/$9.99CAN
___**Sweet Revenge**	0-8217-7879-X	$6.99US/$9.99CAN
___**Lethal Justice**	0-8217-7880-3	$6.99US/$9.99CAN
___**Free Fall**	0-8217-7881-1	$6.99US/$9.99CAN
___**Fool Me Once**	0-8217-8071-9	$7.99US/$10.99CAN
___**Vegas Rich**	0-8217-8112-X	$7.99US/$10.99CAN
___**Hide and Seek**	1-4201-0184-6	$6.99US/$9.99CAN
___**Hokus Pokus**	1-4201-0185-4	$6.99US/$9.99CAN
___**Fast Track**	1-4201-0186-2	$6.99US/$9.99CAN
___**Collateral Damage**	1-4201-0187-0	$6.99US/$9.99CAN
___**Final Justice**	1-4201-0188-9	$6.99US/$9.99CAN
___**Up Close and Personal**	0-8217-7956-7	$7.99US/$9.99CAN
___**Under the Radar**	1-4201-0683-X	$6.99US/$9.99CAN
___**Razor Sharp**	1-4201-0684-8	$7.99US/$10.99CAN
___**Yesterday**	1-4201-1494-8	$5.99US/$6.99CAN
___**Vanishing Act**	1-4201-0685-6	$7.99US/$10.99CAN
___**Sara's Song**	1-4201-1493-X	$5.99US/$6.99CAN
___**Deadly Deals**	1-4201-0686-4	$7.99US/$10.99CAN
___**Game Over**	1-4201-0687-2	$7.99US/$10.99CAN
___**Sins of Omission**	1-4201-1153-1	$7.99US/$10.99CAN
___**Sins of the Flesh**	1-4201-1154-X	$7.99US/$10.99CAN
___**Cross Roads**	1-4201-1192-2	$7.99US/$10.99CAN

Available Wherever Books Are Sold!
Check out our website at **www.kensingtonbooks.com**

Romantic Suspense from
Lisa Jackson